I0818115

Peter

T. R. Robinson

Anickto Publishing

First published in paperback and digital format by T. R. Robinson 2016

This hardback edition first published by Anickto Publishing 2025

(www.anickto.com)

ISBN 978-1-7385435-5-7

Cover by: SelfPubBookCovers.com/BeeJavier

Dedication

In memory of my maternal grandmother
whose strength of character and moral standing
have rarely, if ever, been equalled.

Contents

Preface

Language: British English, including British spelling, has been used throughout.

Accuracy: Where this tale is based upon factual events, I have done my best to represent them truly. Of course, this depends upon the quality of my own memory, which is generally very good, and the memories of those who passed on the stories to me.

Disclaimer: As indicated above, some events in this story are based upon actual happenings. Therefore, in order to protect those still living, the descendants of those referred to and my own family, names of people and places have either been changed or omitted. In the fictional remainder of the tale, any similarity to any person living or deceased is coincidental and not intended.

T. R. Robinson

1

Captivated

She felt the heel of her right shoe slip from the edge of the step as her body spun from the impact. The intense pain in her elbow the least of her concerns for now. She tried to get a better grip with her left foot but it was too late. Her equilibrium was lost. Gravity was pulling her forward. “Oh Noo!” Tensing every thigh muscle and utilising both hips, she managed to force her torso into a backward motion. At the very least, hoping to save her face and bust from impacting upon the hard marble. With arms outspread, as if on a trapeze wire, she attempted to balance and find something to hold. But there was nothing. She wobbled for what seemed an eternity and then fell. Thankfully, she had succeeded in coercing her body back from its forward motion. Much to her embarrassment, she landed buttocks first with a resounding thud, the soft delict flesh stinging from the impact. “Ouch!”

All before her spun uncontrollably at a sickening speed. She desperately tried to refocus and not to vomit. As her eyes cleared, she noticed a solitary, apparently unattached, hand come into her circle of vision.

“I’m terribly sorry. That was very clumsy of me.” Again, she tried to refocus. Her irritation increasing with every passing moment.

“Yes, you oaf. Why did y............” Her words trailed off as she looked up into those amazing, captivating hazel eyes. Looking down upon her was one of the most handsome visages she had ever seen. A cold little shiver passed down her spine while she tried to regain her composure. He continued to offer his helping hand. Feeling rather cross and embarrassed with her undignified position, she was in two minds whether to accept it or not. Then, realising how petulant she would appear and wishing to get up in as dignified a manner as possible, put her hand into his. The strength in his arm was readily apparent as he lifted her without the least effort.

"Thank you."

"My pleasure. I'm so very sorry."

"You should look where you are going. Why on earth were you running down the steps so fast?"

"You're right. I should've been more careful. My friends and I are late for a lecture."

"They only just missed hitting me on their way down, but you....."

"Yes. I can only say I'm sorry again. Are you all right? Are you hurt?"

"Mostly my pride. It was not a very dignified position I ended up in."

"Ha, oh um hum. No. Yes. My apologies."

"Well, no permanent harm done. Just be more careful in the future." She could not bring herself to scold him anymore. He was so handsome and his apologetic sheepishness was so endearing.

"Yes, I will."

"You better get off to your lecture. Your friends are waiting." He hesitated, and hovering for a moment, continued to look at her with those wonderful eyes. Their gaze locked, and she felt her colour rising. He continued to look unashamedly directly into her eyes. She was unaccustomed to such boldness. It confused and flustered her. She had to break it. Compelling herself to leave those magic eyes, she looked down and away, hoping he would not see how unsettled she felt.

"Hum, may I see you again?" The little spinal shiver repeated itself.

"What do you mean?" Secretly hoping he was going to suggest a social outing.

"Would you allow me to take you for a coffee one evening?"

"Um, I do not know. I am on my own here."

"Please. I'd like the opportunity to make up for this properly."

"I am not sure. I have no chaperone."

"Well, why not think about it? I'll ask you again in a couple of days."

"Um, all right."

"Katherine, you can't!" Jennifer was shocked by the very idea.

"He was so nice and polite. He couldn't apologise enough. I cannot see it would do any harm."

"But on your own, with a man, and no chaperone. What will people say? What would your parents say?"

"I know, I know. It's so frustrating."

"Do you know anyone here you could ask to accompany you?"

"No. My parents were hesitant at first about me coming on my own. But they wanted me to have the best training available. Father studied in the same academy."

"Yes, I remember you said he got his degree here."

"Yes. I love my parents and would never disobey them. They told me they trusted me to be sensible and to make the right decisions. I've seen women here out with men on their own. I don't see I would be doing anything really wrong."

"Yes, I've seen them too. Things are so different here in Vienna. It's such a cosmopolitan and sophisticated city and there're people from all over the world, living and studying here. It's obvious the different cultures have brought their influence to bear, one way or another. And some are evidently far less strict than our own."

"Anyway, it's the 1860s, nearly 1870. It's about time women were treated more equally. And I think it is about time we were allowed to choose who we see for ourselves."

"Katherine! Anyway, I'm sure your parents must've already started looking at potential husbands for you."

"Arranged marriages are such a pain. Mind, many appear to work, but then many do not."

"But social, not to mention economic, status is crucial. Especially in families like ours."

"Why? If people love each other, surely that is enough."

"I'm not sure your parents would agree."

"Well, never mind about that now. I am hardly thinking about marriage. What am I going to do? I like him and he's so handsome. Did I mention his eyes?"

"Yes, you did. Several times. How about if I at least come with you?"

"I do not think that would work. We are the same age. Anyway, what is it they say, 'Three is a crowd'."

"What're you going to do? You don't really know him."

"I do not think it can do any harm. I will make sure he does not get over friendly."

"But what would your parents say?"

"They trusted me enough to let me come without a chaperone. And, as I said, to make the right decisions."

"But I'm sure they never thought you'd go out with a man on your own."

"Have you decided?" A couple of days later, in the academy's foyer.

"It is difficult. My family would expect me to be chaperoned."

"You can trust me. I'd never do anything to embarrass you."

"But what if someone who knows me and my family saw us? I am not sure."

"I'll ensure there's always an appropriate space between us. You can trust me. I promise."

"Well, yes, you do strike me as trustworthy." She wondered if she really believed that or was she just being influenced by his good looks and pleasant manner.

"What's it to be then?"

"Oh, why does life have to be so difficult?"

"I promise to be on my best behaviour. Honestly." She could not help but smile at his pleading sincerity.

"Well, um, all right."

"Good. How about Tuesday?" A beam of satisfaction brightening his features.

"Yes. That will be fine."

"Good! I'm glad. I'll pick you up at seven."

She felt that little shiver of excitement again as she watched him approach across the piazza. His confident stride, six-foot frame and glistening dark hair made him stand out. How wonderful he looked compared to the classical figures which adorned the ornamental fountain he was passing. As he drew nearer, she wondered why he affected her so much. More than any boy or man she had ever seen or known. They really did not even know each other. But there was something about him. And not just his good looks or those wonderful eyes. She noticed how several of the ladies glanced back after passing him.

"Hello. I'm glad you're here. I thought you may've changed your mind."

"Oh no. When I say I will do something, I do it. I do not believe it is right to mislead or let people down."

"Well, I'm very pleased to know it. There's a nice little café I know just round the corner. Shall we go?"

"All right."

"Here we are. Do you like it?" A quaint bay windowed building looking a little incongruous amongst the surrounding elegant Viennese architecture stood before them. On the window shelf, between the tied back green and white curtains, stood a selection of mouth-watering pastries.

"Yes. It looks a sweet little place, cosy and friendly."

"I found it soon after arriving in the city. It's now one of my regular haunts." The babel from many conversations struck them as he opened the door for her. She noticed a few raise their heads and give him a nod of recognition. Their gaze then fell on her for a few moments before reengaging with their companions. It was obvious the man standing beside her was very popular. Several of the women, however, were evidently not pleased to see her, their eyes penetrating into her like some oversized corkscrew. With a smile, she acknowledged those who greeted them, having decided it was best to ignore the sharp looks.

"I can see why. Looks like quite a few of your fellow students come here."

"Yes. Not only do you get a great cup of coffee, but their snacks are also really tasty and reasonable. And they make absolutely gorgeous cakes." They made their way to a small vacant table set in a corner between the side wall and bay window.

"It really is cosy."

"What would you like?" The aroma of freshly brewed coffee and warm sweet pastry had set her taste buds going.

"A cup of coffee and a small pastry would be nice, please." They spent the short time waiting for their coffees, looking round. It was obviously a popular place with students. They fitted in just fine.

"We haven't been properly introduced. I know it goes against protocol, but I think I've no option but to introduce myself."

"Yes, I have to admit this does feel a little strange."

"Are you sure you're okay without a chaperone? I know how some families consider it important for girls to be escorted."

"I am. I would not have come out with you otherwise. But I cannot help feeling a bit odd. This is the first time I have been out with a boy, sorry man, on my own."

"Let me assure you I will be on my best behaviour."

"Thank you."

"Well, I'm Richard Palmerstone. I'm here in Vienna studying to be a doctor."

"I am pleased to meet you Mr Palmerstone. I am Katherine Brampton and I am here studying to be a qualified nurse."

"Ah, that's good. Why did you choose Vienna, Miss Brampton?"

"My father studied here and thinks very highly of the place. He wanted me to have the best possible training."

"Yes, it can't be argued Vienna has the best medical academies there are. That's why I came here, with my parents' support of course."

"What made you want to be a doctor?"

"There's so little medical care back home and I frequently see people suffering when I don't think they have to. I wanted to try and do something about that.

Why nursing?" He cocked his head to the left as he asked. She thought it such a cute mannerism.

"As I said, father is medically trained and does what he can to help the less well off. Mother is experienced in the old family remedies and between them they try to provide as much care as they can for villagers. I hate seeing how so many of them suffer and, like you, want to do something to help."

"We've much in common then."

"Yes, I suppose we have." His broad, warm smile sent another tingling sensation through her.

"Where do you come from, Mr Palmerstone?"

"I don't expect you'll have heard of it. It's a small village in the southern regions of my country where we've most of our estates. It's called Farringdon Oaks."

"Farringdon Oaks! Is it high up the side of a mountain overlooking the Lucas Valley?"

"Yes. How'd you know?"

"This is amazing. How small the world can be at times."

"What do you mean?"

"My ancestral home is at Cross Oaks."

"Not the Cross Oaks in the foothills of the same valley?"

"Yes. We are almost neighbours."

"You are joking. It cannot be. You mean we are the same nationality?"

"No, I am not joking. And yes we are. My ancestral home is in the same Lucas Valley."

"What a surprise. Our villages are no more than a mile apart as the crow flies."

"I know."

"Well, I never. How come I've never seen you before?"

"I do not suppose you come to our village often, if at all, and we rarely have occasion to come up to yours."

"But surely we should've seen each other in town. It's not that large."

"Just one of those things." As they chatted about the various places and people they each knew back home, Katherine felt pleased and relieved. Richard was not only of the same nationality, but also from a similar family background. He would therefore be familiar with their traditions and the social etiquette expected. Consequently, there should be no misunderstanding about what behaviour was and was not acceptable. Nevertheless, she ensured, despite the temptation, there was no inappropriate physical contact.

"Thank you for coming. I really enjoyed the evening." Walking through the quiet lamp lit lanes as he escorted her back to her lodgings.

"Yes, I also enjoyed it. Thank you for asking me and for taking me to that nice café."

"My pleasure, I assure you. May I take you out again sometime?"

"Oh! I am not sure that would be appropriate. Once will probably be frowned upon, but we may get away with it. More than once, however, would be considered scandalous by many. After all, I am on my own without a chaperone."

"You didn't come to any harm this evening, did you?"

"No." She smiled within herself. Richard had behaved immaculately. The perfect gentleman in all ways.

"Well?" She had to admit she liked him and would love to see him again. He had been such good, intelligent company. What was she to do?

"Well, we are in a lively city where society is so different. I suppose it would not do any harm. And I did enjoy the evening." She could not help but tremble slightly at the thought of what her parents might say.

"Okay then. How about Saturday? There's usually all sorts of entertainment in the park on Saturdays."

"That sounds nice...... All right."

"Katherine!"

"I know, I know. But he is so nice. He was the perfect gentleman all the time. Not once did he try anything inappropriate. Anyway, as you said yourself, this is a cosmopolitan city with a very different outlook on life."

"Perhaps but.... If anyone back home were to find out, you'd be in serious trouble with your family. Not to mention the old biddies. Some of them would even ostracise you."

"I know, but it all seems so small-minded. Would you not agree?"

"Maybe, but that's how things are, for now anyway."

"Did you hear about those women in America who started having meetings a few years ago? They are trying to get the vote. Apparently, there were three hundred at the first meeting. Even though it has been difficult, they have continued with more joining them each year. As we know, it is hard for women to change attitudes, but they are clearly determined to carry on until they succeed. Why should we not try and change those things that are unfair to us?"

"I'm not sure our society, or your family, are ready for that yet."

"I suppose not." Feeling a little deflated by the truth of Jenifer's statement. "I do love my family and our people, and the last thing I want to do is hurt or embarrass anyone. But we are here in Vienna now and they cannot see. What is that saying? 'What the eye does not see, the heart cannot grieve over', or something like that."

"You're quite determined, aren't you?"

"Yes, I think I am. I have never met anyone like Richard before."

"But that's it. You have only just met. You hardly know each other."

"It does not make sense, I know. Yet, there is something about him."

"Yea, I know. Good looking, wonderful eyes. Blah! Blah! Blah! Ah!"

"No, well, yes, but it is far more than that. It is hard to explain. He has such an open face, is polite and intelligent. Anyway, he was brought up in the same society as us and understands the constraints and demands."

"I give up! I just hope no one from back home is here. There'd be no end to it if you were seen." Secretly, Katherine still had her doubts about the appropriateness of her behaviour. Nevertheless, she allowed her attraction to Richard to overrule her usually sensible head. She was going to see him and that was that. Well, at least for now. The Saturday proved as enjoyable as he said it would.

"You're seeing an awful lot of him." This was some weeks later.

"Just two or three times a week." She could not help her defensive reaction. Though she would never admit it openly, she felt as if she were sinning. And yet!

"Are you falling in love?"

"No! Of course not. We are simply friends. He really is good company and we have such pleasant times together. And I enjoy being able to discuss almost anything in an intelligent manner. He has such a wealth of knowledge and a broad range of interests. It is quite refreshing. And he treats me as an equal."

"Oh, thank you. So you can't have an intelligent discussion with me? Anyway, are you sure that's all there is? I've seen how you look at him. And you hardly ever stop talking about him these days."

"I am sorry. I did not mean we could not have sensible conversations, of course we can and do. I like him as a friend, but that is all there is."

"I'm not so sure." She also wondered whether there was more to it. Every time she saw him her heart leapt a little and there was always that tiny little shiver down her spine. But surely she could not be falling in love. They had only known each other for such a short time. Anyway, what is falling in love? In truth, she frequently felt drawn into him and as if she were being submerged within the golden haze of those wonderful eyes. To her bewilderment, she also found she longed to kiss that manly mouth. These feelings shocked and confused her. What would her parents and people generally say if they could see into her thoughts?

Richard, for his part, had always enjoyed the female attention he attracted. In fact, he relished in it. He always wanted to make love to them, though it was usually a passing sensation that only lasted while they were in front of him. Nevertheless, there were times when he enjoyed a chase provided it was not prolonged, and especially when he was victorious. But now he found himself attracted to a woman in a very different way. There was something about her that excited but also unsettled him. Though, out of respect for her and himself, he would never admit it, he desperately desired to kiss those delicate lips. Excitement arose within every time he considered the prospect. He wondered if he could or would be able to cope with only having a 'friendship' with this lovely, captivating woman. He doubted it. Something would break in the end. But he feared ruining what they had and the possibility of losing her altogether. How did she feel about him? There were times he was sure he saw more in her eyes, but then at other times there seemed to be a reserve. He had little idea of the struggle and turmoil occurring in Katherine's own heart.

2

Spirit Talk

"I won't be able to meet you in the evenings this week. We've a midterm exam coming up, so a few of us are getting together to prepare for it."

"I quite understand."

"How about having lunch with me instead?"

"Yes, all right. I would like that."

"Tomorrow?"

"It will have to be somewhere nearby. I have a late lecture in the morning."

"That'll suit me. I'm attending an autopsy in the afternoon and the pathologist wants to start early."

"Where do you suggest?"

"Meet me by the K. K. Hoftheater as soon as you're free. There's a little place I know close by."

As Katherine approached the splendid building, she wondered why so many women had gathered by the corner at this time of day. The opera usually only gave evening performances. They appeared to be jostling each other to gain a better view of something. Then she noticed the dark shiny head of hair that overreached them all by a few inches. Could it be? Through a momentary gap, she spotted Richard. He was leaning in his provocative manner with one foot bent up behind him against the wall and his hips thrust slightly forward. Smiling his broad smile all round, he was clearly enjoying the attention. She could even see the twinkle in his eyes, though she was still on the other side of the piazza. The sudden spasm of jealousy surprised her. What right did she have to be jealous? They were just friends. There had been nothing to indicate otherwise. Or had there been? The way he looked at her at times made her certain there was more. Yet nothing had ever been said. Besides, he was always flirting and seemed to know several women intimately. More intimately than he knew her for sure. Her own emotions still confused her. Did she simply enjoy his company as a friend? Or, dare she even think it, were her feelings for him deepening to something more substantial? No, she had no rights with respect to him. They were just friends! Imperceptibly shaking herself, she strode out into the piazza and headed for the enthralled group.

She was halfway across the piazza when Richard looked up. As usual, he felt the sudden surge that passed through him every time Katherine filled his sightline. Here she was looking the picture of beauty she always did. Taking his eyes off her for a moment, he looked round the circle of hopeful faces but, for him, there wasn't one to compare. Yes, they were pretty and under other circumstances he'd not have hesitated. But things were different now. Quickly pushing himself from the wall, he straitened and moved out from the group, though they were reluctant to let him pass. As he did so, they turned to see what had caught his attention. A cloud of envy, jealousy and bitterness passed across each face and the corners of their mouths took a downward turn. But he no longer noticed them.

His sudden movement and unusually nervous smile gave her the impression of someone with a sense of guilt. Nonsense, it was her imagination. What did he have to feel guilty about?

"Hello. Hum. I was just chatting to some fellow students." Was that a blush?

"So I see. Quite a gathering. Are they also studying to be doctors?"

"Um... No. Just seen them round the academy."

"I see." She allowed the teasing, wicked smile to cross her features, enjoying his apparent discomfort.

"Yes... Well. How was your lecture?"

"Tropical diseases. There is a visiting professor from Africa who has considerable experience with them."

"Don't expect you'll come across many back home. But never hurts to have some knowledge. Right, the place I'm taking you is just across the street."

During the meal, she relented and surreptitiously allowed Richard's awkwardness to pass. By the end of it, they were laughing together.

"Why don't you come with us?"

"I am not sure. I do not think my priest would like it."

"Go on, Miss Brampton. It can't do any harm."

"But a séance. It seems wrong. We're not supposed to try and contact the dead."

"It'll be fun. As I said, there's a group of us going."

"I do not know."

"It's not as if we're going to sit round a table holding hands. The medium will be on stage while we sit in the audience. It's more of a show, really. Be like seeing a play."

"Give me time. I need to think about it." She was feeling torn between her childhood teaching and her trust of Richard.

"Okay, but it's in a few days. You'll have to make your mind up pretty quickly."

"I know. Please just let me think about it. I will let you know in plenty of time."

"You're joking! You can't be serious?" Jennifer was more than a little taken aback by the idea.

"Richard says it is really just a show, not a proper séance. We will not be sitting round a table holding hands or anything like that. I would not think of going if it was."

"I think you're pushing your luck. Back home they wouldn't be very happy that you've been out with him so many times already but a séance or whatever you want to call it. They'd be horrified."

"Yes, I know you are right. But I trust his judgements and I do not want to upset him."

"I thought you wanted women to be on an equal footing. Whether it would upset him or not shouldn't come into it."

"You know what I mean."

"Yes, and better than you think."

"What do you mean?"

"For all your denial, I think you've fallen for him. You're certainly captivated. Or are you going to tell me it's just an infatuation?"

"Well, no, I suppose not. I really do like him."

"And how does he feel about you? Are you hoping he's going to ask you to be his wife?"

"No! Maybe. Oh! I do not know. You are confusing me."

"Am I!"

"Never mind that now. What shall I do about Thursday?"

"You know what I think. But that won't make any difference. You're going to have to decide for yourself."

"I think you like him too. Do you think he is trustworthy?"

"Yes, I do like him. And yes, I think he can be trusted. But he also has a bit of a wild side and enjoys taking occasional chances."

"That is part of his attraction. He loves to live life to the full. And he has an enquiring mind."

"Just be sure, in yourself, before you do anything. You must make your own decisions and not let him make them for you."

"Are you sure it will be all right, Mr Palmerstone? I am still nervous about going to something like that."

"It'll be no different than going to a fairground fortune teller. It's just a bit of fun, nothing really."

"We are not supposed to go to them either. I do not think my parents or our priest would approve."

"Oh, come on. I don't believe there's anything in it. I certainly don't believe in spirits or ghosts. It's just a bit of entertaining nonsense."

"Well, if you are sure it is all right and safe."

"I am. So will you come?"

"All right, yes I will." Still feeling torn. All her life she had been taught to trust completely in God and the church and not to seek spiritual information or guidance elsewhere. In particular, they were not supposed to try and find out about the future. But at the same time, she had to admit she was intrigued.

"Good. By the way, please call me Richard. I get fed up with all this formalism."

"Oh! Well, I suppose it will be all right when we are alone. You can call me Katherine. But when we are in public, I think we better stick to convention. People would not understand."

"Okay, that sounds fair.... Katherine. Ha! Ha!"

As they walked across the piazza, Katherine could not help but admire the beautiful buildings. The tall classical style pillars supporting the entrances always impressed her, no matter how many times she saw them. And the general architecture of the city continually thrilled and delighted. There were no buildings like these back home in the village or in the little provincial town that served them. Prior to Vienna, their church had been the largest construction she had ever seen. When they reached the other side, Richard turned to the right and led her down a shadowy little side street. The steadily darkening evening accentuating her already uncertain nervous condition caused her to feel vulnerable. She was still unsure if she was doing the right thing. The need for reassurance and a sense of safety led her, without having actual physical contact, to draw as close to Richard as she could. Thankfully, he had agreed they must always behave as if a chaperone were constantly present. This was a large city to which many of their fellow countrymen came to study. They could never be sure who was observing them. Though evidently irritated by it all, he complied because he knew her reputation could otherwise be seriously compromised. He didn't want that. Neither did he want to behave in an untoward manner, though he craved intimacy. It was all so frustrating. Unbeknown to him, Katherine also secretly desired the same. She longed to embrace and hold him close. To feel the warmth and vibration of his body against hers. At long last, she admitted, to herself at least, the love she had for the man beside her. He cared for her also, she was sure. But to what extent?

That was a question in need of an answer. She would have to wait. What if she was wrong? The thought was too disheartening, so she pushed it to the back of her mind.

"Here we are." Richard stopped outside a small building with a simple portico entranceway. It was set back slightly from the street.

"I had no idea this was here."

"Few people do. They tend to only have specialised events and shows here."

"How come you know about it?"

"Anthony Howard, one of my friends, has an interest in psychic phenomena. In fact, he and some other friends research the subject."

"Is that part of their degree?"

"Not really. Most of them are studying medicine of one type or the other. That's how I got to know them. Some of them reckon people's psyche plays a bigger part in their health than we realise. They therefore decided to research more fully. Going to things like this is part of that."

Entering the vestibule, both were taken aback by how many people were milling about.

"Goodness, I had no idea so many people are interested in séances and such things."

"Yes, it's surprising. But then we're in a scientifically orientated city. Good, there's Anthony. He's got our tickets. And there's Andrew. They're my two best friends." Richard led her over to where a short, sandy-haired man was chatting with some other people.

"Hi Anthony."

"Oh hi. You made it then."

"Yes. I'd like you to meet Miss Katherine Brampton. Mr Anthony Howard Miss Brampton. Mr Andrew Reece Miss Brampton. Miss Brampton, Mr Anthony Howard and Mr Andrew Reece." Richard couldn't help but smile at the formality of his introductions.

"Good evening Miss Brampton, I understand you were hesitant about coming."

"Good evening Mr Howard. Yes, I was and to be quite honest, I am still unsure. Back home we are told not to involve ourselves with such things."

"Don't worry, you'll be okay. There's nothing really too serious in it. Allow me to introduce some friends. Mr Mark Augustine, Mr Rick, sorry Richard Stroud. It was confusing having the two of them, so Mr Stroud kindly agreed to being called Rick. Mr Charles Regal, Miss Antoinette Schultz, Miss Margarita Fontan, Miss Isabel Doner."

"Good evening gentlemen. Good evening ladies."

"Good evening Miss Brampton." The men smiled and bowed while the ladies made their customary little bobs. She could not help but notice the latter were less warm in their responses and held her with their unsmiling eyes. As usual, Richard had greeted each of the ladies with a fixed look directly into their eyes. When the formalities were over, the ladies manoeuvred so as to shoulder her out of the way, effectively creating a barrier between her and Richard.

"I think we better go in and find our seats before the crowd." Anthony, smiling at the ladies' slight coolness, had decided to break the moment.

The theatre was medium-sized and looked as if it could seat one to two hundred people. Much to their surprise, despite the crowd still gathered outside, it was already quite full.

"We're in the stalls." Anthony led the way forward. "Here's our row. Please excuse us." As those already sat got up to let them pass.

"These are nice seats. Whenever I do manage to go to the theatre, I cannot afford the stalls. I usually end up in the gods or at best, to the rear of the upper circle." Despite her uncertainty about the whole affair, Katherine was pleased they would be able to see everything clearly.

"Anthony knows the organisers and often brings friends, so they give him a discount. Don't they?"

"Yes. I think we know far too little about our psyche, so I like to take every opportunity to learn more. Even things like this, which aren't really that serious, have the ability to teach us something. Even if it's just about people's superstitions, hopes and fears."

"Is it me or is there an aroma of hot bread and something else?" Katherine asked, doubting her sense of smell.

"No, it's not you. Mediums believe having hot bread and warm soup, or something similar, in the room attracts the spirits. I've never quite followed that as surely a spirit, if they really exist, would be past eating and drinking. But they believe it so always have something about."

"I find this talk of spirits unsettling. I am still not sure I should really be here."

"Come, Miss Brampton. There's no need to worry so. It's just a bit of fun." Richard tried to reassure her.

"Are you sure, Mr Palmerstone?"

"Yes I am. Don't you agree Anthony?"

"Yes. I've never really seen anything that I'd call real, and I've been to a lot of these séances. It's usually just things like someone's grandma wants to say hello and that she's happy where she is. It's so nebulous that it could be anyone's grandma or whatever. I sometimes think it's just the medium's overactive imagination."

"All right, as long as you are both sure."

Katherine settled, and looking round, took in her surroundings. The plush red velvet seats were filling up steadily with groups of people chatting and laughing together. No one appeared troubled or nervous. She wondered if she were being silly, but it was hard going against all she had been taught. Above her head, the ornate gilded balconies with their carved garlands and cherubs glinted in the soft lighting. On the open stage, a large elaborately decorated wood carved chair occupied the centre. The carved images of griffins and eagles, combined with symbols she did not recognise, shone in the candlelight. To either side, set slightly back, were two tables. She could see a loaf of bread on one with a dish next to it. From the rising steam, she surmised this must contain the soup Anthony had mentioned. A variety of different sized candles covered the other table. As the flames wavered in an unseen breeze, she saw thin trails of smoke rise into the dark overhead. The gentle light-hearted ambience together with the cheerful audience relaxed her, and she wondered, with some anticipation, what would happen. As these thoughts were passing through her mind, a small, brown-haired man walked on to the stage. Stopping slightly left of centre, he raised both hands as if surrendering to some highway robber. As the lights slowly dimmed, he angled both his palms to the floor and gently lowered them, as if pressing down on a suitcase that would not close. The audience steadily quietened until there was complete silence.

"Good evening ladies and gentleman and welcome. It is a pleasure to have you with us tonight." Some light applause followed. He bowed in acknowledgment and again indicated for quietness.

"Who is he?" Katherine whispered.

"The medium's assistant."

"Please welcome Alphonso Rygard." Applause erupted as a tall, thin, dark-haired man walked on to the stage. Katherine sensed a cool draught passing through the theatre but upon looking round could not see any open doors or windows. Dressed in a plain black but fashionable suit, Alphonso Rygard momentarily stopped to acknowledge the welcome and then went and sat in the chair. Bowing his head, he seemed to become oblivious to all round him.

"He's the medium." Richard whispered loudly above the applause.

"Now ladies and gentleman if we may have quiet again we will pray." The brown-haired assistant was speaking again. He bent his head and Katherine noticed how many in the audience did likewise. Normally, when in church, she would not think twice about also bending hers when the priest prayed, but here it was so strange and different and nothing like being in church.

"Beloved spirits, we bring you gifts from life into death. Be pleased to move among us and to commune with us. We open our hearts and minds to receive your wisdom." A cool shiver passed down her spine as she listened to this intonation.

The lights appeared to dim further as what appeared to be a shadow passed before them.

"What was that?" Whispered.

"What?" Richard whispered back.

"Something passed in front of the lights."

"I didn't see anything. Must be your imagination. You still feeling nervous?"

"I am sure I saw something." But had she? Was she being hypersensitive? Was it just her imagination?

"Just try and relax. There's nothing to worry about."

Alphonso Rygard, sitting with his head bowed, appeared to pass slowly into a trance. When the assistant finished his prayer, he moved to the candle table. She noticed his left-hand jerk slightly. The sudden flash and bright fiery sparks which leapt from a small dish on the table made her jump. A sweet scent pervaded the atmosphere, subduing the aroma of the bread and soup. Then the faint sound of relaxing soft music filled the air. She was starting to feel calmer when a deep groan emitting from Alphonso Rygard made her start.

"Who is there? Say your name." Speaking in a deep breathless tone, he remained sitting with eyes closed and head cocked to his left. He appeared to be listening to someone or something the rest of them could not hear. "Welcome Marbela. Do you have a message for anyone?" Silence followed for a couple of minutes. Everyone in the theatre seemed to hold their breath. "What is that? The letter R?" Alphonso still keeping his eyes closed, straitened his head and faced straight into the audience. "Is there anyone with the initial R?" Katherine glanced sideways at Richard. No one moved. Several seconds passed. Then a young man near the back stood up.

"Yes. My name is Rodrigues."

"Your grandmother wants to tell you she is happy where she is and not to be sad." Katherine saw an expression of relief cross the man's face and tears sparkle in his eyes. "What is that?" Alphonso asked, again with head cocked and eyes closed.

"Is there a young lady whose name begins with A?" This time a woman sitting two rows in front stood.

"Yes..." Her voice barely above a whisper.

"Someone you loved dearly passed over recently."

"Yes, my mother." Her soft voice filled with emotion.

"She wants you to know there is no more suffering for her now. That she is at peace. And she wants you to be happy and not to grieve for her." The woman's friends reached up to hold her as she dissolved into floods of tears.

"Someone is facing an exam they are terrified of failing." Katherine was beginning to feel a little cynical. In such a large crowd, there was every chance there would be people whose names began with R or A or almost any other letter of the alphabet. It was also highly likely there would have been some family deaths among them. Now, in a city full of students, he could hardly go wrong with this mention of exams. But much to her surprise, only one person responded.

"That's me!" A very young pale-faced boy had leapt out of his seat. He looked like a first-year student.

"Do not fear. The spirits are with you. You have the ability to pass."

"Thank you. Thank you." The boy could barely control his shaking as he breathlessly responded.

"K? Yes, yes K. Is there a young woman with the initial K?" Katherine looked round to see who would respond. No one moved. "K, there is someone here with the initial K." Again, no one moved. Katherine was now in turmoil. She was sure it could not be her. Richard and Anthony both turned and focused on her. She longed for someone to stand. She did not want to be part of this.

"Yes." She found herself involuntarily rising out of her seat.

"What is that Marbela?" Alphonso again put his head on one side and appeared to be listening intently. "Marbela says you have a kind heart, but you must take care. At some stage in your life, you are going to be close to a family where there is death and sorrow. You will be tempted to give more assistance than is due.

Marbela says you should not. If you do, you will regret it for the rest of your life. Take heed and do not treat this warning lightly."

Katherine sat down heavily and neither saw nor heard anything more. Her head was in a fog, and confused thoughts paraded through her mind. Was this really a message for her? Did spirits really exist? If so, could they really talk to people? What family? Whose death and sorrow? What regret? Was this just some sort of game? Was any of this real? Was it all a dream? She slowly emerged from the mist as something touched her hand. Shaking her head in an attempt to clear the fog, she found herself looking straight into Richard's wondrous golden eyes. He looked concerned. She then noticed he was holding her hand. The sensation of his flesh against hers was delightful, but it would never do. She quickly moved her hand away.

"What happened? I feel a bit lightheaded."

"We were worried. We thought you'd passed out."

"Nonsense. I never faint."

"But you didn't seem to know we were here. Neither did you appear to hear us."

"Oh! It felt as if a mist surrounded me for a while. Anyway, what is happening?"

"Are you sure you're okay?"

"Yes, I am fine." She was beginning to feel irritable. What had happened?

"Okay. The meeting is about to come to an end."

"Did anyone else receive a message or whatever you call them?"

"A few. Someone is going to have an unexpected journey. Another's father told him all is well and to get on with living his life. Then one of the men was asked to look after the family. There was even one saying a pet dog was enjoying romps in heavenly grass."

"Oh!" Katherine wondered why she had not heard any of those messages.

"Well, it's all over now. Let's go for a coffee. Coming Anthony?"

"Yea, okay." They joined the departing throng. The earlier confusion of multiple conversations returned, along with the raised lighting.

"Well, that was unexpected." They were sitting at one of the cosy corner tables in the café.

"What do you mean?"

"The last thing I expected was for one of us to receive a message."

"Do you really think it is at all real? Anyone could have made those things up. No offence meant Mr Howard. We are in a city full of students of all ages, so there are bound to have been family deaths somewhere. And it goes without saying some will be worried about exams."

"Agreed, but he was rather specific about people's names." Anthony replied a little defensively.

"With so many people, what are the chances of there not being someone whose name begins with an A or R or K?"

"Point taken, but did you notice only one person responded each time? They knew it was them."

"I did not."

"Didn't you? Why did you stand up?"

"I am not sure. Perhaps because no one else did. Perhaps I felt I should help the man out and not allow him to be embarrassed."

"Was that really why you stood?"

"Maybe it is mass hypnotism."

"Now who is being farfetched?"

"Oh, I do not know. But I can say I did not like it. It all felt so wrong."

"What about your message? What do you think it means?"

"Nothing. It is fairly safe to say to anyone they will, at some stage in their life, know a family where there is death and sorrow. All of us will have to face that at some time within our own families. No, it means nothing. Just a party trick, if you ask me, but on a larger scale. Anyway, I did not like it."

"I said it'd just be a bit of fun." Richard was eyeing her carefully.

"It is all right, Mr Palmerstone. I am not cross. After all, I did not have to go with you. It was my choice. But I do not think I will ever go to one of those things again."

Back in her lodgings, Katherine could not help but think back to what had been said to her. It must all be nonsense. There could be nothing in it. Just some sort of party game. Another way to get people to part with their money. A con, that is what it was. But the doubts pervaded. What if there is any truth in it? How would she know? Best forget it.

3

Knights Serpent

Again she felt that slight but pleasant constriction in her breast as she watched this handsome man walk toward her. Since meeting him, she had experienced sensations previously unknown. They confused and unsettled her, but not unpleasantly. Yet at the same time, she felt she was being ridiculous and inwardly scolded herself for behaving like a silly schoolgirl. But then he was so different, so special. To find intelligence, an inquiring mind, humour and a zest for life together with gentleness and yet manly strength within one handsome man was a new experience. Up to now, the majority of men she had met only displayed, in part, if at all, one or two of these attributes at most.

"Hi, you're looking lovely this evening." She had intentionally worn the green brocade dress that complemented her colouring and set off her features to advantage. He had that mischievous sparkle in his eye.

"Oh! Thank you." Though his familiar tone was a breach of etiquette, it pleased her. She had been aware of the boys back home looking whenever she passed but had never come across such direct, unashamed flirtation before. She had to admit she liked it, even though it made her feel quite wanton. Not an entirely unpleasant sensation. Was she a wicked woman? Was she condemning herself? What would her priest or parents say if they knew? Did it really matter? What was happening to her? She had never been like this before.

"Where would you like to go this evening?"

"Could we go for a stroll? It is such a lovely evening."

"Of course. Would you like to join the evening promenade?"

"That would be fun. I enjoy watching the gentleman and ladies parading in their finery."

"Bit of nonsense if you ask me, everyone showing off like that."

"But it is a good way for people to meet, though they rarely speak. I am told it helps to have seen each other when introduced at balls and dinner parties."

"Well, I don't suppose we're going to be invited to any. We're just visiting students as far as they're concerned. Of no consequence."

"Even so, I enjoy watching." They made their way to the piazza and joined the colourful throng strolling round its perimeter.

"Ronaldo has invited me to a meeting of the Knights Serpent."

"Who?"

"Ronaldo Bettichelli, he lodges in the same house as me."

"What is Knights Serpent?"

"I don't really know. I think it's some sort of philanthropic society where professionals get together."

"What for?"

"Again I'm not sure. But Ronaldo, he's a member, reckons it'd be good for me to go. He thinks I might find useful contacts among them."

"How do you mean?"

"Ronaldo qualified a couple of years ago, but decided to stay here in Vienna instead of returning to his home. He has a position with one of the city's most respected doctors. He reckons the contacts his employer has within Knights Serpent helped establish the practice in the first place and now to maintain it. Some of the most prestigious people in the country go to him. Ronaldo thinks this would have been unlikely without Knights Serpent." Richard's enthusiasm visibly increased as he spoke.

"Why have I never heard of them? If they are that involved with doctors, I would have expected to hear something of them at the academy."

"Apparently, they're a bit secretive about what they do."

"Why?"

"I don't know. It's a bit odd. Every time I ask for any details, Ronaldo puts me off. He says they're not really supposed to talk about it to non-members. The only thing he would say is that they help a lot of people. Perhaps they prefer their charity to be anonymous."

"Perhaps, but how can you possibly know if you would be interested in meeting them unless someone tells you what they do?"

"Well, that's just it. He wants me to go with him to an open meeting. I say open but in fact no one can go unless they are invited by a member. Apparently, the idea is to give those whom might be considered suitable for membership an insight. He tells me I am not even supposed to mention the invitation to anyone, friends, family or colleagues."

"So you should not be telling me."

"Not really. But then I think it's all nonsense, all the secrecy. What harm can it do?"

"I assume, from what you just said, he considers you may be a suitable candidate."

"I suppose so."

"Are you going?"

"I think I might. It wouldn't hurt to have a look."

"Well, take care. I have heard some of these secret societies can be very strange. Some are even rumoured to indulge in occult practices."

"That's just gossip. I'm sure Ronaldo wouldn't be involved in anything like that."

"Well, just take care. Over the years, it has been said that some of the most highly respected and influential men have been participants in such things. And that they will do anything to hide their involvement and their secrets."

"Well, I'll just have to wait and see."

"When is the meeting?"

"In a couple of days, I think." Continuing their promenade whilst chatting about lectures, professors, friends and fellow students, Katherine could not help but notice Richard's behaviour. How he tended to straighten himself to full height whenever one of the young ladies glanced in his direction. Not that he was hunched or ever slouched. Or how he followed the pretty ones with his eyes. She was coming to realise he was a bit of a flirt and loved the attention. Yet, he was not really vain. He just loved life. Neither did she ever have cause to feel neglected. He always paid her due attention, never appearing to notice the cold, hostile, jealous looks bestowed upon her.

~~~~~~~~

"I'm afraid you'll have to be blindfolded."

"What on earth for?" Richard was less than amused by the idea.

"Our meeting places are private. Only members may know where they are."

"How odd."

"That's the way it is. Okay?"

"Okay, if you must." Allowing Ronaldo to place the thick black blindfold across his eyes, noticing how he ensured it was firmly tied at the back of his head. He didn't like the sensation of vulnerability it gave him.

"Hold my elbow so I may lead you."

"This is stupid."

"It's the only way. You are interested, aren't you?"

"Yes. But I never thought I'd have to go through something so ridiculous."

"It won't take long. Just keep hold of my arm. I'll let you know when there are any steps, low beams, or other obstacles."

It seemed they had walked for ever before Ronaldo stopped and removed the blindfold. He had to blink a few times to regain focus. As his vision slowly cleared he looked about, taking in the surroundings. The height of the pillar supported ceiling surprised him, as did the vastness of the chamber they were standing in. Its elegance and opulence surpassed anything he had seen even compared with the large ornate lecture halls and rooms of the academies. The ceiling was
~~~~~~~~

intricately painted with all sorts of images and symbols. Some he recognised as being scripture based. Others depicted folk lore. In between and round the perimeter, a variety of symbols and geometric tools had been painted in. He even spotted a pentagon. Almost subconsciously, he looked for additional occult imagery, anticipating perhaps a goat's horned head, a sacrificed sheep, or other such indications of the dark arts. The conversation with Katherine had obviously stirred up his inner thoughts and imagination. The high walls were adorned with huge paintings. He was no artist, but thought they looked like masterpieces. Between these hung a series of rich tapestries, all reflecting topics similar to those he'd noticed on the ceiling.

"What do you think?" He'd almost forgotten Ronaldo.

"Oh, well, wow! That's quite a collection." He couldn't take his eyes from the splendour on display.

"It's been built up over years. That's not all of it either."

"No! Where's the rest?"

"Spread across a variety of buildings the society owns." He'd been so engrossed with his observations he hadn't, up to this point, really registered the noise. This break in concentration now made him aware of it. Lowering his eyes from the arrayed wonders, he registered the vast gathering. Throughout the chamber, he noted men gathered in groups of varying size, all talking. He reckoned there to be at least a couple of hundred.

"Who are all these people?"

"Members and guests for the evening."

"I hadn't expected to see so many."

"We have a large following."

"Clearly. I'd no idea."

"As I said, we don't talk about ourselves very much in public."

"Gentlemen! Gentlemen!" A commanding voice echoed from the front of the room.

"Come with me. We must find our seats. The meeting's about to begin."

"Who's that?"

"He's the second master. Master of ceremonies if you like. He's calling us to order before the grandmaster comes in." They found their seats a few rows from the back, sat and waited. The din of voices slowly dissipated until there was almost total silence.

"Please be upstanding!" Two ushers dressed in black trousers, white shirts and with small white aprons tied round their waists opened a set of large ornate doors on the left. A silver-headed man of about six feet and wearing an exquisite gold and silver embroidered cloak came striding through. Everyone immediately stood. Ronaldo indicated he should do the same. Without glancing to left or right, the black cloaked man marched to the front, turned, bowed to the assembled audience and then sat in a large gilt adorned chair. The rest of the assembly followed suit.

A series of what appeared to be ceremonial greetings were then exchanged between him and men, who appeared to be dignitaries of one sort or another. Upon completion, he announced the meeting was now open to the floor. Various men stood, and either made reports about some event that had taken place or announced forthcoming celebrations, meetings or gatherings. As far as Richard could make out, these were all to do with some charitable event or other. He found it rather dull, so allowed his eyes to roam round the room. First, he tried to see if there was anyone he knew. Ah yes, there were one or two professors and a chancellor he recognised. There were also a couple of government officials and he was sure he recognised one from the royal household. Then he took in the rest of the room, which, due to his earlier distraction with the paintings and images, he hadn't noticed. At the front and perfectly in the centre was the gilt chair the grandmaster was occupying. Behind this stood a very large gilt adorned table. It reminded him of altars he'd seen in various cathedrals. Immediately above was one of the largest paintings he'd ever seen. It depicted a shepherd separating goats and lambs from each other. But, whereas in most similar paintings he'd seen, the lambs went to the right and goats to the left, this had the goats going to the right and the lambs to the left. It struck him as odd but did not give it a second thought. Perhaps he should have.

The next thing he was aware of was Ronaldo's elbow gently poking into his ribs. He'd drifted off into his thoughts. The jab refocused his attention and, seeing everyone was standing again, followed suit.

"Well, what do you think?"

"Not sure. It just seemed to be people reporting about successful charity events or forthcoming ones."

"Yes. We do raise a lot of money for various causes. It's one of our principal aims."

"I see. So it's principally a charitable institute?"

"Not entirely. There's a lot more to us than that. Amongst other things, we support and help each other in our various businesses, enterprises and vocations. Everyone is expected to reciprocate with their help whenever they can."

"So why all the secrecy?"

"There's more. But I can't tell you about that."

"Well, thank you for bringing me. There're obviously a lot of important and influential men here."

"Did you recognise anyone?"

"One or two."

"I'm sure I can trust you to keep their identities to yourself."

"If you wish. But in view of all the charitable work, wouldn't it help to be more open and public?"

"As I said, that's only part of what we're about. Anyway, the scriptures encourage us not to let the right hand know what the left is doing. Modesty, in other words. Publicity can actually have a detrimental impact upon charitable works."

"Very well. I'll not tell anyone else whom I've seen."

"Thank you. Now I'm afraid I'll have to blindfold you again."

"Really! This is such nonsense."

"I'm sorry, but it's necessary."

"As you wish." Richard permitted Ronaldo to blindfold him again and to lead him back out.

"Well, what was it like?"

"Who was there?"

"Was it interesting?"

"Did they have weird ceremonies?"

"Slow down. I'll tell you what I can in good time. Now I need a coffee and something to eat." As agreed, he'd joined Katherine, Anthony and Andrew in the café later the same evening. Much to their disappointment, he stood by his promise not to mention whom he'd recognised. After listening to his account of the evening's events, none of them could understand the need for secrecy. It did seem very odd.

4

Dark Matters

"You finish in a week or so, don't you?" Rolando asked as they walked toward the academy.

"Yes. We take our finals at the end of this week."

"Then what?"

"I'll be going home."

"Why not stay?"

"Father needs me to help with the family estates and business. He's been running them on his own for too long. But I must admit, I'm going to miss this intriguing city. There's so much going on. It's so different from home."

"You'll come back for a visit, won't you?"

"I hope so. Will have to wait and see."

"I'd be happy to find somewhere for you to stay. I hope we'll stay in contact."

"Thank you. Yes, me too."

"I've been talking with some friends from Knights Serpent. I understand you've really impressed your tutors. Apparently, they consider you to be one of the best students they've had for a very long time."

"Kind of them to say so. I don't think I'm anything special. Perhaps it's just I believe in studying hard and thankfully have a retentive memory."

"No, it's far more than that. In fact, it's been suggested you may like to become a member of Knights Serpent. What do you say?"

"Oh! Never crossed my mind."

"You enjoyed the public meeting, didn't you?"

"It was interesting." He didn't want to upset Ronaldo by saying how boring he found it. "I was impressed by the amount of charitable work they do." Which was true.

"Well? What about it?"

"Would seem pointless. I'm about to leave Vienna for what may be good. I can't see I'd be of any benefit to them."

"The society isn't just limited to this city. There're branches all over the world. I'm sure there'll be one near you."

"I've never heard of any such society in our district."

"As I said, we prefer to keep a low profile, so it's unlikely you would've. And until now, there'd have been no point in telling you."

"I see."

"Membership could be advantageous. Not only with your medical practice but also with the family business. You may find new avenues of trade opening up for you. Members look after each other."

"I'll admit it would be useful to extend our circle of contacts."

"Well, there you go. I've been authorised to propose you formally at the next gathering. What do you say?"

"Well, this is a surprise. Seriously though, I'd never given the idea any thought."

"Well, you've now got the opportunity. I can guarantee you'd find membership useful."

"Very well. Why not. Yes, I'd be happy to accept. What's involved?"

"There'd be an initiation ceremony. Nothing too dramatic. You'd have to take a couple of oaths. Then you'd be declared a knight of Knights Serpent and welcomed into the brotherhood of knights."

"Sounds okay."

"Good. We've our next meeting on Thursday."

"That'd suit me. My last paper is on Thursday morning."

"I'll call for you at seven."

"Good evening Miss Brampton. You look well."

"Good evening Mr Palmerstone. A little flushed, I suspect. My last lecture overran, and I had to rush to get here on time."

"It suits you." His enthusiasm and the way he focused on her mouth embarrassed her. She could feel the colour in her cheeks deepening further.

"Not long to go before you complete your degree."

"No. End of this week. You also finish at the end of the week, don't you?"

"Yes."

"Will you be returning home straight away?"

"I am supposed to, but quite honestly, I would like to enjoy a few more days here. I love this city and may never have the opportunity to return. A few days completely free to enjoy it a little more would be welcome."

"I'm going to stay for another week or two. Like you, I think Vienna's a terrific place. I hope to visit again sometime, but you can never be sure."

"Yes, I think I will stay for a few days."

"Good. We can see all those places we didn't have the chance to before." He desperately hoped she'd agree to spend the time with him.

"That would be nice." Katherine's stomach fluttered at the thought of having more time with Richard. She really ought not to feel this way, but she could not help it.

"By the way, I've been invited to join the Knights Serpent." A puzzled look crossed her countenance. "You remember, that society Ronaldo took me to a meeting of a few weeks ago."

"Oh Yes. You did not think much of them, I recall."

"Well, no, it was rather boring. But Ronaldo thinks being a member will help when I set up a medical practice and also with the family business. It'd also be useful to belong to something so philanthropic. There're many people in our area who could do with some help. An organisation their size would make quite a difference to the help we'd be able to offer."

"Yes, I suppose they would. Their secrecy is a bit off-putting, but as you say, they may be able to help a lot more people."

"The secrecy's all a bit stupid if you ask me. I see no need for it, but they insist. A bit theatrical and immature really, like a schoolboy's secret club. But if they can help, I'm prepared to go along with it."

"You are going to accept then?"

"Yes, I think I will. Ronaldo's taking me on Thursday evening."

"I look forward to hearing all about it."

"Why don't you, Anthony and Andrew meet me in the café afterwards? Let's say at about ten thirty."

"All right. Tell the others I will meet them there."

"Are you ready?" It was Thursday evening and Ronald had called at seven as arranged.

"Yes. I'll just grab my jacket."

"I'm afraid you'll have to be blindfolded again."

"Why? If I'm going to be a member, it doesn't matter anymore that I know where we're going."

"It remains a secret until your final initiation. That's the rules. Sorry."

"All right, but it all seems rather silly." He did his best to suppress the irritation.

"There're reasons for it." Ronaldo asserted as he tightened the blindfold round Richard's head.

"Just make sure you let me know when there're any obstacles. I don't want to fall on my face or arse. I already feel stupid enough with this blindfold on."

"Of course. Now take my elbow."

"Here we are. Now there're some steps to go up." The cool breeze brushing across his cheeks told him they were on an external staircase. Upon entering the building, instead of being led along a level surfaced corridor as he'd expected, he was directed down further steps. "It's a long flight." Ronaldo warned him. He did his best to control his increasing annoyance at being subjected to this blind state again. Fearing the possibility of making a spectacle of himself by falling, he kept a firm grip on his escort's arm.

"That's it. We've reached the bottom. No more steps."

"Good. Now, will you take this wretched blindfold off?"

"Sorry, but until your final initiation ceremony it has to stay on."

"Why?"

"Until you take the final oath, you're not a member and therefore may not be privy to our secrets."

"It all sounds stupid and unnecessary to me. But if that's the way it has to be, so be it."

"You'll understand later."

"Okay." The hum of many conversations told him there were a lot of people gathered.

"I better explain what's going to happen."

"I'd appreciate it."

"The members will go into the chamber in a moment. We'll wait here in the antechamber while the preliminaries are gone through. Someone will then call for the initiate, that's you, to be brought in. I'll lead you in, you'll remain blindfolded."

"Damn nuisance."

"Maybe. I'll then hand you over to one of the more senior knights of the order."

"You're not going to stay with me?"

"No. I'll have to take my seat with the other members."

"Oh."

"It's all right. You'll be quite safe. The knight will lead you round the chamber to four different masters. They'll each pose a question you must answer. Once you've responded satisfactorily to each, you'll be led to the centre."

"What if I don't answer the way they want?"

"You will. Basically, you'll be agreeing to keep certain promises. They're easy enough to understand. No need to worry."

"Will I still be blindfolded?"

"Yes. As I said, you'll remain so until after you've taken the final oath."

"I feel a right idiot."

"We've all been through it. Now listen. Once you've arrived at the centre, the grandmaster will ask you to respond to what he asks with an oath. When you have, the blindfold will be removed and you'll officially become a knight of the order. Do you understand?"

"Yes. Seems a lot of hocus-pocus nonsense."

"Don't take this lightly. These are serious matters. There's still time to change your mind if you'd prefer not to become a member."

"No. I'd still like to join. Just I'm not used to such things."

"All right. Here we go. The doors are opening."

"Who stands without?" A load firm voice echoed from within the chamber.

"One who requests admittance to the sacred congregation?" Ronaldo responded in an equally firm tone. Richard's hand was removed from his friend's arm and placed on to another silk covered one. Without a further word, his new guide led him forward a few paces and then stopped.

"Who seeks entry into the sanctuary?" A short incantation in Latin had proceeded this. An older man's voice.

"Richard Palmerstone." He responded, not feeling his usual confident self because of the blindness. His guide then led him to the right. Another short incantation in a language he didn't recognise followed.

"Will you acknowledge the Grandmaster, together with the masters under him, have full authority?"

"I will." He was then taken to the left. Yet another incantation.

"Will you accept those who shall be your fellow knights as blood brothers?"

"I will." He felt foolish. Nevertheless, it appeared he'd given the correct responses so far. Again, it all reminded him of childhood games. Turning him to the right, his guide led him forward several paces.

"Will you acknowledge, respect, and abide by our spirit guides?" He thought it a rather odd request, but decided to play along. What harm could it do anyway?

"I will." He was then turned about face and led slightly to the left to what, judging by the distance, he thought must be the centre. His guide then turned him about face again. A sickly sweet smell he couldn't identify struck his nostrils. It reminded him of body odour, and yet it wasn't.

"Kneel." His guide commanded. What now? But he obeyed. Someone then unbuttoned the top of his shirt and, pulling it aside, exposed his chest. His instinct was to resist such interference with his person, but something told him to remain still. Then what felt like the tip of a dagger was pressed into the flesh just above his heart.

"On pain of having tongue and heart cut out, are you prepared to take the oath of allegiance?" He was taken aback. That's a bit rich. No one told me about this. Well, now I've come this far, why not?

"Yes." Did his voice quiver? He hoped not.

"Do you swear by all that is holy to keep the secrets of Knights Serpent and never to repeat them to an outsider?" Is that all? A sense of relief swept over him.

"I do."

"Do you swear to abide by the rulings of the Grandmaster and his under masters?"

"I do."

"Remove the darkness from our brother knight." Someone loosened and removed his blindfold. He blinked for a few moments as the light from the multiple candles engulfed his blurred vision.

"Stand knight of Knights Serpent. Welcome brother." The grandmaster embraced and kissed him on each cheek. Not being quite sure what to do now, he remained standing on the spot. An older man dressed in a long black and blue silk cloak stood just behind him. He'd evidently been his guide round the chamber. He then placed a cloak across Richard's shoulders and indicated, with a move of his head, for him to follow. As he did, he noticed the Grandmaster, together with a handful of others, wore a sword at his belt. The rest of the assembly held daggers aloof. His recollection of the dagger point piercing the flesh above his heart made him involuntarily shiver. He followed his guide to an empty chair next to Ronaldo, who greeted him with a broad, beaming smile. Feeling embarrassed and a little foolish, he, without really thinking, automatically and quietly sat down.

"Welcome our new brother my fellow knights."

"Welcome!" the gathered men chorused as they lightly applauded. He turned his head in all directions, nodding in acknowledgment.

"Now to order." The Grandmaster commanded.

He now had the opportunity to take in his surroundings. They weren't in the same room as before. The fact they had gone down a long flight of stairs should have told him. This was a cavern of a place. He surmised they must be in the subterranean part of a very large building. Again, there was a high roof, but this wasn't adorned with the elegant frescos he'd seen before. The walls also lacked the adornment of rich paintings, though there were a few heavy tapestries. Presumably these helped keep the damp icy chill of such a place at bay. The seating, which was arranged in an oblong, was filled to capacity by men wearing rich cloaks of black and blue. He could see each bore the embroidered emblem of a silver sword entwined by a cobalt blue serpent over the heart area. The Grandmaster's cloak and those of the men sitting near him were more elaborate. The Grandmaster's was heavily embroidered round the edges with a unique design in thick gold and silver thread. He was sure it included geometric symbols. The others only had silver thread boarders. These must evidently be the hierarchy. Each also wore a cobalt blue sash across his chest. Continuing to look round, he noticed a handful of men, standing near the entrances, who did not wear cloaks. Instead, they were dressed in black suites with open-necked white shirts. In addition, each wore a small white apron and white cotton gloves. Clearly, there was still a lot for him to learn. The tiled quadrangle between the seats was dominated by a large, broad gold encrusted table upon which massive candles burned. Some were of an unusual deep red colour. To the left stood an ornate golden chair, more a throne really. To the right was a black standard that bore, in larger dimensions, the same embroidered image as he had seen on the cloaks. As he was taking all this in, the Grandmaster started to chant.

"Come Arastoth. Come ....." A series of names, most of which he couldn't hear clearly, followed. The Grandmaster kept repeating the same chant over and over in a soft voice, adding an 'amen' at the end of each phase. Continuing to listen, he thought he recognised one or two of the chanted names, though he had his doubts. Surely he must've misheard.

"What's he doing?" Whispered to Ronaldo.

"Shush. You mustn't speak. He's summoning our spirit guides." He thought he felt a chill draught pass through the room. But no, it must've been his imagination. No one else appeared to have registered it. A deep, almost deafening silence fell over the assembly. Nearly every head was bowed.

"Welcome. We are your servants." The Grandmaster bowed.

"Share your wisdom with us." One of the more official looking men who sat in the seats to the left of the Grandmaster had stood and spoken. He held something in his hand.

"Do you have any message for us?" The Grandmaster again. The other man then let what he held fall from his hand. It was a silver pendulum hanging from a silver chain. It began to swing from right to left. A murmur rose as its swing increased in strength and distance.

"Silence. Let us hear our guides." He noticed the pendulum move more distinctly to the left. The man was obviously controlling it. However, he noticed the man's hand and fingers remained dead still. It must be some sort of trick.

"There is someone here who has been asking whether to move into business with a fellow knight. The answer is yes." He hadn't anticipated anything like this. It rather reminded him of the séance he and the others had gone to.

"Does anyone seek direction from our guides?"

"Yes. Should I be leaving Vienna now?" A young man further along the row they were sitting in had risen. The pendulum distinctly swung to the right this time.

"No. You have work to do here." The young man sat, clearly contemplating the consequence of this reply.

"It will be a good marriage, combining joint fortunes for the good of all." This appeared to be a message for another person.

"You have made the right decision." For another? Further similar messages, if that is what you'd call them, followed.

"Do you have anything for your new servant?" The Grandmaster turned slightly so that he faced in their direction. Richard looked at Ronaldo.

"They always ask when there's a new initiate. It's an important part of it all."

"Beware. You have a positive outlook on life at present, but a kindness, where it is not necessary or warranted, will be repaid with sorrow, pain and more. You have been warned!" A moment of silence followed.

"Thank you .... for being with us this evening. We bless you for your kindnesses to us. Go in peace." The Grandmaster had again spoken the series of names as he uttered this closing prayer. He held his hands outstretched and his head bowed as if in homage.

"Wow! That was some message for you. Have you any idea what it means?" Ronaldo asked, turning to fully face his friend.

"Not in the least. I didn't realise you did things like this. Reminds me of a séance I went to a while back."

"It's far more than that. We believe the spirits guide us through life and require us to do their bidding always."

"Do you really believe that?"

"Of course. Why else would we take the oath to acknowledge, respect and abide by our spirit guides?"

"Yes, of course. I see." He decide it best not to vocalise his serious doubts.

"Come, I'll introduce you to some others." The congregation having left their seats were conversing in small groups or milling around the chamber.

"May I introduce my very good friends, Mr Peter Lucca, Mr Andreas Faber. Mr Lucca, Mr Faber, my friend Mr Richard Palmerstone." They greeted each other with the usual bend of the head. However, Richard thought there was something very sinister about Peter Lucca. There was a darkness in those eyes which was not improved by the black circles beneath them. He did not like him and it appeared from the man's dark look this feeling was reciprocated. It was the first time he'd taken an instant dislike to someone.

"Allow me to greet you as a brother knight, Mr Palmerstone." Peter Lucca moved forward embraced and kissed him on each cheek. There was something false and unpleasant in it.

"Thank you, brother knight." He did his best to sound as sincere as possible. But he couldn't shake it. There was just something about this man. He just wanted to get away from him. Thankfully Ronaldo then introduced him to some others who were passing. When he looked round again, Peter Lucca had disappeared. While his friend chatted, other knights came up and greeted him with the now accustomed embrace and kiss on both cheeks. He reciprocated as custom appeared to demand.

Ronaldo was now in deep conversation, so Richard took the opportunity to stroll round and take in his surroundings further. As he moved between the chatting groups, he could not help but overhear some discussions; 'I'll introduce you tomorrow.' 'He'll be happy to give you a list of contacts in Prague.' One group of five or six caught his attention. Peter Lucca was standing in the centre with the rest huddled round him. Unlike the other groups, they appeared to be talking in lowered voices. Whispering, it seemed to him. He was intrigued, and surreptitiously moved closer.

".... full moon in two days."

"We'll meet in the forest at the usual place."

"All right. I'll be there."

"Simeon has already set the altar up. He's got everything ready for the mass." There was no mistake. The men were definitely whispering.

"Good." One of the others moved to tap his companion on the shoulder in acknowledgement of his statement. As he did so, his cloak moved away and Richard noticed a gold pendent embossed with a goat's head bearing two large horns hanging from his belt.

"… … sacrifice?" He hadn't caught all the words.

"Quiet. Not here." Peter Lucca noticed him listening and gave him a very black look. Alter in the forest. A mass. Goat's head. Sacrifice. This sounded like a black mass. Could it be occultism? Though he liked to live life and experiment whenever possible, he really was not sure about this. He decided to ask Ronaldo.

"Well, what do you think?" Ronaldo appeared alongside him.

"To be honest, it was a bit weird. I thought this was just a philanthropic society, but that business with the pendulum was divination. I hadn't expected that."

"It wasn't divination! Well, not really. We're a believing people. The pendulum just helps us focus."

"Well, whatever you want to call it, I wasn't expecting it." In view of his friend's defensive attitude regarding the divination, he decided it best not to ask about the possibility of occult practices.

"What do you think of your fellow knights?" Ronaldo looked a little unsettled and had clearly decided to redirect their conversation.

"They seem a decent bunch."

"Yes, they are. I'll introduce you to some of the medical practitioners another time. You'll find them helpful as well as useful. I expect some of them will know people near your home."

"That'd be great. By the way, when I was at the front with the Grandmaster, there was a sickly sweet smell I couldn't identify. Do you know what it was?"

"Oh, that'll be the red candles. They're made differently to the others."

"How do you mean?"

"Blood is used in their manufacture. It's a life source that attracts the spirits. Apparently, it makes them feel welcome."

"I see." He was a little horrified by the idea, but considered it wise to remain silent. While they'd been talking, the gathering had started to break up.

"Time for us to leave."

"Okay."

"I'll let you know when the next meeting is to be held. We can come together if you like."

"Yes, I'd like that. I think there's still a lot for me to learn. Thank you for bringing me and for nominating me. I appreciate it very much, brother."

"Ha! Ha! I see you're getting the idea."

"Yes I am. No need for a blindfold now, I hope."

"Oh no. You're a knight now and sworn to secrecy. Remember your oaths and never break them. The penalty is severe for anyone who does." He then led the way up the stairs and out of the building.

"I'd never have guessed we were in this place." On exiting, he found they had been in one of the more elaborate official buildings just off the piazza.

"No one ever does." Richard, looking back to take in the impressive façade, saw Peter Lucca staring at him with an intense black look of hatred. There's something really evil about that man. I better watch out. How strange that we two, who don't even know each other, can have such an immediate mutual feeling of dislike. There was no mistaking it was mutual.

5

Escape

"To be honest, it was all nonsense. A bit like some stupid schoolboys secret gang. I know I keep repeating myself but it really is like that." Richard, Katherine, Anthony and Andrew sat at a corner table in the little café.

"What do you mean?"

"I was blindfolded again, but this time it was left on when we entered the building."

"I would not have liked that." The very thought of being made to feel so helpless and to be at the mercy of someone else sent a shiver through Katherine.

"When we entered the main chamber, I was handed over to another person. Ronaldo wasn't allowed to stay with me. It was a bit off-putting, having to trust someone you don't know when you're so helpless. This person then led me round the room. Every now and then, we'd stop in front of someone else. I believe, from what Ronaldo told me beforehand, each was one of their masters, or hierarchy. I've still to learn all about the structure and who's who."

"Where you still blindfolded?"

"Yes. The man we'd stopped in front of would then chant some incantation, sometimes in Latin, sometimes in another obviously ancient language. They'd then ask me to respond to a question. Well, it was more like I had to take an oath. All a bit melodramatic, if you ask me. Once I answered, my guide led me to the next person. This went on for a while. It must have been twenty or so minutes. By the time we finished, I'd had to answer four questions and then take a final oath before the Grandmaster."

"And you were blindfolded the whole time?"

"Yes. I have to admit it was getting on my nerves. But then, when I was about to say I'd had enough, someone removed the blindfold."

"Oh, thank goodness." Katherine let her held in breath escape with a sense of relief. She had got quite caught up in the tale.

"The Grandmaster, dressed in all his finery, stood before me. He and his under masters, well I think that's what they're called, along with their elaborate cloaks, wore sashes across their chests. The majority simply wore long black and blue cloaks with the emblem of Knights Serpent embroidered on them. That's a silver sword with a cobalt blue snake wound round it. There were a few without cloaks who stood by the doors. They had little aprons on and seemed to be like some sort of staff or servants."

"When you say sashes, do you mean like royalty?"

"Yes, very similar. The hierarchy also wore swords on their belts while the rest held drawn daggers."

"Not real ones!"

"Oh yes, they were real all right. I'd the point of one pushed into my chest."

"That's terrible." Katherine could hardly believe what she was hearing.

"Not really. It's all part of the ceremony. I had to swear, to the Grandmaster himself, on pain of having my tongue and heart cut out, not to reveal the secrets or ceremonies of the society. As I say, all very childish. I think the drawn daggers were supposed to act as a reminder or threat."

"How horrible. Was there anything else?"

"Nothing much. The Grandmaster welcomed me as a knight and brother, and then I was taken to an empty seat next to Ronaldo. The Grandmaster then uttered a strange prayer to some spirits or other. After that, there were messages for some people and others asked for guidance. It was a little like that séance we went to."

"Oh!"

"I was surprised, too. It wasn't what I expected. But then I think there's something strange going on that I've not been told about yet. Ronaldo says there is a lot for me to learn."

"What do you mean 'strange'?"

"When the Grandmaster was praying, welcoming the spirits, I'm sure I recognised a couple of the names. I couldn't hear most, but I'm sure I heard Beelzebub and Lucifer."

"But those are evil names. You must be mistaken."

"I don't think so. Later on I said to Ronaldo I hadn't expected divination. One of the men had a silver pendulum which swung when messages were being passed on or questions asked. He, that's Renaldo, got a bit agitated and denied any such thing. So I didn't think I could ask him about the names. Anyway, once the formal ceremonies were completed and a closing prayer said, we moved round the room. While I was being greeted by other members, knights I should say, I'm sure I overheard some of them talking about an altar in the forest. One even had a pendant with a goat's head on it. I think some of them may be into the occult."

"That is terrible. Surely you must have been mistaken. I thought you said it was a purely philanthropic society."

"Yes, I did, and so I thought. But I'm now wondering. Ronaldo did say there's a lot I haven't been told yet, which will apparently explain why they prefer their activities to remain secret. I find it hard to believe he's involved with the occult. He never struck me as someone who would be. But I think I'm going to have to be on the lookout. I don't want to get into anything like that." They were so engrossed in their conversation none of them noticed the two young men listening intently at a nearby table. Each bore a furious, vindictive expression.

"Will you go to any more meetings?" As usual, Richard was escorting her to her lodgings. "Not sure. It was really all rather stupid. However, Ronaldo keeps on about making useful contacts. So I may go for a while and see if anything comes of it. Anyway, I'm a knight now."

"Oh, excuse me Sir Knight." Katherine made a mock bow and laughed.

"Mock if you will, but I've the cloak to prove it." He desperately tried to keep a straight face.

"So it is official then. Sir Knight." This time giving him a short curtsy but finding it increasingly difficult to control her amusement.

"Enough of your irreverence lady." But he couldn't suppress his own laughter.

"Hum, sorry Sir Kn......" Laughter again got the better of her. "Sorry. Now, to be more serious." She struggled to keep a straight face and to subdue her hilarity. "By contacts, do you mean other doctors?"

"Doctors, surgeons, pharmacists, academics, officials, businessmen, and so on. I'm particularly interested in medical professionals. We don't have many back home. I think they'd prove useful, if there are any."

"My father is a doctor. I am sure he would be happy to help you with anything you need. Anyway, are there really so many medically trained people involved?"

"It appears so." They were so absorbed in their conversation neither had noticed the two men following them.

"I can see how it would help. Father often says how he would like the opportunity to discuss symptoms and such with other qualified men."

"Yes. And it wouldn't do the family business any harm to increase our number of contacts. Here, let's go down this lane for a change. It's a bit of a shortcut."

"Are you sure? I have never been down there before."

"Yes. It comes out just a couple of streets away from your place."

"All right. If you are sure." They carried on chatting about Richard's experiences, frequently laughing together at some of the antics he described. She really did enjoy his company. Was she being wicked? The thought of what her priest and parents would say if they knew still troubled her.

The street's lamps created occasional pools of glistening golden light on the cobblestone surface as they made their way along. In between were eerie darker patches, but as it was a cloudless night, the moon and stars made it possible for them to see clearly. The lane turned out to be rather doglegged, with many darker alcoves and corners. She would never have dreamt of coming down here on her own, but with Richard beside her felt safe. They were rounding yet another corner when the echo of running feet reached their ears. Looking back, they saw a man running full pelt toward them. He appeared very agitated and instinctively both knew something was wrong.

"Run!" Richard earnestly whispered whilst still looking back.

"Why? What is wrong?"

"Run!" Noting his urgency, she did as he commanded. He ran alongside but kept looking back over his shoulder. The clatter of their shoes on the cobbles combined with those of their pursuer resounded on their eardrums. All of a sudden Richard went flying. She stopped to help him up, but then noticed a man standing in the shadows. He had evidently tripped Richard with his outstretched foot. Snarling at her in a most grotesque manner, as if to say 'you dare come near' he dived toward her companion's prone form.

"Look out!" Her scream came too late. The man was on top of Richard, pummelling him with both fists. She thought she heard the word 'traitor' but was not sure. Richard, however, was having none of it. Using the full length and breadth of his frame and all his muscular strength, he managed to throw the man off and to leap to his feet.

"Run Katherine! Get away from here!" But she was too stunned by the suddenness of it all to comply. She stood motionless, not quite believing what she was seeing. The man who had been running after them caught up and immediately joined the other in beating, kicking and generally laying into her friend. A sudden flash of light caught her attention. It was a dagger!

"Look out, he has a knife!"

"Tongue and heart forfeit! Tongue and heart forfeit! Tongue and heart forfeit! Tongue and heart forfeit!" The second man manically and continually uttered. Had she really heard correctly? She shivered. What should she do? How could she help Richard? She was worried the two would overpower him. However, and thankfully, he was taller and broader than both. Grabbing the second man's neck, he pulled him off balance. The first meantime regained his footing and was moving to help his co-conspirator when Richard kicked out. A screeching cry followed. His booted foot had connected with the man's groin, causing him to double over. A resounding crack followed by a cry of agony echoed from the walls. Richard had kneed the man full on the chin. He sensed he had gained the upper hand, but then a sharp, almost sweet, pain darted through his lower arm. The other had sliced him with the dagger. Responding instinctively and with a broad sweep, he struck his attacker hard across the cheek. Then, as the man fell forward, rabbit punched the back of his neck. The man fell next to his companion. Both remained motionless on the cobblestones.

"Come on, let's get out of here before they recover." He grabbed her hand. It was as if an electric shock passed through her whole being. This was their first real physical contact. The thrill and excitement of his touch, enhanced as it was by adrenaline, almost subdued her fear. Subconsciously, her sense of wantonness returned. Nevertheless, she did not withdraw her hand. The confusion of sensations dizzied her. They ran without speaking until clear of the lane, then stopped to regain their breath.

"Who were they?"

"I reckon they're from Knights Serpent. Did you hear one say something about tongue and heart?"

"I was not sure I had heard correctly. I think I also heard the other one call you a traitor."

"Yes. You remember I told you how I had to take an oath, on pain of having tongue and heart cut out, never to reveal the societies' secrets and practices?"

"Yes. Oh! You cannot be serious!"

"Clearly they are. It never crossed my mind anyone would take those words literally. But obviously they do. They must've overheard me talking to you all in the café."

"What are you going to do?"

"If the knights really take it that seriously, I'll have to watch out. They won't be the only two after me. And I really would prefer to hang on to my tongue and heart." He tried to make light of the situation for her sake.

"Those two are bound to tell some of the others. They will all know who you are. It does not look like it will be safe for you to remain in Vienna."

"I was just thinking the same. It won't be safe for you either now they've seen us together."

"But I have nothing to do with them. Surely they cannot view me as a threat?"

"I'm all new to this and have no idea how they operate. But if tonight is anything to go by, they're clearly fanatical. We'll have to assume they'll stop at nothing to protect their secrets, if you can call them that. I think you'll also have to leave Vienna."

"What about Anthony and Andrew? You better warn them."

"Yes, I suppose I will. That can wait until morning. I doubt those thugs know where any of us live. For the present at least."

"Ronaldo does."

"I don't think he'd give me away."

"I hope you are right. That really was frightening." She had not realised until now how hard she was shaking.

"I'm sorry. More trouble I've got you into. First, I knock you down, then I take you to a séance and now I get your life threatened."

"It is not your fault. Well, maybe the first was, but that is immaterial now. Is that blood?!"

"Yes. Nothing to worry about. Just a scrape. He caught my arm with the dagger. I'll see to it later. Now I'll see you home safely. We can decide in the morning what to do."

"Are you sure you are all right? There is a lot of blood on your shirt."

"Yes. It really is just a scratch. Looks worse because it's soaked into the fabric." He'd been concerned a vein or artery may have been caught, but the blood flow had stopped quickly.

"I can clean and bandage it when we get to my place."

"There's no need. I've got all I need at my lodgings." They continued the rest of their walk in silence, both occupied with their own thoughts.

"I can't go home yet. Ronaldo knows where I come from and may say something. I haven't told him about last night, but he's bound to hear soon. I'll have to disappear for a while." It was the next morning. They sat in a small off the beaten track café having decided it unwise to return to their favourite place.

"Oh! I was hoping we would travel back together."

"No, I'm sorry. Anyway, I don't want you involved anymore. None of them know you and I'd rather they didn't. Even those two last night may not recognise you again, or at least I hope they won't."

"But surely it will be safe back home. They are not going to chase you all that way."

"I've no idea what they may do. They may contact someone over there. Ronaldo told me there're branches all round the world. Possibly even near home. They'll certainly have one in the city. No, I better let things settle for a while."

"Where will you go?"

"Some friends from Sweden have been asking me to visit. It's about time I accepted."

"Will it be safe?"

"I think so. No one knows about them and, as it's another country, they're unlikely to think of me going there."

"I will miss you."

"And I you. More than you know. I'll try and write whenever possible." 'More than you know.' The phrase pleased her.

"How long do you think you will have to stay?"

"At least a couple of months, maybe longer. Hopefully, they'll forget all about me after that. It's all so childish."

"Yes, it is. But they appear to be rather serious and determined about it."

"I'll come and see you as soon as I return home."

"I would like that. It is going to be strange not seeing you for so long. You are such a good friend." That was not the word she wanted to use, but decorum told her to be circumspect. She noticed a frown quickly pass over his features, but just as quickly, his smile returned. "When are you leaving?"

"First thing in the morning. There's no point delaying it. And as I've taken my finals, there's nothing to hold me here or make it necessary for me to remain." Damn! Not what he meant or wanted to say. "Well, you know what I mean."

"Yes. I understand."

"Have you decided when you're going?"

"As you know I planned on staying for a few days. However, I think it would be wise if I also leave as soon as possible. I will see about booking passage later today."

"I'm sorry Katherine. This is the last thing I expected or wanted. Me and my foolish ideas."

"There is no need to apologise. It is not your fault. Perhaps Ronaldo should have explained better. But that is all in the past now. We have to deal with what is."

"This will be the last time we see each other until I get home."

"Oh! I thought we may meet this evening."

"Better not. We don't want to take any chances. I'm going to stay in my rooms for the rest of the day."

"So this is goodbye then."

"Let's say au revoir, as the French do, rather than goodbye." Can't, won't, resist any longer. Bending, he kissed her full on the mouth. The excitement of the moment pulsed through his veins. Her initial shock, at this break in protocol, hit her like a tidal wave, but quickly passed as she allowed herself to melt into his embrace. Her arm, it seemed automatically, circled up and round his shoulder until her hand rested on the nape of his neck. She did not want the moment to end. "I'm sorry. I just couldn't resist any longer. I've wanted to do that since the day we met." Breathlessness and confused senses of pleasure and guilt prohibited any response. A couple of minutes passed before she was able to recover any sense of composure.

"It is all right." Her faint voice almost inaudible. She was still battling to calm her beating heart and coursing blood.

"I didn't want us to part before making sure you knew how I feel about you."

"Well, yes..." Confusion still getting the better of her.

6

Expectations

Opening her eyes to the morning light, her thoughts immediately turned to Richard. Perhaps they had been there all night. She did not feel rested despite the sleep. He would be well on his way to the north by now. Better get up. She had her own arrangements to make. Despite the potential danger if she remained, she felt a wrench at the thought of leaving. Was it for Vienna, a city she loved and had been happy in? Or was it at parting from Richard? Was it both? She would never be able to think of Vienna without thinking of him. In her mind and heart, the two were now inextricably united.

"I was hoping we would go together Jennifer."

"I can't really afford it. Anyway, the journey takes so long I'd have to start back almost immediately. You know I have another year before I get my degree."

"I had forgotten. We have been friends for so long it seems as if we have always been together."

"Yes, it does. But the year will pass fast enough and then I'll be home for good."

"I suppose it will. I am going to miss you, and Vienna. I really have enjoyed being here." She had agreed with Richard it best not to tell any of their friends what had occurred on the previous evening.

"And those 'wonderful' eyes, no doubt." Jennifer smirked.

"You really can be quite wicked at times."

"Only telling the truth." The smile spreading across her face.

Katherine sat by the carriage window, watching the passing scenery. The snow-capped mountains and lush green hillsides with grazing cattle were delightful. There was nothing like this at home where the fields were dry and aired for most of the year. Cattle only really survived well in the northern regions and, therefore, as they lived in the south, they had to rely on their goats and sheep for their milk. She would miss the taste. The initial disappointment of not having Jennifer with her now turned to gratitude. She needed time to think. So much had happened in Vienna and there was now the added complication, was that the word, of Richard. Never had she experienced such feelings and emotions. They confused and bewildered her. No one had affected her in such a way before. But surely it was all rather silly. After all, they had only known each other for a few weeks. And yet! It was as if he had always been there. The sensation of guilt at having blatantly ignored convention and protocol muddled her thoughts further. Her parents would be cross, if not angry, once they knew. She would have to tell them. She would not lie. Their anger would dissipate once assured nothing untoward had happened. That they were never inappropriately alone together. That they were just friends. Were they? Except for that last night, it was all true. But that night had been something else. No need to worry them by telling. It had been a one off. Anyway, had the kiss meant anything? Had it simply resulted from fear and adrenaline? But then what were these feelings? Why was there such bewilderment in her head? Had she done anything wrong? No! Not really. This was the eighteen sixties after all. If women in America can freely step up and demand the right to vote, why could she not go out unchaperoned? But then hers was a very traditional society steeped in customs from the past.

A young man entering the carriage broke her train of thought. He smiled as he sat on the seat opposite. She had to admit he was quite good looking. The blond hair flopping over his forehead enhancing the intensity of his blue eyes. Much to her unsettlement, he continued to smile, making no secret of his flirtation. She felt her cheeks reddening. Why? It was not as if she were unaccustomed to such behaviour. Richard had constantly flirted with her. So had one or two of the others. If a stranger could do this to her, then what were her real feelings with respect to Richard? Had it just been a passing flirtation? Was it simply the fact someone had taken such a deep interest in her? Confusion and uncertainty mounted. Pull yourself together, you silly girl! She turned back to the window and tried to forget the young man sitting there.

So what were her true feelings about Richard? Was it love she felt? Or was it infatuation with a handsome and fun character? How did he feel about her? Did he mean what he said that last evening? What about that kiss? Was it just his way? After all, he flirted mercilessly with all the girls and was always amiable with them. Had it just been a thing of the moment? Would it be a case of 'out of sight, out of mind'? Ah! It was so frustrating not knowing for sure what her own and his feelings were. But from the moment they met there had been something special and different. It was true she had never met anyone like him before. Well, at least no one who affected her so much. If only she could be sure.

Glancing back into the carriage, she found the young man still looking and smiling at her. He had such a pleasant, open face. She could not help but smile back.

"Hello, I am Alfred." Despite her bravado in being a modern woman, she found his boldness in addressing her so directly and against all convention unsettling. Nevertheless, not wishing to appear rude and as there was no chaperone to speak on her behalf, she returned his greeting.

"Good afternoon. I am Katherine Brampton."

"Good afternoon Miss Brampton. I apologise if I have shocked you. Allow me to introduce myself properly. I am Alfred Charles."

"Good afternoon Mr Charles. Not at all. After all, there is no one here to make formal introductions."

"So refreshing to meet someone with such a modern attitude, Miss Brampton."

"I have been in Vienna for a few years."

"Ah, I see. A beautiful city and very modern in its outlook. People stand less on convention there."

"Yes."

"Why were you there?"

"I have been studying for a nursing degree."

"And you're now travelling home?"

"Yes. I completed my studies recently."

"Successfully no doubt." Again he gazed directly into her eyes, making clear he found her attractive. And again she felt unsettled by it, though could not deny it was flattering. So silly, after all she had been accustomed to in Vienna. But somehow the teaching of her early years still influenced her subconscious. Did her reaction mean she was shallow? Was she fickle? Were her supposed feelings for Richard simply the result of living in a free, perhaps immoral, society? Confused thoughts engulfed her again. She really needed to sort out what was going on before arriving home. How else could she reassure her parents she had behaved properly? That she had not thrown her modesty aside. Or ruined her reputation. If she could not convince herself, how could she possibly convince others?

"Hello darling. It is so good to have you home again."

"Hello Mama, I am glad to be back. I have missed you." Running into her mother's open arms, she kissed and hugged her. It had been so long. Her childhood sense of security flooded back. Tears of joy stood in both their eyes.

"Now come on dear, enough of that. You must be tired from your long journey. Sit down while I make some tea."

"That would be nice. How is everyone?"

"We are all okay, thanks be to God. Father had a severe bout of influenza, but he is much better now. "

"Where is he?"

"He had to go and see to a patient. He should not be very long."

"Good. Do you have any idea what my friends have been up to?"

"Well, let me see. Rachel's engagement to Michael is now official."

"About time. Their parents agreed the marriage when they were toddlers. I am glad she likes him. It would have been awful if they did not get on."

"That is how it is dear. I never knew your father before we married."

"I am not sure I agree with the idea of arranged marriages. What if they do not like each other?"

"Then it is up to them, usually the woman more than the man, to make the best of it."

"But it does seem cruel. Did you and Papa like each other?"

"As I said, we did not know each other. But as the months passed we became very fond of each other. It must have been about a year after our marriage I fell in love with him. I think he also fell in love with me at the same time."

"That was good."

"Yes, we were fortunate. I do know several people who have not been so lucky. Some have had to put up with very brutal treatment and others are treated as servants or worse."

"Well, what else has been going on?"

"Mark Dennis asked Angelina's father for her hand."

"Goodness, I never thought he would ever find the courage."

"He surprised us all. He must really love her. You know she was supposed to be betrothed to Arnold Mann."

"Yes. So what did her father say?"

"Well, Arnold had been away for some time. I am not sure where. Anyway, when he returned, he had changed. He is not a very nice person and no one really likes him. Besides his rudeness, he is also a bit of a bully. I feel really sorry for his poor mother."

"Oh dear. What changed him?"

"No one knows. He never talks about his time away."

"So, what did Angelina's father say?"

"Of course socially and financially, Mark's family are not on a par. Nevertheless, he agreed. We were all surprised. When asked, he simply said he could see they were deeply in love. Consequently, he was sure Mark would look after his daughter."

"Good for him. Anything else?"

"Roger Harris has gone off to study somewhere. I am not sure where or what."

"Probably politics. He was always a bit of a rabble raiser."

"You are probably right. Anyway, enough of that for now. I want to hear about Vienna."

"It really is a lovely city."

"Your father always said so. He enjoyed his student years there very much."

"Yes, it is very cosmopolitan with people from all round the world. I found it very interesting." They went on to discuss the city, her studies, her friends and the people generally.

"Without a chaperone!"

"It was all above board. He was the perfect gentleman. We always made sure we were in public and never had physical contact." Forget that last night.

"We trusted you to behave!"

"I did! Was I supposed not to mix with other people or students? Vienna is very different from here."

"Your father will not be happy."

"I did not do anything wrong. You both told me you trusted me to make right decisions. I think I did."

"We better keep this quiet. The rest of the village will think you behaved like a loose woman or worse as a harlot."

"Mama! For goodness sake. We always behaved." At that moment, her father entered the drawing room.

"Hello Papa." Leaping up she greeted him with a hug and a kiss.

"Hello dear. You look well."

"Yes I am. I was just telling Mama how much I liked Vienna."

"Ah Vienna. It seems to have liked you too."

"That is as maybe, but do you know what she has been up to? She has been out with a boy on her own. Without a chaperone!"

"Have you dear?" A stern expression replaced his smile. Despite his broad experience and education, he remained very much of a traditionalist.

"We did not do anything wrong. I have been explaining to Mama how he was always the perfect gentleman. Never once did he behave inappropriately. And we were never on our own together." Lying again. But it was only the once, and the circumstances were unusual.

"We trusted you to behave as a young lady. Not to flaunt yourself in front of society."

"I did not 'flaunt' myself. What was I supposed to do? Remain locked in my room when not attending lectures?"

"You could have gone about with other female students."

"I did. But Richard was ...."

"You are on first-name terms?" His countenance darkened further.

"Sorry I mean Mr Palmerstone. He is a very intelligent man, and we were able to have in-depth conversations about all sorts of things."

"That is no excuse for seeing him on your own. What must people have thought?"

"From your own experience Papa you should know how different Vienna is. Most people there do not think it is wrong for a woman to go out unchaperoned."

"I am not concerned about what 'most' do. We expected you to behave as befits your position in our own society."

"I am sorry if I have upset you Papa. But we did nothing wrong, and he was always the perfect gentleman. I think you would like him."

"I doubt I will ever meet him."

"Well, actually you may. His family home is in Farringdon Oaks."

"You did not tell me that Katherine." Her mother said in an accusing tone.

"I was about to when Papa came in."

"What is his name?" Her father appeared taken aback by the information.

"Richard, sorry, Mr Richard Palmerstone."

"I see. It so happens I know his parents. They will not be very happy when they hear he has been leading you astray."

"He never led me astray, as you put it." She had decided not to tell her parents about the séance or Knights Serpent. They would definitely not approve. Nor did she want them to worry or to think badly of Richard. Though cross that, in their opinion, she had acted with such poor judgment they believed her. In truth, they trusted her but would not admit it openly in the current circumstances.

One afternoon, shortly after her return, they were relaxing on the terrace after a light lunch. Though eager to begin her nursing career, she would have to wait. No one engaged new staff during the holiday season. Unable to sit idle, she occupied the days helping her mother run the house, her father, whenever possible, with his patients and visiting the sick and poor.

"Katherine."

"Yes, Papa."

"When you were very young, your mother and I sort of agreed with Mitchell and Norma Compton that you and their son would get together."

"Do you mean Gregory and I would marry?"

"Well, yes."

"But I do not like him."

"We think he is nice. And they are a decent family."

"You mean well-off."

"Well, yes. There is nothing wrong with that, is there?"

"No. But this whole arranged marriage idea is so old-fashioned."

"That has always been the way for families like ours. We only want the best for you."

"I know you do, and I appreciate it. But...."

"You like this Richard Palmerstone you told us about." Her mother interjected.

"Well, yes, I do."

"Are you expecting him to call on you?"

"Um, well, yes, I hope he will. We got on very well. I think he also likes me."

"Katherine!"

"I cannot help it. I really do like him. May I write and invite him to dinner one evening?"

"Certainly not! That would be considered very forward."

"But...."

"No! If he wishes to see you, it is up to him to call." Had they really not accepted her word that nothing had happened, and he was trustworthy? Their refusal, however, highlighted another concern. She had been back six weeks and not even a note had arrived. He should have written by now. Had he forgotten her? Was it just a passing phase while students? She felt belittled and sad by her parent's reaction but knew she had no choice but to accept their ruling.

"We have invited Gregory and his parents for dinner this evening." Her mother announced excitedly one morning.

"Mama!"

"Your father is insistent."

"Very well. But I hope neither of you expects me to change my mind."

"You have not seen him since before you went away. He really is a pleasant young man. You might be surprised."

"I doubt it. I am not saying he is not a nice person, but he is not for me. He was always a bit like a wet fish."

"Well, wait and see. Anyway, whatever happens, you will have to obey your father."

"I thought you loved me. Surely you will not force me into a loveless marriage."

"It is only dinner darling. We are not forcing you into anything. At least please try to be polite."

"Of course I will. I have no wish to offend anyone. But I will not pretend to feel something I do not."

"I think you should wear one of your nice new dresses." Her mother bringing the discussion to an end.

Her thoughts were anywhere but with the dress slithering down her slim, taught body. Richard must have thrown her over. Perhaps he met someone else at his friends. She was behaving like a silly schoolgirl again. Nothing had ever really been said about romance or any such thing, despite that kiss. Maybe he was like that with all the girls. A spur-of-the-moment thing. But? No, it could not have been. It was obvious, at least to her, there was more to it. Or had it been one sided? No, she was sure he had feelings for her. But who knew how deep a man's feelings went? With a heavy heart, she descended the stairs, tears gathering. No, must not let them fall. Would not be fair. Drawing them back, she forced a smile, hoping it did not look as false as it was.

"You look lovely darling. That blue complements your eyes."

"Thank you Mama. You look nice too." Her mother wore the satin mist grey dress she had brought as a present.

"Well, look at you two. The perfect ladies." Proclaimed her father as he entered the hall.

"Thank you Papa." A knock at the front door interrupted them.

"Kathy, please let our guests in." Kathy, so called to avoid any confusion with Katherine, emerged from the kitchen and sped to open the door. She was the household maid.

"Mitchell, my dear friend, so good to see you. Please come in. Good evening Norma. Good evening Gregory." Her father clasped his lifelong friend's hands between his own while her mother and Norma embraced. The glint in her father's eyes when greeting Gregory did not go unnoticed. She hoped he was not going to make things difficult.

"You remember Katherine." He waved her forward.

"Of course. Good evening Katherine. You look well. Vienna obviously agreed with you." She curtsied in acknowledgment.

"I am sure you remember Gregory."

"Yes. Good evening Mr Compton." She gave the shortest possible curtsy, not wanting to encourage him unnecessarily in any thoughts he may have. He bowed in return.

"Good evening Miss Brampton."

Politics, farming and updates on local businesses and neighbours dominated the dinner table conversation. Throughout, she tried to ignore her father's conspiratorial glances and Gregory's irritating puppy dog looks. After, when in the drawing room, they asked her to tell them all about Vienna, the latest trends and, of course, the prevailing fashions. Her mother shot an unnecessary warning look to avoid details of her personal life. She was hardly going to tell them any of that. The conversation then returned to more general topics, her boredom increasing with each passing moment. How she missed the lively debates with Richard. Would he ever come or had he forgotten her? No, must not think of that. Never do to betray her emotions in company. At long last, the time for their guests to leave arrived.

"Thank you for a lovely evening." Mr and Mrs Compton chorused together.

"We must not leave it so long in the future." Her father again clasped his friend's hand whilst the ladies embraced and kissed each other on the cheek.

"Good night Miss Brampton. It has been a genuine pleasure to see you again." Gregory bowed a little deeper than usual.

"Good night Mr Compton." She curtseyed and bent her head in acknowledgment.

"Good night." The parents each echoed as the Compton's carriage drove off.

"Well, that was a pleasant evening. Do you not agree Katherine?" Her mother turned an enquiring eye upon her.

"Yes mother, it was all right."

"But darling, you make it sound as if it were tedious."

"I am sorry."

"What did you think of Gregory? He has grown into quite a presentable gentleman. Do you not think?"

"I suppose he has."

"Would be a good catch for someone."

"Mama!"

"Well he would. Why do you not like him?"

"He still reminds me of a wet fish. And all evening he kept looking at me like some forlorn spaniel."

"I think he has always been a little in love with you."

"Just a schoolboy crush."

"I am not so sure. I think he is still in love with you."

"Well, I am sorry to hear that. I cannot return the sentiment. I feel nothing for him."

"Oh Katherine! You can be so frustrating."

"Just the truth Mama. There is no point in pretending otherwise."

"Your father still has hopes of you two getting together. He will be very upset if you turn Gregory down."

"Do you mean you expect him to propose?"

"That is my understanding. Both your fathers expect it."

"Oh dear. This is going to be so awkward. I cannot, I will not marry him. It would be a marriage without love. On my side at least. What hope is there that we could ever be happy together?"

"Many marriages survive without love."

"Could you have survived?"

"I would have accepted my lot and got on with it. That is how we were brought up."

"Maybe, but you have both taught me to think for myself."

"I sometimes wonder if we made a mistake doing so. Society is not ready yet for your radical ideas."

"But really Mama, would you have put up with it?"

"Yes. I would not have wished to offend or upset my parents. However, I have been very fortunate to have a husband who loves me and whom I love."

"You understand then. If I marry, I also want it to be to someone I love and who I believe loves me."

"Remember dear, you also have to uphold our position in society. You cannot just marry any so so."

"What do you mean 'so so'?"

"I mean anyone below your station."

"For goodness sake. It is time we got past all that nonsense."

"Is it nonsense?"

"I believe it is. It is the eighteen sixties. It is time we freed ourselves from some of these old-fashioned ideas."

"Katherine! Please think carefully about what you are saying."

"I have."

"Oh well, sleep on it dear."

Frustration and irritation at being placed in such a position prevented a settled night. She felt as if in a cage with no door. If only Richard would write or, better still, visit. Her parents were bound to like him.

"Good morning dear."

"Good morning Papa." He was already at breakfast.

"Well, what did you think of last night?"

"It was nice to see Mr and Mrs Compton again."

"And Gregory?"

"I have not changed my mind about him."

"He likes you."

"May be. However, I cannot reciprocate the sentiment."

"I think he is going to ask for your hand."

"I sincerely hope not. But if he does, I hope you will refuse."

"It would be a good match."

"But it would be a marriage without love. On my side at least." It was irritating having to repeat all that had passed between her and her mother.

"Are you sure? I have held expectations of this for many years."

"Papa, you may order me to marry him if you wish. I hope you will not. Nevertheless, I would not disobey you, though I would feel I was condemning myself to a life of unhappiness." She meant every word. However, her father had earned her respect very early on and had never lost it.

"I will think about it."

She had now committed herself. Whatever her father decided would be. If it was to marry Gregory, she would have to put all thoughts and memories of Richard out of her head and heart. She almost burst into tears. Would he really force her into such a marriage? She returned to the quiet of her room to try and calm herself.

It had been so long with no word from Richard. She must have been wrong. Were men really so deceitful? Was he just laughing at her all the time? No, she could not accept that, but what other explanation could there be? A firm, load knock at the front door broke her chain of thought. What time was it? Eleven. Right time for a morning visitor, though they rarely received one. Kathy's footsteps echoed as she went to answer. Then a familiar voice caught her ears. It cannot be? Yes, it is! She almost rushed out of the room and down the stairs, but quickly thought better of it. Her parents would have disapproved of such unsophisticated and uncontrolled behaviour. She must wait to be called.

An hour seemed to pass before she heard Kathy's gentle knock on the bedroom door.

"Come in."

"Excuse me Miss, but there is a gentleman asking to see you. The master says you are to go to his study."

"Very well Kathy. I will come straight down." Quickly checking her hair and dress in the dressing mirror, she followed Kathy. She knocked on her father's study door.

"Enter!"

"You sent for me Papa."

"Yes my dear. A young man has asked to see you. He is in the drawing room."

"Who is it?" For a moment she feared it may be Gregory. But no, it had not been his voice.

"His card states he is Mr Palmerstone."

"Oh!" She did her best not to beam too much or to faint from the exhilaration passing through her.

"Would you like to see him?"

"Yes, if you approve."

"He is the young man you knew in Vienna?"

"Yes."

"I should really have him chased out of the house for having put you in such a position there."

"Please do not Papa. He really is quite respectable."

"Um. I am not sure I should allow you to see him. It is quite improper. We have never been introduced."

"Would you at least speak to him. I think you will like him. I can wait here. Then if you approve, you can call me, or if not, he may leave without us seeing each other."

"You really are quite taken with him?"

"Yes, I think I am. Everything I told you was the truth. He is a gentleman. He is intelligent. And nothing improper happened."

"Very well. As I already know a little about his family, I will speak with him. I make no promises. I may send him off with a flea in his ear, never to return. I may forbid him from ever calling again or from trying to see you. You understand?"

"Yes, Papa I do. But I hope it will not come to that."

"We will see." Her father left the room.

Nerves and excitement combining to torment she could not settle. What if her father took a dislike to Richard? No, he could not. Richard was so likeable. The murmur of masculine voices reached her through the study door. What were they talking about? What was her father saying? What were Richard's responses? She worried the turmoil in her stomach would result in her vomiting all over her father's ornate carpet. She paced back and forth between the picture window and her father's desk. Then she circled round the room, brushing against the wall to wall bookcases, not even seeing the books. She stopped in her tracks. The voices had ceased. She dared not breathe.

"Come with me." Her father held the door open. Though she searched, there was no hint of what had happened in her father's eyes or expression. With trembling everything she passed through the door.

"Well, young man. Here is my daughter."

"Good morning Miss Brampton. I am pleased to make your acquaintance again."

"Good morning Mr Palmerstone." She curtsied.

"It is sometime since we last met. I hope I find you well."

"Yes, thank you, sir. I hope you are also well."

"I am thank you." All this time she was aware of her papa viewing them both with a critical eye. He was an astute man, and she was sure he could see how genuine a gentleman Richard was.

"I am glad to hear it. You were to visit friends in the north, if I remember correctly."

"Yes I did. I enjoyed seeing them again, and the country round their home is very beautiful. By their insistence, I extended my visit."

"It appears to have agreed with you."

"Thank you. When I returned, my father required me to attend to some of our estates. Consequently, I have been rather dilatory in remaking your acquaintance, for which I apologise."

"No matter, sir. You have obviously been very busy."

"Well, there we are. Thank you for calling Mr Palmerstone." Her father interrupted, indicating it was time for the interview to end.

"Thank you Sir. May I call again?"

"Please send a note beforehand and I shall see if we will be 'at home'."

“Good Day Sir. Good Day Miss Brampton.” He bowed as he backed toward the door. She just caught the little wink he gave her with his right eye. Thankfully, her father had not seen it. Once he had left the room, she turned to her father.

“I told you he was a gentleman.”

“You did my dear. But it is still all very improper.”

“Oh, Papa.”

“Do not try getting round me with that little girl’s voice and your antics. I know your tricks.” She felt a little thrill when she saw a smile pass over his lips.

“Of course not Papa. Will you allow him to visit us again?”

“We will see.”

7

Venice

Waking with the dawn chorus, she stretched, luxuriating in a sense of joy. She had barely slept, excitement having gained the better of her, but did not feel the least bit tired. Like a fresh faced school girl, she glowed with happiness at the prospect of a life with Richard. It was early and though, due to the summer heat, her marriage would not take place until early evening, she could not relax.

"Good morning dear. You are up early."

"I am too excited to stay in bed."

"You really love him."

"Yes I do. I never thought it possible to care about someone quite so much."

"I am glad you are happy. He is a nice young man. Your father and I have rather taken to him, despite our earlier reservations."

"I cannot possibly convey how grateful I am for that. I thought father was going to forbid our marriage. Gregory is nice enough, I suppose, but he definitely was not for me. Our marriage would not have been a very happy one."

"Well, you never know what may have been. Look at your father and I. As you know, we found love though we did not know each other to start with."

"Yes, you were fortunate. Many have not been so. Look at Hannah Conrad and Margaret Symons. We all know how unhappy they are."

"Yes. But they really should not make it so obvious. We were all brought up to make the best of our situations and to respect our husbands, no matter what we felt. They bring shame on their families by behaving so badly."

"It all seems so false and artificial. I do not think it is fair."

"Fair or not, society expects a woman to behave and to be quiet. But then we have been liberal with you. I should not be surprised by your outlook."

"Yes, I am grateful to you and Papa for teaching me how to, and for allowing me to, think for myself rather than insisting I be dictated to by convention in all matters."

"Well, enough of this philosophising. It is time the rest of us got on with the preparations. Now I do not want you tiring yourself. Have some breakfast and then rest before having your hair done."

"I am too excited to relax. Please let me help."

"Are you sure? You do not want to be worn out before this evening."

"Yes I am. I will only fret and get myself all worked up. It would be better if I do not have time to think. I have to admit the thought of being the centre of attraction in the middle of so many people makes me a little nervous."

"There really is no need to worry. I am sure you will be fine. All right if you insist you can help with the place settings, but that is all. I want you to be fresh for your wedding?"

"Of course. But I think I will go mad if I just sit round doing nothing."

Standing with her beloved, happiness radiating like the beams of a brilliant sunset, every part of her tingled. The simple white satin dress tapering to her slim waist and then falling in folds to the floor combined with her bouquet of white lilies and peach coloured rose buds further enhanced her features. Could she really be this happy?

"I now declare you man and wife." Loud applause erupted as he bent and kissed her delicate lips. Such happiness! Would her heart hold out? To stay forever with his lips pressed to hers would be more than enough.

"Come on sweetheart, people are waiting." Their wedding was very much a local event. Both families not only held high status in the locality generally, but were also very much respected. Consequently, residents from the entire district, as well as all their estate workers and staff, had gathered. Some were even forced to stand in the church doorway peering in.

"Oh! Yes. All right .... husband." My husband! The realisation dazed and thrilled. Was it true? Yes, it was! Would, could, her heart survive the knowledge? He led her as those gathered round the door parted to let them and the guests following through. Stopping on the top step, they waved and smiled at the gathered crowd. Cheers, laughter and loud applause greeted from every direction. Determined not to allow anything to spoil the day, she chose to ignore the jealous looks in some of the women's eyes. No matter what, he was hers now. The rush of emotions nearly overcame her. Sensing his firm grip on her hand, she followed as he carefully led her down the steps.

"Here we are sweetheart. Time for us to lead the dance." The air suddenly resounded with lively notes as the small group of musicians gathered to one side struck up.

"Oh Richard! I am so happy. I love you!"

"And I love you sweetheart. To be honest, I wondered if this day would ever happen. You really are the love of my life. I'm not sure what I'd have done if I couldn't have married you."

"Darling! That would have been too cruel."

"Now come on, no time for ourselves. People are waiting." Placing his arm round her waist, he spun her off. Others, similarly taking their partners, followed as they led the dance through the streets. By this means, those too frail to attend the ceremony were able to participate in the celebration while sitting on their front porches or steps. Laughter, happiness, clapping and music resounded everywhere. Congratulatory shouts and faces full of joy greeted them at each turn. At long last, they were one! Could it get any better? Their euphoria infected all. No one could mistake their happiness. The reception continued into the early hours with no one really noticing, all so happy to be there.

Time for them to leave arriving, they kissed their respective parents and in-laws. Nervous anticipation thrilled through her as she observed the mischievous sparkle further brightening those captivating eyes of his. Her heart would surely burst. It was so full.

"Happy sweetheart?"

"Yes darling. I never knew I could be so happy." At last she could let herself melt into his broad chest. Now at long last she could give herself to him totally as she had longed to almost from their first meeting. The long abstinence of physical contact was over. Her controlled, subjugated passion was now free to flow. She sensed he was also feeling the release. She allowed these sensations to sweep through her unhindered as he gently took her in his arms, laid her on the bed, and unbuttoned her dress.

She woke to bright sunshine and a sense of fulfilment she had never experienced before. There on the bed next to her lay her husband, the only man she had ever loved or wanted. Life could not be better. Richard stirred as the sunlight passed across his eyes.

"Good morning sweetheart." His sleepy, contented tone excited her.

"Good morning darling."

"Why don't we stay here all day?"

"I would love to Richard, but we have to get going. It is a shame we cannot go to Vienna. I would have liked to see it again. I am surprised by how much I have missed it."

"Me too. But I think it'd be too dangerous. I don't expect they've forgotten or forgiven. Someone may recognise me."

"Do you really think so? It has been so long."

"Yes, I'm afraid I do. Many of them come from families that traditionally never forgive. I've heard some of their feuds continue through several generations."

"That is ridiculous. Surely they must forget after a while."

"Apparently not. Anyway, I don't think we should take the chance. And I don't want to endanger you. It's hard to believe grown men can be so childish. What harm did it do me telling you and the others? Well, whatever, that's the way things seem to be."

"Well, if you really think it would be that dangerous. Such a shame. I have so many lovely memories of the city and our lives there."

"I'm sorry sweetheart. I wish I'd never heard of Knights Serpent. It was just the idea they might've helped with various things. Well, can't go back."

"No, sadly. You are sure you are safe here?"

"I think so. Before coming home, I checked if there were any branches in the area. Thankfully, there aren't. As far as I can make out, the nearest is in Portside. That should be far enough away. Shame though, it would've been useful to have some professional contacts here. Anyway, Venice sounds like fun."

"I have heard it is a very beautiful and unusual city."

"So have I. They have canals instead of streets. It'll be interesting to see somewhere so different and novel." Leaning over, he pulled her toward him, kissing her neck, shoulders, arms slowly making his way down. Oh! What would another hour matter?

~~~~~~~~

They spent their days luxuriating in each other's company. She could hardly believe her happiness. Was it all a dream? The warmth and masculine aroma of his body next to her said otherwise. To think they could have been prevented from marrying if her father had insisted upon tradition and convention. It was hard to imagine life without the man beside her. The man she loved! Settling into his firm yet gentle embrace and the softness of the velvet gondola cushions, she allowed herself to gaze upon him. His dark hair glistening in the sunshine combined with the Romanesque nose, strong mouth, rugged chin, broad shoulders and athletic build, still catching her breath. The beauty of the moment swept over her while the gondolier's love song rebounded off the rose and sienna facades of the palazzos they were passing. Looking down on their cuddled forms, he could not mistake their adoring love. Intense happiness occupying her thoughts, she barely noticed the city they were floating through. Nevertheless, it would not concede, its uniqueness ultimately demanding her attention and enchanting her with its beauty. Were those who occupied these magnificent palazzos as happy as
~~~~~~~~

her? Hopefully. She pressed further into her beloved. He is drawn from his contemplation of the engineering it must have taken to erect these elegant buildings by the sensation of her closeness. Turning, he is lost within those adoring eyes. His inner man stirs with thoughts of love. His loving smile thrills and enthrals awakening further her longing for him.

"Shall we go back to the room?" His voice husky and intense with desire.

"Yessss." Her breath catching with anticipation. She dissolves further into his embrace.

The sweetness of her lips. The fresh scent of her hair. The depth of those sea-green eyes. The gentle, soft pliability of her pale flesh. All combine to urge him beyond control. He wants her so much. He is near to madness.

"You're beautiful." He whispers in her ear.

Gazing into the pools of his wondrous eyes, she yields to his earnestness. They are no longer part of this world.

Lying in his arms, she feels vibrant and full of life. The soft baritone voices of the gondoliers as they sing their love songs fill the air. There is nothing else she could wish for but to be with him forever. Just to remain where they are, not to move, ever. They remained like that for a while, just drinking in the joy of each other's body and breathing in the moment.

"Shall we go for dinner in St Marks?"

"Um. Oh. Yes. That would be nice." Reluctant to stir from his embrace. To leave the intimacy of his naked body.

Having bathed and dressed, they hail a passing gondolier. Taking in the spectre of St Mark's as they float toward it, they see the square is, as usual, full of people enjoying an evening promenade. The air vibrates with the stir of fluttering wings as pigeons rise to avoid being trampled. The gentle chaffing of gondola against gondola as they gently bob beside the pontoons combines with the music of distant chiming bells. Could life get any better? She doubts it. The suddenness of Richard violently pulling her arm breaks the moment. An intense look of worry clouds his face as he drags her behind a pillar.

“What is wrong?!”

“Those two over there.”

“The two men standing under the arch?”

“Yes.”

“Who are they?”

“Knights Serpent.”

“Are you sure?”

“Yes. I recognise them from the meeting. The taller one is Peter Lucca. He’s a friend of Ronaldo’s. I don’t know the other’s name, but I definitely recognise him.”

“Do you have any idea why they are here?”

“Damn, I’ve been a fool. I should’ve thought. Knights Serpent’s original roots are here. It was started by some of the Medici merchants in secret.”

“Why secret?”

“Some of their relatives weren’t happy about them using part of their fortunes to help the poor and downtrodden.”

“Why?”

“They feared they’d lose control and the people might rise up against them. They had a tendency to use their workers as slaves. Anyway, I’d forgotten some of the men in Vienna are Venetians. They must be visiting their families. I just hope they didn’t see us.”

“Would it matter if they had?”

“As I said, they don’t forget or forgive. I’d rather not take any chances. And that Peter is a nasty piece of work. Damn, I think they’ve spotted us.” She looked up to see the taller one earnestly talking to his companion and pointing in their direction.

“Yes, I think you are right. What are we going to do?”

“Better make a run for it. From their expressions, I don’t think they’re going to be friendly.” As he spoke, the two men started jogging toward them. Grabbing

Katherine's hand, he pulled her after him. Taking the first side lane they came across, he rushed her down the narrow footway bordering the canal.

"This is crazy Richard!" Despite herself, she was trembling.

"I know, but I think they're still out to kill me. Tongue and heart. You recall?" She shuddered at the remembrance.

"I am not sure I can outrun them."

"Look for a gondola. Preferably one with a canopy."

"There is an empty one, but it has no canopy."

"Never mind. It'll have to do." She beckoned the gondolier to cross to them quickly. Before it touched the side, Richard leapt in, bodily lifting her in after him.

"We're in a hurry! Quick man!"

"Where to sir?"

"Anywhere! Just away from here. Go down there." He pointed to a canal on the other side that was at a tangent to the one they were on. The gondolier, looking bemused, just shrugged his shoulders as if to say 'mad tourists'.

"Quick man, quick!"

"I go as fast as can, sir."

"Stay low Katherine. Let's hope they don't spot us." Pushing himself as far down into the seat as he could, he pulled her after him. As they turned into the adjoining canal, he chanced a peek over the back of the plush seat. The men had just arrived at the water's edge. The look on Peter Lucca's face even succeeded in sending a shudder down his spine. It was pure evil. The men frantically looked round, but thankfully, the gondola glided out of sight before there was any chance of them being spotted.

"I am scared Richard." Fighting to hold back her fearful tears.

"It's okay darling. I think we've given them the slip." Holding her tightly to his chest.

"I'm sorry about dinner darling." Sitting in their rooms having safely returned.

"Oh Richard. Are we always going to have to run from them?"

"I suspect so. But I'll make sure not to go anywhere near one of their meeting places in the future. I'm afraid we won't be able to come here again. We can only hope, with the passing years, they will forget all about me or at least won't recognise me. 'Out of sight, out of mind'. Well, I hope so anyway. I hope Ronaldo hasn't told that Peter where I live. He's pure evil."

"What do you mean?" A note of fear returning to her voice.

"There's something really sinister about him. I saw it the first time Ronaldo introduced us. I never liked him. And it was obvious he didn't take to me either."

"Oh!"

"Don't worry. I'm sure he didn't see us in the gondola, so won't know where we are."

"What are we going to do? We are supposed to have another couple of days, but do you think we should leave straight away?"

"No, damn it. I'll not let them spoil this for us. But we better stay away from the centre." Struggling to subdue his anger, not wishing to agitate her further. "I know. I'll take you to the Lido tomorrow. We should be safe enough there."

"This is foolish. How can gown men behave like that?"

"Grown or not, many remain immature. As I said at the time, it was all rather childish. If only Ronaldo had explained to me fully. I hadn't expected divination and occultism or the evil hatred."

"I doubt it would have stopped you if he had. You know how you enjoy an adventure. You would have just thought it another fun thing to do."

"I suppose you're right. I've never really taken these things seriously before."

"Well, now you know better. And you better take them seriously or you will have me to answer to."

"Oh dear, I'm so scared." Both felt tension leave as they laughed and fell into each other's arms, the residue of fear intensifying their passion.

"This is very different to the city. So much more open. You can breathe here." Good to his word, Richard had taken her to the Lido.

"It is nice."

"Are you sure that man will not be here?"

"I can't see why he would be. He's more than likely to visit people in the city. Anyway, as far as I know, there's no branch here on the Lido. Too small for them, I reckon."

"I hope you are right. I am getting tired of having to run every time we see one of them. Will we be safe at home?"

"I am perfectly sure of that. There's no branch in the district added to which none of them know where we live. Let's forget about it and enjoy the day."

"All right. It is silly to let them spoil this for us."

"Yes it is. Now why don't we go for a stroll and see the sights. After all, we are tourists."

"Ha! Ha! Yes we are." With arms affectionately round each other, they headed down the wide street that crossed the island. "These shops are just as nice as those in the city. And this Venetian glass is so beautiful. I cannot see enough of it."

"They're very proud of it. I've to agree though the styles may have changed over the years, it's still all rather marvellous."

"I would like to buy a few pieces more. Not just for ourselves, but also as gifts."

"Okay, but before you load us up with packages, let's got for a walk along the shore. I enjoy the sea and we're so far from it at home."

"All right. But we will come back here after?"

"Yes, of course."

"Good." Continuing along the street, both were taken by the brilliance of the blue horizon, sea and sky almost indistinguishable.

"Let's go this way." He led her along the shoreline.

"What is that?"

"What?"

"Over there." She pointed a little distance ahead of them.

"Don't know." Let's have a closer look. "Oh. Never seen anything like it before. People are swimming in the sea."

"Are they?!" She strained her eyes against the strong and yet misty sunshine. "So they are. But there are so many together."

"Just a minute. I think I read about this somewhere. It's what they call a bathing facility."

"What does that mean?"

"It's where a lot of people can gather together to swim safely. The organisers provide changing booths down by the waterside. That way swimmers don't have to spend much time exposed in their costumes."

"You mean people can see each other!? Men and Women!?"

"I think so. But the idea is to give them little chance of a proper peek."

"Oh dear. I am not sure I would like that."

"Well, you don't have to worry. We haven't got any bathing costumes with us. Come to that, we don't have bathing costumes." That mischievous twinkle sparkling in his eyes.

"Richard. Sometimes you are incorrigible."

"Only sometimes?" Leaning in, he kissed her passionately.

"Behave yourself." Another pleasant, not quite the word, night was clearly coming.

"Why?" That mischievous sparkle still there. "Come on then, let's get back to the shops before they close. You'll never forgive me if you don't get those things you want."

"True." They headed back at an easy pace. The shops would not be closing for a while yet.

"Have you decided?"

"There are so many different styles. Look how intricate they are and all the colours. Then there are the enamelled ones and those with threads of gold going through them. I am not sure which to choose."

"You can't buy them all so better decide."

"Perhaps one of each style for us. And would you mind if we bought some of those wonderful paintings?"

"No, but remember, you already bought some the other day."

"Yes, but these are different."

"All right." He couldn't deny her the pleasure. Anyway, she rarely spent much. This was special after all, and they'd probably never come back. Seeing Peter Lucca in the square had seen to that.

"Thank you darling."

"If you've got everything, I think we've time for a coffee before heading back. I saw a nice café by the sea when we arrived. It's not far from the jetty, so we're not in danger of missing our ride back."

"That sounds just right."

"What is it darling?" They had been enjoying the view across the lake together with a coffee and light Venetian pastry when he'd suddenly sat bolt upright.

"Cover your face quick!" As suddenly as he'd sat up, he now slid down into his seat. Picking up one of the packages, he pretended to read a non-existent label.

"What is it?" She whispered, while pulling the rim of her hat down.

"Peter Lucca. He's in that passing boat." She moved her head to look. "Don't. He might spot you. Blast, can't we get any peace?"

"What are we going to do?"

"Stay still. Try not to draw attention. They'll have gone in a few minutes. Thankfully, he's looking straight ahead and not over here." He pulled the rim of his own hat further over his face. She held her breath. He discreetly watched from behind the package in his hands. "Okay, they've gone." He breathed from under his hat.

"I thought you said he would not come here."

"I didn't think he would. Well, he didn't really. They were clearly heading somewhere else."

"Are we going to be safe?"

"Yes. Tomorrow's our last day. Then we're out of here. We'll be fine once we put a little distance between this place and ourselves."

“I hope so. This is getting annoying. I have a good mind to find him and give him a piece of my mind.”

“I bet you have. But it’ll do no good. Okay, the boat’s arrived. Let’s board before he comes back. We’ll sit behind one of the awnings, just in case.”

8

In-laws

"Thank you dear, these are exquisite. They will look perfect on the sideboard." Katherine had just presented her mother-in-law with a pair of Venetian glass vases.

"Now come with me." Richard's father semi-commanded with a friendly smirk. Moving from the drawing room, he led them down the corridor into the east wing.

"Where're you taking us father?"

"We thought you and Katherine may prefer to have some privacy from the rest of the household. So we took advantage of your absence to refurbish the east wing." Katherine, Richard and his parents would, as was traditional, be living in the same house.

"That is very thoughtful of you sir."

"Please call me George Katherine. We're family now. There's no need for such formality between us."

"Thank you sir, I mean George sir. Oh, sorry. It will take me a while to get used to it."

"Ha! Ha! That's all right. Now, here we are." Opening the door to their right, he ushered them through.

"We thought this would make a nice little drawing room for you to enjoy together." Richard's mother declared with a beaming smile. A couple of comfortable looking armchairs with a delicate occasional table set between them stood in the centre of the room. Above a small writing table set against the wall to their right hung a magnificent painting. It depicted a view of Venice that included one of the canals they had enjoyed gliding along. Large gilt-edged mirrors adorned two of the other walls. A plush richly coloured Turkish carpet combining with the penetrating sunbeams gave the whole a warm, cosy, luxurious feel.

"I hope you like it. George brought most of the furniture from Vienna when he completed his degree."

"Oh yes! It is wonderful. Thank you."

"Come and have a look at the view." Opening the French doors, George ushered them onto the large balcony. A vast broad open fertile valley spread before them. To their right, in the distance, the aqua blue sea glistened in the sunlight. The backdrop of majestic purple mountains had lost none of its impact. It was the same panoramic vista Katherine had admired on her first visit to the house. She was enchanted. A bedroom to the rear of the house with all other amenities shared had been all she expected.

"How can we ever thank you? This is all so marvellous. Thank you very, very much." Her face bright with unreserved delight.

"Yes sir. Thank you. You've both been very generous." His father waved away the compliment.

"Let us continue." Purposefully striding across the room and out the door. They dutifully followed. Opening the door of another room, he indicated for them to precede him. Katherine's eye was immediately drawn to the large honey coloured maple four-poster. In truth, she could hardly miss it. Cuddling into the warmth of Richard's arm, she was unable to stifle the small giggle that arose within her. He looked down with that mischievous glint in his eye. Then recalling his parent's presence straitened his features.

"I really do not know what to say. This is lovely!" She was truly taken with the beauty of the room. The rich thick lace curtains that hung round the bed softened the brilliant sunshine as it bounced off the dressing table, water stand and chairs appropriately dotted round the room.

“We wanted you to feel you had your own home separate from the rest of the house. There is also a changing room and a small study further down the corridor.”

“You have thought of everything. We can never thank you enough.”

“No need. We are just pleased you like it all.”

“The rest of the rooms will make nice nurseries.” Her mother-in-law added with a twinkle in her eye. Katherine giggled again. She could not help but feel as if she were a little girl having the ways of nature explained to her for the first time. “I hope you will not mind, but we wanted meals to be a family time. So we have not provided any separate utility rooms.” Helina further added while smiling broadly, having really taken to her new daughter-in-law.

“You have been so thoughtful. I really do not know how to thank you both. It is all wonderful. And of course we would love to have meals together.”

“Good. I am so pleased. Martha has already sorted out which of the staff will look after your needs.”

“Oh dear. I do not want to be a nuisance or cause any inconvenience.”

“You are not. I always insist all rooms are cleaned regularly even if they are not in use. So it is not going to make a great deal of difference to them.”

“Thank you and you sir, sorry George, you are so considerate.”

“Yes, thank you Mother and you, Sir. I hadn’t expected anything like this.”

“I cannot tell you how much pleasure it gives us son. We are very pleased to have you both living here with us in the family home.” Relief flooded through Katherine. She had expected, as a new bride and as tradition dictated, to have to share everything with her mother-in-law, without being allowed to live a separate existence. She had often overheard newly married wives complain about how difficult they found their new existence with their overbearing mothers-in-law. Thankfully, Helina appeared to be of a different disposition and someone with great understanding. Of course, it made it easier that there was a household staff, though she was pleased to note they were treated more like family members than servants.

She spent the afternoon familiarising herself with their new home. There was little she wanted to change. George and Helina had decorated and organised everything to her liking, as if they'd been inside her head. She simply put her own stamp upon it by adding knickknacks and ornaments bought in Vienna and Venice. The Venetian glass, set off to advantage by the ornate furniture, fit perfectly. Some pictures she replaced with ones bought in Venice and a couple of childhood favourites her mother let her have. Hopefully, they would become favourites with her own children. To finish it all off, she added some of the china purchased as part of her wedding trousseau. Stepping back to admire her finished work, she again found herself surprised by how happy she was.

Sitting at the dressing table brushing her hair on this first night in their new home, she wondered. Would she ever come to terms with how happy she was? None of this could have been truly envisioned. Was she really living this existence, or was it all some fantastic dream? Her reflection in the mirror and that of her husband crossing the room told her it was all real. With just a couple of his long strides, he reached her, bent, and kissed the back of her neck. His firm, powerful hands resting on her shoulders were so reassuring. Closing her eyes, she leaned back into him, extending her neck to its full length, exposing the sensitive areas. She languished in the sensation of his lips as they caressed her delicate flesh.

Stepping back a pace, he gently turned her. As they looked into each other's eyes, she felt, and certainly not for the first time, as if she were being submerged beneath some wonderfully warm golden liquid. Those eyes, those wonderful eyes.

"I've never told you how from the first moment I looked into your eyes I never wanted another woman in the same way."

"Really? You could have fooled me what with all the flirting." Intense joy percolated through her. Leaning in again, he recommenced his kissing of her neck. She felt the strength of his desire for her as it pulsed through his shirtless torso. Her own mounting passion threatened to suffocate. She wanted him! She wanted him NOW! He sensed her opening up to him like a fresh flower in early sunlight.

Lifting her in his muscular arms, he headed for the demanding four-poster that would see the birth of their four children.

"I want to make lots of babies with you."

"Uh uh. But not too many." Her voice, with its soft, far-off smoothness, aroused him further.

"We'll see." Her hair fell across his arms in rich, if tangled, waves, all thought of brushing it forgotten. Gently placing her on the bed, he removed his remaining clothing.

"Sweetheart..."

"Darling..." Time ceased to exist. There was no one else in the entire universe.

9

Dorcas

"Before we get the clinic up and running, I better get to grips with the family business. That way, we'll have a clear idea of how much time I'll have available."

"Yes, I suppose so. I would have preferred not to wait. But what you say makes sense. I will just have to be patient." He spent the following weeks with his father and the estate manager. She occupied herself helping Helina run the house and with visiting the sick and poor. In particular, ensuring their estate worker's families had all they needed.

"I hope you realise Richard will not have very much spare time. I hardly ever see his father during the day except for the occasional lunch." A note of concern infiltrating Helina's words.

"I am beginning to appreciate it."

"Do you really want this clinic? You are the one who will have to deal with it and the patients for most of the time."

"Richard and I have discussed it at length and agree we want it. There would have been no point in us both training otherwise. We realise I will have to deal with most of the patients and paperwork, but as long as he can see to the more serious cases, I do not mind." Her motivation had always been to help as many people as possible, whether well off, poor, or destitute. The thought of anyone suffering was anathema to her.

"As long as you understand."

"I do, but thank you for your concern."

"I am prepared to help if I can. With the organisation and paperwork, I mean. Not with patients."

"I would appreciate that. I would also value your help with the old family remedies. Mother has taught me everything she knows, but perhaps you know of others."

"All right. But I doubt I have more knowledge than Andrea."

"Thank you. Now, if we have finished here, I think I will visit the ladies for a while."

"Yes, I think that is everything done for today. You will be back for lunch?"

"Yes I will."

Following the path as it wound round the large outcrops of rock, she could not help occasionally stopping to enjoy the vista. The valley never ceased to impress her with its beauty and variety. The few walnut and cypress trees scattered across the valley floor reminded her of sentinels, each guarding the fertile fields spread below them. Labourers rested in the shade, escaping the intensity of the summer sun. What a shame they had to work in the open fields during the hot days. But what choice was there? Everyone relied upon the harvests for their survival. At least she could help relieve some of the anxiety of such a demanding life by providing for their families.

Rounding the final bend, the joyful laughter of children playing on the green greeted her. How good to have such considerate in-laws who had arranged for the cottages to be built on this little plateau just a little further down from the house. In her mind's eye she imagines how lively the green would be during Mayday, national and holy day celebrations. The children's innocent laughter and high spirits as they run round the well dominating the far side of the green is infectious. She bounces along with a light step.

"Good morning, Peggy!" Standing on the threshold of the open door, she peered into the darkened interior.

“G’d moning miss. Com in, com in.” Peggy’s pale, timid, fearful form slowly materialised next to the kitchen table.

“Katherine please.”

“Oh! Ok .... Kath..rin.” Commotion suddenly erupted from the rear of the cottage.

“Goodness, what is going on?”

“T’s only th chilrn playin.”

“How many have you?”

“Five nother on way.”

“Goodness. How do you put up with it? I think the noise alone would drive me mad.”

“Oh no. I lov aving em bout me.”

“Really? I do not think I could cope with so many.”

“Thm no bther really. Jus plaful. But I worris bout em. Wat I’ll do if any of em bit by snake or av bad fall?”

“Well, with the noise they are making, I doubt any snake would come near. But should it ever happen, which is unlikely, there are antidotes.”

“But I man’t get em sen to in time.” Her ever present worry lines deepened.

“We are only just up the hill. Send for one of us whenever you need to. Richard is a qualified doctor, and I have studied many illnesses, including snake bites.”

“Ave ee! Tha good.”

“You understand? Remember, any time of the day or night.” She noticed how much thinner Peggy looked and how her dark auburn tangled hair lacked lustre. Her constant worrying and stress was obviously taking a toll.

“Ye. Tank ee. Yee kind.”

“Nonsense. That is why we trained. We want to help when we can. How is Martin?”

“E’s in nortrn filds tody. Tol me som tees needs loping. Wat if e falls?”

“I doubt he will. He is very experienced, I believe.”

“Ye e is. But wat if e’s hurt? Or killd? Wat woul chilrn an I do?”

"Come along Peggy, you are being a bit melodramatic."

"Am Is? Is alwys worris soming'll appn."

"No matter what, Peggy, Richard and I will always make sure you and the children are looked after."

"Yee's kind. But wat woul I do?"

"Peggy! That is enough. Nothing has happened, nor is it going to happen."

"If yee's say so miss."

"Katherine please."

"Kath..rin...." Starring into the distance, a mist clouding her eyes. As if in a trance, she rose from her seat and returned to the sink. Where, appearing to have forgotten her guest, she continued preparing the family meal.

"Are you all right Peggy?" No response. It was as if she were invisible. Keeping her voice calm and soft, "Peggy, nothing is going to happen." Still no response. Probably best to leave her to herself for now.

"Good morning Dorcas. How are you all?"

"Fine, thank you Katherine. And you up at the house?"

"We are all well, thank the Lord."

"Good."

"You are getting large. When is the baby due?"

"Soon, couple of weeks, I reckon. When's yours due?"

"Oh! How did you know?"

"I've been around enough expectant women to recognise the signs."

"Well, yes, you are right. I am expecting. I have not told Richard or the family yet. I have only just become sure myself."

"Congratulations. Your first. Are you excited?"

"More nervous really."

"Nothing to worry about. This is my sixth and I've never had any problems."

"I hope you are right."

"You look the picture of health. You'll be fine. When you going to tell the others? If you're anything like me, you'll start showing soon and won't be able to hide it much longer."

"I know. Over dinner this evening, I think."

"They'll be thrilled. I've often heard Mr Palmerstone say he wants to see the birth of an heir."

"I really do not mind what I have, but for his sake I hope it is a boy."

"That's in the Lord's hands. What will be will be."

"Yes it will. I have just been to see Peggy. She is in quite a state worrying whether one of the children might get bitten by a snake or have a bad fall or her husband having an accident. I told her not to worry so. I also assured her we would always look after her and the children, no matter what. But she just would not be calmed."

"Peggy's always been like that. Can't forget how she and her mama struggled after her papa died. They did have a rough time of it until Mr Palmerstone, Mr Palmerstone senior I mean, kindly employed them. And now she's married to Martin their future is reasonably secure. But she just can't seem to stop her fears. We all do our best to keep her calm."

"I had no idea."

"No reason you should."

"I do not really like to say anything, but do you think her mind is in order? She behaved a little strangely before I left."

"Acting as if you weren't there?"

"Yes."

"Don't concern yourself about it. It's just tiredness. The children and her constant worrying wear her out at times and she just drifts off for a moment. We'll keep an eye on her. Nothing for you to worry your pretty head about."

"As long as you are sure. You will let me know if there is ever anything I can do."

"Yes. But I doubt you'll be needed. Having her next door makes it easier for me to keep an eye on things. I can just nip over whenever necessary."

"Very well. I will continue to visit as usual, but leave the rest to you."

"She enjoys your visits. We all do."

"I am so glad. I sometimes wonder if I am being a nuisance."

"Not at all."

"I better get going. I am expected for lunch."

A deep sigh escaped as she made her way back up the hill, her thoughts turning to her beloved. How she missed him. There was so much to learn and understand that most days he left before she was up and rarely returned before late evening. There had been the odd lunch time when he would unexpectedly surprise them, but these were rare. She longed for the time when he would not be away so much. Lost in these thoughts, the sudden grasp on her shoulder made her jump.

"Hello sweetheart. I've been missing you." He covered her mouth with his, preventing any response. The tangy aroma of his masculinity sent a delightful shiver down her spine.

"Richard! I did not expect to see you until this evening." She pulled back a little and gazed into those wonderful, captivating eyes. Would she ever get over the effect they had on her? Did she want to?

"I know. But I've missed you so much today. Let's go to our room." He couldn't restrain his mischievous, wicked smile.

"But it is almost lunchtime. Helina is expecting me." Despite herself, she felt the desire within responding.

"Plenty of time." The sensuality of his voice awaking her passion further. She followed him to their room.

"I'm sorry it's taken so long, but I finally feel I've got a grip on the business." They were enjoying an after lunch stroll in the garden. He'd decided to take a rare afternoon off.

"I am glad darling. You have been working so hard."

"We can get on with establishing a clinic now if you like."

"Yes I would. I have been dying to get going."

"Okay, but I now know I'll not be able to give it as much time as I hoped. That means you'll really be the one running it. Are you going to be okay with that?"

"Yes I am."

"As long as you're sure. I don't want you getting stressed or overtired."

"I will be glad to get it up and running. And there is no need to worry about me. I doubt we are going to be inundated with patients. As long as you can see to the more serious cases, I will be fine. I have seen a lot of need when visiting. Some just need general hygiene guidance, but others really could do with more positive medical care. Having the clinic will help a lot. I have done my best with old family remedies, but sometimes having access to the more robust modern medicines and equipment would be useful."

"Okay. I'll go and ask father if we can have one of the unused buildings."

"Father."

"Yes son."

"Would you mind if I use the old stable office for a clinic?"

"No, not at all, but do you think there's really a need for one? Most doctors make home visits. Would anyone bother coming to a clinic?"

"What you say is generally true, but most doctors are in town. Katherine and I would like to provide something for the estate workers nearer to home. And somewhere the poor of the district can come without embarrassment. In addition, Katherine's father is getting frail and intends to give up his practice. He's told her he plans to refer his patients to us. Some of them like to discuss problems discreetly, away from prying eyes and ears. They would be able to pretend they're visiting us."

"You realise the estate workers and, of course, the poor would not be able to pay you?"

"Yes. But we hardly need the money. Anyway, there'd be less working time lost if our staff have more immediate help. And don't forget that we employ a lot more at harvest times."

"I suppose so. All right, you may have the old office. I still doubt it will get much use, but you can have it."

"Thank you sir. You may be right, people may not come, we'll just have to wait and see. Anyway, it would be a shame for all the training both Katherine and I've had to be wasted."

"What about medications, equipment, etcetera? Where will you get them from? Do you know what you will need to have on hand?"

"There's a supplier in town. You probably know him, Mr Johnson?"

"Yes, of course. I do not really know him, but understand he stocks quite a range of products."

"Initially, we'll just keep a selection of medicines to treat the most common illnesses along with bandages and such. I'll keep an eye on medical journals and if any new disease comes to light, I can get some of the appropriate medications in. We won't require very much equipment. Mr Johnson should be able to supply what we need."

"You have obviously thought this out."

"Yes, Katherine and I have been talking about it since we got back. I just wanted to familiarise myself with the business before launching into it. She's been itching to get started."

"So I understand from your mother. I must say you have married quite a woman there. And you have certainly grasped the fundamentals of the business. But will you have time for both?"

"I think so. I won't be able to dedicate as much time as I thought to the clinic, but I've worked out a schedule and am fairly sure I can do it. Anyway, it's more than likely Katherine's nursing expertise will be needed more than my analytical services. She'll look after the clinic when I'm out working. I can always be sent for if needed urgently."

"Father's agreed to us having the old stable office."

"Oh good. It will suit the purpose well. A small consulting desk with a couple of chairs, a water stand and cupboard will fit nicely. The little room at the back will be ideal for examining patients."

"Well, you seem to have that all organised. Just need to get it cleaned and painted. Now, you really do understand you'll be on your own for much of the time? And as father ages, I'll have to dedicate even more time to the business."

"We have already discussed this. Anyway, as I said before, I doubt we are going to be overrun. There are bound to be long periods when there is no one. I can use those times to dry and prepare herbs for the home remedies."

"You won't be able to see the clinic door from the shed."

"I have already thought of that. If your father will not mind, I can use one of the outhouses opposite. The office door is visible from them. That way I will be able to use all my time effectively rather than just sitting rounding waiting for people to turn up."

"I'm sure he won't mind. Well, that's all settled then. There's something different about you. Have you done something to your hair?"

"No. But there is something I want to tell you. I was going to wait until dinner this evening, but I think it only fair I tell you before the others."

"Tell me what? There's nothing wrong with you, is there?" Anxiety shadowing his features.

"No, I am fine. But I did not want to say anything until I was sure."

"Sure of what!?"

"Sometimes, for a doctor, you can be a bit dense. I am pregnant."

"You're what!?"

"Pregnant."

"Oh, darling, that's great!"

"I thought you might be pleased."

"How long? I mean, how long have you known?"

"I have been reasonably sure for a couple of weeks or so, but I wanted to wait before telling you, just in case."

"I wish you'd told me. Now we must take care of you. This isn't the time to worry about a clinic. We'll put it on hold."

"That was one of the things that has been bothering me. Everyone making a great to-do about it. I am not fragile. I am just pregnant. Most women survive it without any problem."

"Yes, but this is our first. I want to make sure you're okay."

"I am. Now stop fussing. I would prefer we did not tell anyone else until your parents know. I thought we could tell them over dinner this evening." However, he couldn't contain his excitement. No matter how often she tried to quieten him, he insisted on telling anyone who happened to be around. Gardeners, stable staff, general labourers, anyone. Back in the house, he immediately called for his parents and breathlessly imparted the news. So much for a calm announcement over dinner!

"Oh darlings! I am so happy for you both." Helina cried, just as beside herself as her son.

"Are you okay Katherine?" George was the only one who did not appear bowled over by the revelation. Though she spotted a discrete, broad, satisfied smile when he thought no one was looking.

"Yes, thank you. It is hardly a new experience for a woman."

"I was saying I thought we should put the clinic on hold."

"Please stop fussing. I am fine. I am not going to break. Anyway, do you expect me to sit round for the whole time doing nothing?"

"Well......."

"As a doctor you should know better. We pregnant women need exercise if we are going to be fit enough to give birth properly." Oh! Goodness! Pregnant! Full realisation hit, sending a shiver down her spine and releasing butterflies in stomach.

"Katherine is right dear. She does need to keep active."

"Yes I know. But I don't want her over taxing herself."

"Please stop. I want to get this clinic up and running. And I want to continue helping where I can. No more argument please." Keeping her frustration in check was becoming difficult.

"If you're sure sweetheart."

"Yes I am."

"They've finished cleaning and painting. It's almost ready for use." A week had passed since Katherine's announcement.

"Good. We will be able to help more people now."

"Father said we could take any of the old furniture we wanted from the store at the back."

"I have already had a look. There is a nice desk for you and an old washstand. There are also a couple of cupboards I think will do once they are cleaned up. Your mother has also offered a rug that is no longer used. The only thing outstanding is an examination couch. I think you will have to buy that."

"Okay. Why don't we go into town tomorrow? I reckon I can be spared for a couple of hours or so."

"That would be ideal."

"Johnson stocks a wide range. He should have everything we need, including dressings, splints and whatever else you think necessary. We could have lunch while we're in town. Make a change."

"That would be nice. We better stock up with medications while we are there. The old remedies cannot heal every condition."

"Okay then, it's a date. Now I better go. It looks like the west meadow may have to be drained. Wretched nuisance."

"Ready?"

"Yes." He gingerly lifted her into the carriage. She could not help laugh at how cautious he was being. "I am not made of china darling. I really will not break."

"Can't be too careful. I want you both well."

A pleasant warm breeze caressed their faces as the carriage gently bumped along. The road taking them along the edge of the valley now enabled her to admire the familiar vista at eye level. Sunlight glancing of the yellow, brown, green and purple crops enhanced her delight as she took in the misty grey and purple mountains on the far side. Was there a more beautiful place?

"Here we are. Shall we go and order what we need before having lunch?"

"Uhuh."

"Not too tired, are you sweetheart? Was the journey too fatiguing?"

"No, I am fine. It is just the pleasant drive and warm sunshine have made me feel quite relaxed."

"Good. I don't want you overdoing it."

"Richard, please stop fussing." Trying but failing to look cross, she secretly rejoiced he cared so much. Despite her remonstrations, the pregnancy combined with her vomiting had been tiring her. Consequently, she had had to refuse his advances most nights. Concern for the frustration he must be feeling troubled her. After all, he was a very physical man.

"We better get to Johnson's before he shuts for lunch." She cradled his arm in the pretence of needing support as they headed for the store. But in truth just wanted to feel the warmth of his body against her own and to breathe him in. If only she did not feel so tired at nights.

"That's everything sorted. I'll take you to lunch now."

"Where are we going?"

"I thought 'Berties'. What do you think?"

"Mmmm. I have not been there for a long time. They always have a nice selection."

"Okay, 'Berties' it is."

"It is nice to have time together like this again."

"Yes it is. I'm sorry I've been so busy. But we should have more time to ourselves now."

"Good, I am very glad. I have missed these outings." She had often recalled their times in the Vienna café with affection. They had been such happy days. Yet, though those memories were precious, she was almost unbelievably far happier now.

"Katherine!"

"Jennifer! How good to see you." They eagerly kissed and embraced each other. "When did you get back?"

"Oh, I've been back for a while but mother hasn't been well and I couldn't leave her. She's getting a little better now and I was hoping to visit you in a few days."

"It is so good to see you. Richard, you remember Miss Denis."

"Yes, nice to see you again Miss Denis. I hope you are well."

"I am thank you Mr Palmerstone."

"We are just going for lunch. Will you join us?" Though she had been looking forward to it just being the two of them, her excitement at meeting Jennifer overruled.

"That's kind of you. I'd love to if Mr Palmerstone wouldn't mind."

"Of course not." Delighted at the pleasure Jennifer's appearance was giving his wife.

Arriving at Berties, they found a table on the shaded terrace.

"Now tell me all about Vienna, our friends, and what everyone is up to."

"Well, there's no need to ask what's happening here. When's it due?"

"Oh!" A schoolgirl giggle escaping. "Not for a little while yet." While they were talking, Richard suddenly stood and, saying nothing, went to another table where he greeted people he obviously knew. It was impossible to miss how the ladies in the group, as well as others sitting round, brightened at the sight of him. Neither did she fail to see the sparkle in his own eyes. She was not naïve. She knew she had been anything but the first woman he had been with. In Vienna they had always flaunted themselves in front of him and it had been obvious he had not always resisted temptation. Now, knowing she had been unable to satisfy his physical needs, she worried he may be tempted again. The attention was clearly feeding his desires. It had been a long time since she had experienced anything like jealousy, but here it again rose its ugly head. Did she have anything to fear? He still loved her? Well, she thought he did. His attentions recently said he did. Or was that just because of the baby? No, she must stop being so silly. Becoming aware she had tuned Jennifer out, she forcibly drew her eyes from Richard and back to her friend. "Oh, yes, please come over soon. I would love to catch up." She hoped Jennifer had not noticed her distraction.

"Come on dear, another push."

"Agh! No more!"

"Come on, almost there."

"Aghhhh!"

"There I can see the head. Come on, another push." She was exhausted and just wanted to curse and swear. Yet excitement at the prospect of seeing her child overrode those negative impulses. Gathering the little strength left her, she pushed and pushed.

"Almost there. You are doing well. Deep breaths now. Come on, just a little more. Come on, dear."

"Damn! Oh sorry."

"No need to apologise. One more push should do it."

"Aghhh!"

"Well done darling." She lay back exhausted and enquired with her eyes.

"You have a lovely daughter."

"Let me see her!" The thrill of cuddling her new born was unlike anything she had ever felt before. Her initial emotions for Richard had been exciting and wonderful, though they had also confused and disorientated. It had never crossed her mind there could be anything to compare, let alone surpass. But here and now, she discovered an instinctive love for the little bundle in her arms.

"Well done dear. She is beautiful. How are you feeling?"

"I cannot believe how happy I am. I love her. She is gorgeous."

"Shall I call Richard in?"

"Yes please. I want him to see his daughter." Within seconds, the new father was at her bedside. Eyes sparkling with love and excitement.

"Are you all right sweetheart?"

"Yes. Do you mind she is not a boy?"

"Of course not. She's beautiful, just like her mother." She lifted her precious bundle up to him. Hesitantly, he took his daughter from her arms.

"She's lovely." He whispered, looking down upon the screwed-up face of his newborn.

"Come on now. Out with you. They both need to rest." Gently removing the little bundle from his arms, his mother shooed him out. Nevertheless, he insisted on kissing his wife and child before leaving.

"I love you sweetheart." Whispered into her ear. She waited for him to leave the room before falling back on the pillows, feeling totally drained.

"You need to rest dear. Martha and I will clear up and then leave you to sleep."

"Thank...you..." Her voice trailing off as she fell into a deep slumber.

10

Temptation

The small wicker basket of herbal remedies and modern medicines swung from her arm as she increased her pace. The approaching dark clouds promised a rare summer shower. If only it would clear the heavy humidity that had troubled them all morning.

"Hello Peggy. All well?" She called, passing the cottage door.

"Ye tank ee Kath..rin." At long last, she had become accustomed to addressing her by name.

"Good afternoon Mary."

"Oh! Hello Katherine. Nice to see you."

"How are you all? Do you need anything?"

"We're okay, thank you, and have everything we need."

"Good, I am very pleased to hear it. Hello Johnny. What have you got there?" Mary's toddler son lifted a small twisted branch.

"He's forever bringing things like that home. I think he likes the different shapes and patterns."

"What is wrong with his neck?" A sore looking rash descended from his left ear into the top of his collar.

"I'm not sure. He's had it for days. Just won't go."

"Let me have a look at your neck Johnny." He dutifully drew closer and allowed her to lift his chin.

"Do you think it's anything serious?"

"No. If you look closely, you will see there is ground in dirt. You just need to wash him regularly with clean water. It will soon go. Washing frequently, even if it is only with plain clean water, will help prevent a lot of sores and diseases. Daily would be best."

"Really! Okay, I'll do as you say and wash him every day."

"And yourselves. Everyone should wash regularly."

"Oh! Okay. Thank you for telling me."

"It should clear up in two or three days. Let me know if it does not. Now I better get going. I want to call in at Dorcas's and some of the others before returning home."

"Good afternoon Dorcas. How are you?"

"Well, thank you Katherine. And you? I see you're due again. How long?"

"Yes. Not too long now. I am hoping this will be a boy. When Ellen was born I had been concerned Richard's father may resent her for not being a boy but, thankfully, he really does love her. Nevertheless, you were right. Though he never says anything, he really does want to see the birth of an heir. I think he is worried he will die without it happening."

"He shouldn't be worrying about things like that at his age. He's got a long time to go."

"I told him that, but he is concerned. In fairness, though, he has, for some reason, been feeling the years more recently. I have to admit, he does look frailer these days."

"We all go through times like that. I'm sure it'll pass quickly enough."

"I hope so. I have just been to see Mary. It is nice to see her so happy. She really is a breath of fresh air."

"Yes. Such an innocent. Though Peter is a lot older, they are very happy together. He has a tendency to mollycoddle her, which I'm not sure is really good. But there, what can you do. He really loves her. She still thinks life is easy and I suppose, in fairness, it has been for her so far. But as we all know, difficulties are bound to arise at some point. I'm not sure she's really equipped to deal with them."

"Let us hope she is one of those who does not have to face anything too serious. But if she does, we will just have to make sure she survives."

"Yes, we will. As you say, all we can do is hope nothing too awful happens."

"I better get back, otherwise they will worry. They fuss so much. I keep telling them I am fine and will not break."

"You're the lucky one. No one fusses over me. Make a nice change if they did, but I expect I'd get annoyed with it. Mind you, I'd not mind trying it for a while." Both laughed.

"Sweetheart." Leaning over, he embraced her. Desire pulsing through his naked body like lightning.

"I am sorry darling, but I do not really feel up to it." For some time the baby had lain heavily on a nerve but, because of their tendency to fuss, she had told no one. A flash of annoyance darkened his features as he turned away. "I am sorry." No response but to move further to his side of the bed. Feeling terrible, but knowing she could not have coped, she lay as still as possible. At least she could let him sleep in peace. While listening to his rhythmic breathing, anxiety took hold. He was such a physical man whose needs required regular satisfaction. Something she had been unable to do recently. Would he get fed up and start looking elsewhere? His flirting had intensified lately.

"The Jacksons have invited us over. They're going to have a ball for their daughters eighteenth."

"That will be nice. I have not seen them for a while."

"The ball's next Thursday."

"Time enough for me to find something suitable that will fit."

"Ha! Ha! No need to worry. You look great." Was he just saying that? Was it all about the baby? She knew he was excited at the prospect of another child. No doubt, together with his father, hoping for a boy.

“Well, thank you, kind sir.” Giving him a mock curtsy. Deciding to believe he was being genuine or, if not, to at least play along.

She felt heavy and tired. The baby had been kicking for some time and continued to lie on the nerve. All she wanted was to go home and lay down. However, it would be rude to leave so soon. Helping herself to a cool lemonade from the buffet, she moved to the open French doors. Just looking out over the pleasant green lawn refreshed her. It was a real treat amid the surrounding arid sunburnt fields. Glancing back into the room, she noticed Richard in a corner with one of the pretty local girls. As she watched, the girl drew closer to her husband, who towered over her petite form. Then on tiptoe she whispered in his ear. The girl giggled and he laughed. Was she in danger of losing him? Did he find her pregnant state unattractive? She felt anything but attractive with the continuous sickness, flat limp hair and added weight. Not to mention the constant discomfort and tiredness. Or was he bored of their marriage? In her current vulnerable state, she was not sure what to think. But he appeared to pay less attention to her these days and was constantly flirting. Then, in fairness, she had to acknowledge they were always flirting with him. Something she had got used to. You could not have such a handsome husband and expect no one to pay him attention. Should she go over? No, that would appear churlish. Anyway, in her present condition and inability to meet his needs, she could hardly blame him if he looked elsewhere.

“Are you okay Katherine? You look a little depressed. Well, perhaps not depressed but concerned.” It was the next morning and she was on one of her visits.

“I am fine, thank you Dorcas. Probably just tired. The baby is due soon and I think I may have been overdoing things a little.”

“You need to take care dear. You’re not as robust as the rest of us. You don’t have to do everything. Me and the others can help.”

“I know, but I hate sitting round. I am all right really, just a little tired. Please do not worry about me. Anyway, you have enough to contend with seeing to Peggy and your own family. I can rest when I get back.”

“Just take care. We don’t want you being ill. You also need to think of the baby.”

Dorcas had been right. She did feel depressed. And, despite her family and friends, rather lonely. Why? With the baby weighing even heavier, she was finding it a labour to get back up the hill, so sat on a convenient rock. As always, she found pleasure in the view. The green, gold and amber of the ripening vines delighting. The tall corn with even taller sunflowers wavering in the breeze refreshing. The sunlight bouncing from the bell towers and rooftops in the villages climbing up the foothills on the other side uplifting. Yet her despondency would not be alleviated. All was fine with the baby and the clinic. So what was it? Richard. Was she losing him? Did he no longer love her? He spent far more evenings at the café than he used to. Came home later and later. Did she detect other women's scent on him? His kisses at night had become peripheral, just a quick peck on the cheek or forehead as if she were a child. The way he turned from her when in bed. How she missed physical contact with him and the cocooned sense it gave her. If she tried to touch him, he moved further away, not even turning his head to look. Then there had been his flirtation at the ball. Had he really tired of her? Did he want other women now? Was she becoming paranoid? In her hormonal state, she failed to control the tears, glad there was no one nearby to see. When they ended, she glanced up. Goodness! The sun had moved some distance. Helina would start to worry and may send someone to look for her. Shaking her head clear she stood, wiped her tear-stained cheeks, and continued her weary way home.

"You look tired dear. Have you overdone it again?"

"I am all right, but I do feel tired. I will go and lie down for a while."

"Martha can bring lunch to your room."

"Thank you Helina, but I am not hungry."

"No matter. You have the baby as well as yourself to think of. You must eat something."

"Very well. Just a little light soup and a salad. I really do not think I could stomach anymore."

"Are you sure you are all right? You do look rather drawn."

"Just a little tired. I will be fine after a rest." She would not trouble her mother-in-law with her concerns. Anyway, Helina loved her son and believed he could do no wrong. At least, for the present, she could use her pregnant condition as an excuse. But not for ever. How would she cope if he turned to other women? Would have to somehow. All too depressing to think of now. May feel better after a rest. Perhaps she was being silly and reading more into situations than existed. Doubts continued to assail, but for the sake of her daughter and the baby, she must put them aside. For now, at least.

~~~~~~~~

"I've to go up to the city for a couple of days."

"Oh."

"We've had the offer of a substantial contract. Father doesn't feel up to making the journey and has asked me to go and close the deal."

"Where will you stay?"

"Sandra Nola's. Andrew's friend. Do you remember her?" All too well. There had been no mistaking his attraction and the way he would move close to her. Closer than was appropriate.

"The pretty blond?"

"Yes, that's her."

"Yes, I remember her." She hoped her tone held no hint of bitterness. It should not. She was simply feeling insecure, not bitter.

"Why don't you come with me? It'd be nice to have a couple of days away together." Did he mean it? Or was he just playing the game, knowing she had not been feeling too bright?

"It would be nice, but I do not think I am up to the journey. The baby has been lying heavily this time and often on a nerve."

"Are you sure? It'd be great to have some time away."

"Yes it would, but I honestly do not think I am up to it. You better go on your own." The thought of him and Sandra worried her, but she had to face facts.
~~~~~~~~

Travelling at this stage of her pregnancy added to her worn condition would not be wise.

"If you're sure."

"Yes I am. Talking of Andrew, it is about time we invited him to visit."

"Good idea. But after what happened I didn't think it wise to retain contact. But I suppose it's been long enough now. We'll see when I get back."

"All right. It would be nice to see him again."

"Hello Jennifer. So nice of you to call."

"Good morning Katherine. My, you're looking big. Can't be long now."

"No, just a few weeks, I think."

"I saw Richard outside. Looked like he was off somewhere."

"Yes, he has to go up to the city to settle a contract. His father's not too strong these days and I did not feel up to making the journey."

"I should think not in your condition. Ah, here's little Ellen." Her young daughter came bouncing into the drawing room, but stopped suddenly upon seeing Jennifer. "Don't be shy Ellen. See what I have for you."

"Oh! Jennifer, it is beautiful. What do you say Ellen?" Reaching out, the little girl grasped the doll Jennifer held out to her.

"Th..ank you.." Her little shy voice almost inaudible.

"You should not have. But thank you. It really is lovely."

"Nonsense. I love giving her things."

"Well, thank you. I must say you are looking sprightly and pleased with yourself today."

"Am I? Well, I suppose I've reason to be. Do you know Roger Harris?"

"Yes. Mama told me he had gone away to study. Politics in Munich, I believe."

"Yes, that's him. Well, he's back. He's proposed."

"Jennifer! You never told me you were seeing him."

"I didn't want to build my hopes. I wasn't sure if he was serious or not. You know how some of these men can be."

"Well, I am surprised. But you look so happy, so I assume you like him."

"Oh yes! I've liked him for a long time."

"I understand he is really into politics and wants to stand for election. How do you feel about that?"

"I think that may've been one of the things that brought us together. My degree in philosophy and his politics degree seem to complement each other. I can stop him rushing off at a tangent, he can be over enthusiastic sometimes, and he helps keep my feet on the ground."

"I can see how that might work. Well, congratulations. I am happy for you."

"Roger was saying he'd like to get together with Richard. While he was away, he joined some sort of society. He thinks Richard would find it beneficial if he also joined."

"How do you mean?"

"It's called Knights Serpent." No! This cannot be! She desperately hoped her shock was not visible. "Roger says it's primarily philanthropic, you know, charity and all that. Apparently, they help a lot of people. But in addition, each of the members, or knights as they call themselves, help each other with their businesses and careers. He thinks Richard may find it useful for the family business."

"It is kind of him to think of Richard. But I do not think he will be interested in joining something like that." Doing her best to suppress the tremor in her voice.

"Well, Roger's planning on asking him. We'll have to arrange to meet up when Richard's back. I can introduce him to Roger then."

"I will ask him when he returns." They then chatted about Vienna, their friends, and their future expectations.

When Jennifer left, Katherine retired to her room to think. They had not told anyone about Knights Serpent. It was just something they both wanted to forget. But what were they to do now? They had thought it was all in the past, never to bother them again. She would have to wait for Richard. Thinking of him, she could not help but also think of Sandra. Knowing how frustrated he was not having his physical needs met, she worried. Would he be tempted? Would his desires take control? Would the temptation be too much for him? Sandra had always made it obvious how attractive she found him. And, as awful as it was to think it, she knew she was not the most moral of people. But there was no point getting herself into a state now. She did not have the energy. She would have to wait until he returned and then try to work out if anything had happened. On the other hand, did she really want to know?

~~~~~~~~

He found the cool of the marble bench refreshing after his morning stroll through the city. Revisiting old haunts had brought back so many fun memories. How long had it been? Too long. He'd only just turned eighteen when he'd last been there. Would he like to return to those days? Life had been different then. But probably not. Despite recent recurring frustrations, he was actually very happy with life. Debating whether there was time for a coffee before his appointment, he glanced up at the church clock on the other side of the square. No! It couldn't be! What the hell's he doing here? He'd spotted Peter Lucca entering from the east corner. What to do? Mustn't let him see him. But how to avoid it? Sitting in the centre he was surrounded by open space. Whichever way he might try to go the wretched man was bound to see him. Looking round for any possible means of escape, he noted a group of Asian students. The leader, who he imagined must be a lecturer or professor, held a flag above his head. He knew from his time in the academy this was a favoured means for ensuring students didn't get lost. It was chancy, but what else he could he do? With his six-foot broad frame, he would tower over the group. However, the leader was local and of a similar height. What if he stayed beside him and used the open flag as a shield? Not ideal, but what other option was there? Couldn't stay where he was. The blasted man would be on top of him in a matter of minutes.

Standing quickly as the group came alongside, he manoeuvred to place himself beside the guide. Damn! He'd stopped to draw the students' attention to various points of interest. Lucca would be on them at any moment! Should he run for it? No, that would only draw attention. Have to wait and hope. Come on man, quicker! Finishing his talk, the guide led the group on. Phew! Chancing a look
~~~~~~~~

round the flag, he saw no sign of the wretched man. Where was he? Perhaps he'd gone down a side street. Good. Continuing to move with the group though still looking back, he stepped on someone's foot.

"I'm sor....." Turning to apologise, he found himself face to face with Peter Lucca.

"You!!"

"Oh! Hi."

"So this is where you've been hiding."

"I've not been hiding. Let's talk."

"Me talk to you, a traitor? No way. Your tongue and heart are still forfeit."

"For God's sake, this is stupid. We're grown men!"

"Yea! So what! You broke your oath and you're going to pay!"

"I only mentioned a few things to my friends. Of course, they were interested. What else was I supposed to do? It really did no harm."

"You were told never to tell." He hissed. "There're reasons for that. An oath is an oath." As he spoke, his hand moved to his hip. You're joking! An all too familiar dagger handle came into view.

"But it was so long ago. Anyway, I haven't told anyone else a thing. Let's forget it. Okay?"

"No! There's a price to pay, and I'm going to make sure you pay it. By Beelzebub, I'll see your tongue and heart on his altar." His voice full of menace.

"Come on, this is stupid. We're not kids."

"You're going to pay the penalty! You're going to die! This is your last day on this earth!" His eyes darkening, he withdrew the dagger from its sheath. No mistaking the pure evil and vengeance in that look. Have to make a run for it. Which way? They'd been moving along with the group whilst talking, and he noticed a side street coming up. That would have to do.

"This is ridiculous. Surely we can talk it through."

"Nothing to talk about. You broke your oath. That's it. You're going to pay!" HIs voice escalating with each statement.

"What harm did it do? I didn't give any real secrets away."

"You said enough." The blasted man's got a one track mind. No hope of a sensible discussion. Where are we? Ah, right, here goes. Taking a deep breath, he shot off down the side street. The sudden movement catching his antagonist off guard. But not for long. Pushing the dagger back into place, his enemy quickly followed in pursuit. Bugger! Didn't think he was so fit. Pushing himself further, he zigzagged down street after street, lane after lane. If only he could lose him in the maze of crisscrossing streets and lanes. At least he knew his way round, which he doubted his pursuer did. A striking clock reminding him why he was here, he chanced a look back. Good, no sign of him. Diving down yet another lane, he headed in the direction of his appointment, confident he'd now lost the determined knight. Stopping to catch breath, he straightened his clothes then crossing the thoroughfare before him entered the contractor's office.

Stepping back on to the pavement with a sense of satisfaction at having settled the contract, he looked round. Now what? Better abandon any thought of a further reminiscent stroll. Shame. Suppose be best to go back to Sandra's.

"Oh! Hello Richard. I didn't expect you back so early. Is everything okay?"

"Good afternoon Miss Nola. Yes, thank you. The meeting went well, and we concluded our business quickly. Everything has been agreed and the contracts are all signed."

"That's good. So you've a free afternoon."

"Not really. I'll need to get ready to leave in the morning."

"I thought you were going to stay for a couple of days." Disappointment registering.

"That was my original plan. But as everything's been settled so quickly, there's no need for me to stay on."

"Oh! I'd hoped we'd spend some time together. You know, catching up etcetera." A bright lustre shining in her eyes.

"I'm sorry, but it'd be best if I get back as soon as I can. My father isn't too well these days and my wife's expecting our second child soon."

"So you married her then."

"Yes, I thought you knew."

"No. I had no idea. I thought you were still single." Irritation and disappointment this time.

"No more. We married shortly after I returned from Sweden." Best ignore her annoyance. "Thank you for allowing me to stay. Please thank your father for his kindness. He told me he'd be out until late tonight, so I won't see him before I leave."

"Are you sure you couldn't stay another day?" Since his arrival she'd made obvious how happy she'd be to give herself to him. Tempting. Katherine's present condition was making life difficult. Could do with some relief. Perhaps?

~~~~~~~~

"Hello sweetheart." He gave her a quick kiss on the cheek.

"Hello darling. How was your trip? You are back sooner than I expected." She subconsciously looked for any signs.

"Eventful." Fear rose as she observed his dark, clouded expression.

"What do you mean? What happened?" Something was wrong. "Ouch!"

"Are you all right? You don't look too good."

"I think my waters are breaking. Ow!" She grabbed his arm as the pain caused her to double over.

"Mother! Martha! Quick!" Both came running into the hall to find Richard holding Katherine in his arms in an attempt to stop her collapsing on the floor.

"Take her to your room. The babies coming. Hurry!"

Richard, his mother having banished him from the room, paced up and down the corridor, almost wearing a hole in the carpet. As before, his sweetheart's screams of agony tearing at his stomach and nerves. A sudden silence alarmed him. What's happening? Why had no one come out to him? The thought of how many died giving birth crossed his mind. Then, through the heavy silence, he heard a baby's first cry. He couldn't help but leap for joy and with relief.
~~~~~~~~

"Congratulations darling. A baby girl. You can go in now." Almost knocking his mother over, he rushed through the open door.

"Sweetheart! Are you okay?"

"Uhuh. She is beautiful. Look." She gazed down at the little bundle resting on the bed beside her. Then gently pushed the blanket down so he could see the little wrinkled face.

"Yes she is. And so are you. Well done sweetheart."

"Come on, now, out with you. Katherine needs to rest."

"Okay mother. They're both okay, aren't they?"

"Yes dear. Both are fine. But now they need their rest."

"All right, I'm going."

Mother and daughter remained in their room for a few days with Richard, his mother, and Martha in constant attendance.

"Now I want to know all about your trip. You were going to tell me something when Andrea decided it time to come into the world. Bless her." She had not forgotten his look of horror. Not wanting to alarm or burden her after the birth, he had said nothing about his encounter with Peter.

"That can wait. You just get better."

"I am fine. Something is troubling you. I want to know what. I will only worry if you do not tell me."

"If you're sure."

"I am."

"Well ... Are you sure?"

"Richard! Tell me! You are frightening me."

"Okay. You remember Peter Lucca. The one from Knights Serpent in Vienna and then in Venice?"

"You mean that nasty man who chased us?"

"Yes."

"What about him?"

"I saw him. In the city."

"Oh no! Did he see you?"

"Yes." He then described what had happened.

"How awful. At least he does not know where you live. But it is worrying. Could have been nasty."

"I know. I was lucky to get away. He's quite fit. It took all my strength and cunning to escape. I don't understand why he would be in the city."

"He is not likely to come down here. Is he?"

"I don't see why he should. There's no branch anywhere near us."

"Talking about him. I have something to tell you as well."

"What is that sweetheart? Are you sure you're okay? You look tired. Perhaps I should leave you to rest."

"No, I am fine. The day you left, Jennifer came to see me."

"I thought I saw her on the path."

"You know Roger Harris?"

"Yes. He and I went to school together."

"Well, he has been in Munich studying politics and only returned recently. He has proposed to Jennifer, and she has accepted. Bless her, she was so happy and excited. Apparently, she has always liked him."

"Never mind that. What about him?"

"While in Munich, he joined Knights Serpent."

"You're joking!"

"I wish I was. Jennifer told me how he wants to talk to you about joining. You know, for making contacts and so on."

"You didn't tell her anything?"

"Of course not."

"Damn, this is going to be awkward."

"We will just have to pretend we have never heard of Knights Serpent."

"I wish I never had. Well, nothing for it. Just have to play it by ear."

"Yes, and please do your best not to become irritated or cross when he does broach the subject. You are going to have to act the innocent."

"Yes, yes, I know."

"Good. Now I think I could do with a rest."

"Okay sweetheart." Bending and kissing her on the forehead. He daren't go for her mouth, certain he'd be unable to control himself. She was still weak and tired from the birth.

The birth had in fact taken a lot out of her and it was several weeks before she felt anywhere back to her normal self. Richard was thrilled with his new daughter and, though obviously frustrated, had been more understanding. She still worried and feared because the physical strain was clearly visible at times. Though on occasion he appeared free of it. She wondered why, but decided to ignore the question. However, once recovered, their intimate relationship was as meaningful as before. Whether he played away or not, surely he stilled loved her. Would he be such a considerate lover otherwise? It could not just be the physical pleasure which made him so. Could it?

11

Gypsy

"Congratulations Katharine."

"Thank you Dorcas. I am sorry it has been so long since I came to visit."

"Don't be silly. We heard you were poorly. I assume you're better now."

"Yes I am. Thank you. How is everyone here?"

"All well, thankfully."

"Remember, you can come up to the house whenever you need to, even if the clinic is closed. No one will mind."

"You've often said so, but we don't like to bother any of you unless it's really necessary."

"I understand, but please never go without anything you need. We would be cross if you did."

"Thank you. Now, have you named her yet?"

"Yes. As we had already named Ellen in honour of Helina, we decide on Andrea, after my mother."

"That's a nice name. Did Mrs Palmerstone mind you not calling Ellen Helina?"

"Not really. I explained I thought it would be too confusing having two Helinas in the house. To my mind Ellen is close enough and, thankfully, Helina is happy with it."

"That's good. Did they mind it being another girl?"

"Well, I think they probably did. But they love her and for me that is all that matters."

"Maybe next time."

"I hope so. I do not want too many children. I certainly do not intend continuing in the desperate hope of a boy. Someone I know did and ended up having six girls before they gave up. That is too many for me."

"The more the merrier as far as I'm concerned. I love having them round me."

"I think you are very brave. I am not sure I could cope with so many, even with Martha and the others' help. Now, if you will excuse me, I better get back. Some new medicines are due to be delivered to the clinic later."

"You still doing most of the work I take it."

"Unfortunately, Richard has to be out on the estate or in town more often now. Sadly, his father cannot do very much these days. But I do not mind really. We had realised this would probably be the case even before setting the clinic up."

~~~~~~~~

"Katherine!" She had been about to go into the house after closing the morning clinic.

"Hello Jennifer. What a nice surprise."

"Good morning Katherine. I'd like you to meet my fiancé. Mrs Palmerstone, Mr Harris."

"Good morning Mrs Palmerstone. I hope we find you well."

"Good morning Mr Harris. Yes, thank you. It is sometime since we last saw each other."

"Yes. Strange how we can live in such a small community and yet go for so long without meeting. I am very pleased to remake you acquaintance Mrs Palmerstone."

"And I yours Mr Harris. I was away in Vienna for some years and since returning, have not ventured far from the family estates. I understand you have been studying in Munich."

"Yes. I only returned recently."
~~~~~~~~

"Allow me to congratulate you on your engagement."

"Thank you. You're very kind."

"Not at all. I can see how happy both of you are. I must admit you make a handsome couple."

"You'll have me blushing in a minute Katherine."

"Nonsense, you know it is true." Jennifer's shy giggle had them all laughing within seconds, breaking the formality of first introductions.

"Jennifer tells me congratulations are also due to you, albeit a little late."

"Thank you. We have been blessed with another lovely daughter. Please come in and have a cup of tea."

"Thank you, Mrs Palmerstone, but I have an appointment in town. Jennifer insisted, as we were passing nearby, we call in. She wanted us to renew our acquaintanceship before the wedding."

"I am glad she did."

"Well, if you'll excuse us, we must be going. See you soon, I hope. Regards to Richard."

"I am sorry he is not here. He will be sorry to have missed you." No, he would not, but politeness demanded the courtesy. "If you are free, would you care to join us for dinner on Friday? I know he will be here then." They would have to face it at some stage, so why not get it over with.

"Thank you. We'd love to."

"Good. We will see you then."

"Look forward to it. Goodbye." Before she could launch into any further conversation, Roger Harris took a firm grip of his fiancée's hand and led her away.

"Good evening Miss Denis. Good evening Roger. Good to see you again." Richard was the first to greet their guests.

"Good evening Mrs Palmerstone. Good evening Richard. It has been a long time."

“Yes. As you know I was in Vienna for some years and then spent some time with friends in Sweden. You, I understand, left for Munich just before I returned.”

“So I believe. We’ve a lot of catching up to do.”

“Before that, come and greet my parents. They’re waiting for us in the drawing room.”

“Good evening Mr Harris, good evening Miss Denis. I understand congratulations are in order.” George rose and extended a hand of greeting.

“Good evening Mr Palmerstone. Good evening Mrs Palmerstone.” He bowed in the traditional manner for greeting his seniors. “Very kind of you. I am a very lucky man to have Miss Denis condescend to be my wife.”

“You both look so happy. It is lovely to see.” Mrs Palmerstone senior enthused with one of her broad warm smiles.

“Dinner is ready, Mam.”

“Thank you Martha. Come, let us go in.” The general chit chat of congratulations continued as they made their way to the dining room.

“How did you find Munich?” Having enjoyed his time in Vienna when studying, George liked to hear about other places people had been to.

“It is a very stimulating city. So much going on and such mixed society. I am pleased to say I made many friendships which I think will last through the years.”

“I found Vienna, which is where I studied as a young man, similar. I still have contact with several friends I made then. Though these days it is restricted to letter writing. My days of travelling are over, I am afraid.”

“I’m sorry to hear that sir. But it is nice you still keep in touch.” The dinner conversation followed similar themes with Richard, Katherine and Jennifer sharing their own experiences. Naturally, Richard and Katherine were a little circumspect about what they shared. Once dinner was over, they returned to the drawing room for drinks. Seeing some movement outside, Richard went to the French doors to investigate. Just one of the stable grooms on his way home. Turning to re-join the others, he found Roger standing beside him.

"I was hoping to catch you on your own for a few minutes."

"What can I do for you Roger?"

"It's more what I can do for you."

"Oh! I don't understand."

"While in Munich, I was introduced to a useful society. In fact, I became a member, or knight, as they like to call us."

"Really, sounds interesting." Fighting to suppress his agitation.

"Yes it is. They're called Knights Serpent. They help a lot of people. You know charity events and giving, that sort of thing."

"Very kind."

"Yes, but there's more to it than that. Most of the members, knights I should say, are professional people. They make a point of helping each other with their businesses. You know, contacts with people who can smooth the path of a transaction or provide introductions to those in positions of power or influence."

"I expect you'll find that useful with you political career."

"I hope so. I intend to rise as high as possible. Never know, I might even become premier one year."

"Well, you can't be accused of not being ambitious."

"No. You should know that from our school days. I always wanted to get into positions of power and authority. But then prefect was about the only thing to aim for."

"Yes. Ha! Ha! I remember well."

"I was thinking you might find it useful to join. You could find people to help with your medical career and with the family business. It's amazing how many highly influential men belong. I'd be happy to propose you."

"Thank you Roger, you're very kind. But I really don't see any point in it for me. The practice, such as it is, is fine, and the business is going great strengths."

"Maybe, but you could expand. The society has members in virtually any country you can name. Just imagine the contracts you could get."

"Thank you Roger, but I don't think it's for me. I'm quite happy with how things are. I've little enough time now for the family. I don't want to lose what I have." He didn't enjoy deceiving his friend, but what other choice was there if he was to keep his family and himself safe?

"Why not think about it? I can propose you at any time."

"Thank you Roger, I don't think so."

"Well, just think about it for a while." In view of his persistence, he decided to play along rather than risk the possibility of any suspicions arising.

"Okay, I'll give it some thought." Hoping the depth of his reluctance and frustration was not manifest.

"What were you and Roger whispering about?" They had just got into bed.

"Oh, just this and that."

"Come on, I know you better. Something he said is bothering you."

"I didn't want to worry you with it. As expected, he was asking me to join Knights Serpent."

"I thought so. What are we going to do?"

"Nothing. I tried putting him off, but he insisted I give it some thought. I'll thank him and tell him again I don't have time. I'll also repeat I don't consider it would be of any help with the clinic or business. That should hopefully satisfy him."

"Do you think it will? I remember when he was a boy, he could be like a dog with a bone. Never giving up on something he wanted."

"Yes, you're right, he was. But I think I can handle him."

"I hope so. I am frightened he may find out."

"I don't see how. There's no branch near here and he was in Munich, so I don't think he would've met any of the Vienna lot."

"I hope not."

"Now let's forget about it all. Come here, you beauty."

"Sorry darling, I really do not think I am up to it." Bother! Feeling more than a little annoyed by her constant need to reject his advances recently. Admitted the menstruation was unusually heavy and painful. And there were the frequent headaches and wearisome tiredness in her limbs. Yet, though these often heralded the onslaught of some illness, she was sure, besides the menstruation, there was nothing wrong. She missed the sensation of his bare flesh against hers. The sense of fulfilment after. But now just the thought exhausted her.

"Are you okay? You always seem to be tired or something these days." His frustration palpable.

"Yes, I think so. Perhaps it is just because it is that time of the month."

"That doesn't usually bother you."

"No, but it has been heavier and more uncomfortable than usual."

"Okay." Turning over, he moved away. Something that had become habitual lately. What should she do? There was no denying his increasing dissatisfaction. But surely he understood? Again, she worried he would look elsewhere for fulfilment. Though reasonably certain he still cared some evidence, instead of cross looks and irritable sighs, would be welcome.

"How you feeling today?" No 'sweetheart,' she noticed.

"Fine. Why?"

"The fair's arriving tomorrow. I thought we might go."

"That would be nice."

"You sure you're up to it? You've been a bit off recently." The sharpness hurt. Was he hoping she would decline?

"I know, I am sorry darling. But I think I could cope with the fair. It would be nice to have an evening out,"

"Okay. I'll let my parents know. We'll go together." He couldn't help think 'she can go to a fair but not give me what I want.'

She enjoyed looking at all the different articles for sale. So many came from other countries, reflecting the uniqueness of each culture. The Swiss clocks particularly intrigued her with their beauty and intricate mechanisms.

"Hello dearie." She turned to find a gypsy woman offering her a small bunch of heather.

"No, thank you."

"It will bring you good luck."

"Thank you, but no." As was usual with them, the woman was not going to give up easily.

"Are you okay?" Richard reappeared by her side.

"Yes darling."

"Why don't you buy some heather for the lady? Give you both good luck."

"All right, as long as you go away and leave us alone. Here." Giving her some loose change.

"You've both kind faces and I can see dominant bright blue auras that show your generous natures. At some stage, you're going to want to help someone you feel some responsibility for out of a difficult situation. You'll be tempted to offer more assistance than is required, but you shouldn't. You'll regret it if you do."

"Go away woman. You've got your money. Now leave us."

"Don't forget. Don't help them." Neither missed the warning look in her eyes. Then, handing over the small bouquet of heather, she turned and marched off, looking for her next target.

"Oh Richard. I thought we left all that behind in Vienna. In fact, I had almost forgotten. Why are we constantly being told not to help others? After all, you are a doctor and I am a nurse. How can we not help people? Anyway, I want us to help wherever we can."

"I'd forgotten. Bloody nuisance."

"But it keeps coming up. What do you think it means?"

"Nothing, load of mumbo jumbo. Anyway, there's never anything really specific. Don't let it worry you. Let's find the others."

"Why don't the three of you grab that table while I get us something to eat?"

"Are you all right Katherine? You are looking pale. Has this been too much for you?"

"No, no. I am fine, thank you Helina. It was just something that gypsy woman said."

"Ignore them. They always tell you they can see your future. All nonsense. Just a way of trying to make money out of the gullible."

"Yes. I am sure you are right." Anxiously watching her husband's back as he headed for the barbecue area. Was her inability to satisfy causing him to lose interest altogether? The endearing 'sweethearts' and embraces were often missing. At night he firmly remained on his side of the bed, the gap between like some un-crossable chasm. A comforting cuddle would be welcome. It was not her fault she felt so unwell.

"Richard is taking his time. Where is he?" George was becoming impatient.

"It looks like there are a lot of people queuing. I cannot see him, so he is probably at the front being served. Ah, here he is." With his usual long strides, he headed toward them, balancing a series of plates. Two young giggling women walked alongside him, their doe eyed looks unmistakable. And, she noted, he had a definite spark in his eye and was clearly feeling frisky. Jealousy and fear in equal measure arose, the sensations worrying her. She was not usually given to the ugliness of jealousy.

"About time." George's impatience getting the better of him.

"Sorry. There was a long queue."

"Here you are Katherine. I got you some extra vegetables."

"Thank you!" To her surprise, she was finding it hard to be civil to him. She felt hurt, uncertain, angry and frightened. All so silly. She should be accustomed to his flirting by now. She was. But his behaviour and looks a moment ago implied something different. His frustration was becoming dominant. Will it lead him away? Could she blame him if it did?

The next morning, while strolling with his long confident strides, he couldn't help notice how the pretty young women would look as he passed. Unconsciously, he straitened his back and shoulders that little bit more, enjoying the attention. One or two really were quite beautiful. He felt desire pulse throughout the length of his body, from brain to toe. The tension in his abdomen and lower proving particularly difficult. Involuntarily glancing down, he checked he was not showing his trousers having become considerably tighter. Nevertheless, his thoughts were primarily of Katherine. Why was she behaving as she had been recently? Why hadn't they made love for so long? Was she ill and hiding it from him? He'd watched and visually examined her, but had detected nothing. Perhaps she'd reached that stage where sex no longer interested her? Bit young for that, but it happened. He may love her, but he couldn't go on living with his needs unmet. Maybe a mistress or at least an affair would be in order? The thought troubled him. He didn't want to cheat on her, but relieving himself wasn't fulfilling his needs.

"Richard!" Turning, he saw Roger crossing the street toward him.

"Hi."

"Where you off to?"

"The feed merchant. I need to up our order. The livestock have been producing at quite a rate recently." Roger's look of envy both surprised and shocked him. But then, he'd always wanted to be at the top of the tree in whatever he was engaged. He knew Roger's parent's estates weren't doing as well, so he shouldn't be surprised. Roger hated being second in anything.

"Have you thought anymore about what I said?"

"What was that?" He decided playing ignorant, or at least forgetful, was the best option.

"About joining Knights Serpent."

"Oh that. Yes, but I don't think it's for me."

"It really could be very beneficial to you."

"Roger, as I said, I've little enough time at home now besides which the business is doing very well. I've quite enough work and really don't want anymore."

"You could always employ more managers. Besides, you and your wife like to help people. There'd be more opportunities for charitable work through them."

"Thank you Roger for the invitation, but no, I think not. We're able to help a lot of people through the clinic and Katherine keeps an eye on the local poor. I think we're meeting what need there's here."

"Before you make a final decision, I'd like you to meet a friend. I've invited him to stay for a few days. He's been a member far longer than me and can tell you more of what's involved."

"It wouldn't make any difference. I really am too busy." He desperately hoped his increasing irritation would not lead to him losing his temper.

"Will you at least meet him? We, Jennifer and I, would like you both to come to dinner when he's here."

"If you wish, but I don't think it's going to make any difference."

"Good. I'll send a note once he's confirmed the dates. I better get a move on. I've an appointment with the mayor."

"Okay. See you sometime. Give your wife our regards."

"What are you going to do?" He had just told Katherine about his conversation with Roger.

"We'll have to play along. We must take care not to raise any suspicions."

"But what if they recognise you?"

"It's unlikely to be anyone who knows me. Roger was in Munich. I doubt he's met any of the Viennese lot."

"I hope not, but then we had not expected to see any of them in Venice or in the city."

"No. We're just going to have to take our chances."

"I am scared. If they find out where we live, we will never be safe."

"I know, but what else can we do? Roger's no fool. I'm doing my best to put him off without raising questions."

"I realise that darling. But I am frightened."

"I'm sorry I ever got involved. I wish Ronaldo had explained more to me beforehand."

"When is Roger's friend visiting?"

"He's not sure yet. He's going to send a note over once they confirm dates."

"So, there is no immediate threat?"

"No. Not at the moment."

“Good.” Relief registering as she looked into her beloved’s eyes.

“Now then darling.” With a mischievous smile.

“I am feeling much better.” She sparkled back.

Despite keeping busy with the estate and clinic, neither quite shook the concern from the back of their minds.

12

Bitter Sorrow

While cleaning up after dressing a deep wound on a worker's arm, she worried. Though a couple of months had passed with no word from Roger about his friend's visit, she knew it must come sooner or later. What were they going to do? She doubted playing innocent would enable them to sidestep the issue. It was inevitable Knights Serpent would come up. Would they accept Richard's explanation and refusal? Or would they continue to press him? Was there any chance they may discover what had happened in Vienna? If they did, would Richard and the children be safe? Dorcas's unexpected appearance at the door broke her troubled train of hypothetical questions.

"Hello Dorcas. It is unusual to see you up here. Is there anything wrong? Are you all right? You look tired."

"Hello Katherine. I'm okay, thank you. I've come about Mary's little Johnny. He's not been well for a couple of days. We thought he'd just caught a cold, and it'd pass, but he seems to be getting worse instead of better. Please come and have a look at him when you have time. I think it may be advisable to bring Mr Palmerstone, your husband, with you."

"Richard is here today, so I will not have to wait for him to come home. You are obviously very concerned, so I will go for him straight away. We will come down shortly."

"Thank you. She'll be relieved. The poor dear is so worried. I have to say I think it may be with good cause. Peter isn't handling it too well either. I suppose, being that much older, he's frightened for his only son. There's not much to leave, but he wants an heir for what there is, and it's unlikely they'll have any more children."

"Now, before you go, are you sure you are all right? You really do look tired."

"I'm okay, it's just tiredness. I'm having to spend a lot of time with Peggy. Johnny's illness has got her worrying one of her children will get sick. She's become quite hysterical. You know what she's like. I'm doing my best to keep her calm. Most of the time she just wanders round, twisting her hands and crying, but then, at other times, she almost smoothers one or more of the children trying to stop them from going outside. I'm having to clean and cook for them as well as for my family. I also have to get all the children up and dressed in the morning and then into bed at night."

"That is a lot on top of your own family. You will make yourself ill if you are not careful. Cannot some of the others help?"

"They all have their own families to look after. And some don't have any patience with Peggy. Mary would help, but of course she's Johnny to look after. He really does seem to be quite unwell."

"You really must look after yourself as well as the others. Who is going to help your family if you cannot? Is there anything I can do?"

"It's kind of you to ask, but no, there's nothing. As I said, it's just tiredness."

"All right, as long as you are sure. I will close up and find Richard. We will be down shortly." Dorcas left.

Her father had now retired from his medical practice and, as promised, was directing patients to them. Richard had been correct in his assumption that some liked to discuss their little problems in private without anyone else's knowledge or suspicion. And as anticipated, some came upon a pretence of visiting. To facilitate this, he had adopted the habit of working in the nearby estate office for two hours on Wednesday and Friday mornings, something they discreetly let be known. They had additionally posted notices round the village informing residents the clinic was up and running and available to anyone who wished to call upon their services. This was a Friday, so she locked up and went straight to the office.

“Good afternoon Peter. Mary. Where’s Johnny?”

“Over here, Mr Palmerstone. Very kind of you to’ve come.”

“Not at all. After all, Katherine and I trained and set up the clinic to help whenever someone is unwell.”

“We thought he’d just got a cold, but it doesn’t seem to be going.”

“What symptoms has he had? Fever, chills, shortness of breath, cough?”

“He’s had most of those. Sometimes he lays quietly but not for long before his coughing disturbs him.”

“I’m just going to listen to your chest Johnny, okay?” The boy gave him a weak nod. He then listened to his chest and lungs and felt round his small body.

“Okay Johnny, I’ve finished. Sorry about my cold hands.” The poor child attempted a weak smile.

“What do you think?” She had a good idea, but thought it best to let her husband, the ‘doctor’, announce it.

“I’m think it’s Bronchopneumonia.”

“No!” Mary’s sharp cry made them all jump. Peter almost fell backwards and then just slummed into a chair, holding his head between his hands. Pneumonia was a well-known killer.

“It’s okay. There’re some excellent medicines we can treat him with. Have you got some of those new antibiotics with you Katherine? As usual, she had brought the wicker basket with her.”

“Yes. Here you are.”

“Good. Now, Mary, you must give him one of these each morning. Keep him comfortable and warm. I don’t expect he’ll want to, but he mustn’t get up for a few days. And certainly he’s not to go outside. You understand?”

“Yes. Will he get better?”

“He should be all right. He’s a strong lad, and these new medicines are very effective.” He did his best to reassure her whilst hiding his actual concern. The pneumonia appeared to have taken quite a firm grip on the boy.

"Try not to worry, Mary. Remember, you can send for us any time, day or night. We will come down each day anyway."

"Yes, we will. And if there's any change in his condition, no matter how small, send for me straight away. As Katherine says, it doesn't matter what time it is."

"Thank you. You've both been so kind."

"Now Peter." Peter, still sitting in the chair cradling his head, didn't appear to hear. "Peter!"

"Uh. Oh. Ye." It was as if he were only half conscious of their presence.

"Listen Peter. You've got to come and get me at any time if Johnny's condition changes. Do you understand?!"

"Uh. Ye. Ye. E goin b ok in't e?"

"We'll have to wait and see. He's a strong lad, so I'm hoping for the best."

"Alrit." His vagueness was hardly reassuring, but there was little else they could do.

"Looks like it'll fall to you to get me if necessary, Mary."

"Yes. Okay. Johnny's his life. His illness has been a great shock. I'll look after them both. Thank you for coming. And for the medicine."

"Right, Katherine and I have to go now. But we'll be back in the morning. Now remember, any time you need to, send for us."

"Thank you." Tears coming into her eyes as Katherine embraced her.

"Do you think he will recover, darling?" Having seen how ill Johnny really was and her husband's concern. His mask may hide it from others, but she saw through it. They sat on a rock, taking in the valley view spread below them.

"I'm not sure. The pneumonia really has got a hold of him. I think it may be effecting both lungs."

"Oh dear. If anything happens to him, Mary and Peter will be devastated. He is their world."

"And I think you're found of him too."

"Yes, he is a nice boy. He is always friendly and cheerful. I suppose he gets that from Mary. She is always like a breath of fresh air. I really hope he recovers."

“We’ll just have to wait and see. I’ll keep an eye on him.”

~~~~~~~~

“We did all we could.” Responding to Peter Woodcote’s accusation. She had been attending to the herb beds.

“E wer alrigt til ye com.”

“You know that is not true. He was very ill.”

“Ye and tha dam uband of ye’s kill im!”

“No, we did not. You know the pneumonia had already taken a firm hold by the time we saw him. We tried everything we could, but it just would not shift. I am sorry, Mr Woodcote.”

“E twre me only son. Ye kill im!” She watched, horror stricken, as he raised the scythe he had been hiding behind his back above his head. Surely not! The cruel curved blade looked as if it had been freshly honed. Brilliant sunshine reflecting off the hostile weapon partially blinding her, she instinctively stepped back. Though unseen, the swish of the ferocious blade as it cut through the air caused her mounting terror to escalate. What to do?!

“Come, there is no need for this. I appreciate how upset you must be, but......” Should she run? No, no point. He would have no difficulty catching her. Best to try to placate him.

“Upst! Ye’ve no ida! Av ye evr los cild?!” Tears stood in his eyes, whether from anger or sorrow, she was not sure. Probably both. Richard having gone across to the northern perimeter with most of the others, she was on her own. She must calm him down.

“No. But I think I can sympathise. Killing me will not bring him back.”

“Mayb no but meas ye’ll no kill no on els!”

“Please, Mr Woodcote stop! You know this is not going to achieve anything. What would Mary say?”

“Don’t giv dam wa anone sa! Ye kil me son and ye gon pay! An ey fr an ey!”
~~~~~~~~

Coming round the corner of the stables, Richard quickly assessed the situation. Holding a hand up, he indicated for her to avoid drawing attention to him. The man had been shouting so loud he'd not heard the footsteps.

"Please, Mr Woodcote, put the scythe down. Think of your family, they need you. Who will look after them if you are not here?" Intentionally raising her voice in the hope of covering her husband's footsteps as he crept closer.

"Don car, ye no gon kil non els's son!" He again swung the vicious instrument at her. She stepped back a couple of paces, hoping not to fall in the process.

"Come on, Peter" Perhaps a more personal approach would mollify him. "I know you are upset, but this really will not achieve anything."

"It'l giv me satfactn to know ye ot t way." Richard quietly crept nearer.

"We really did do all we could. I am very sorry your son died."

"Wat's it to ye. As fa e concnd on mor por cild out t wa."

"Peter!, you know that is not true. I cared about Johnny." Leaping forward, Richard grabbed the scythe swinging arm. Peter, taken by surprise, froze momentarily but quickly recovering from the shock wrested his arm free.

"Ye! Goo! Can kil ye bot now!" Launching toward his attacker, he brandished the weapon in wide one hundred and eighty degree arcs. Richard quickly leapt back out of range.

"Come on sir, there's no need for this."

"Sas oo! Ye! Murdre!"

"You know very well we did all we could to help your son."

"E wern tat ill til ye medded. Ye kil im!"

"I know you're upset. I would be. But don't do something you're going to regret."

"Kilng ye tis las ting I regret. I'm goin to mak ye pa for wa ye did! Me son! Me son!" Uncontrolled deep sobs arose from within him.

"Peter, please put the scythe down. You know this is wrong." Struggling, despite her intense fear, to keep her tone soft and calm.

"Do I….?" His voice trailing off as distress engulfed him. Taking advantage of the lapse, she stepped forward and placed a compassionate hand over his free one. His shoulders sagged as he allowed tears to stream down his face. Moving quickly and quietly, Richard removed the scythe from the now limp right hand. Sagging even further, he slumped onto her shoulder. Uncertain how to respond but feeling sorry for the poor man, she gently embraced him. Convulsions shook his entire frame as his grief took full rein.

"Oh! Thank goodness you're alright. I was so frightened when they told me." An out of breath Mary ran toward them. Gently disengaging herself, Katherine moved aside so Mary could hug her distraught husband as she, too, dissolved into floods of tears. Richard, placing a protective arm round his own perturbed wife, discreetly moved them away, allowing the couple freedom to grieve in comparative privacy. Ten or so minutes later, Mary, recovering herself, left Peter sitting on a wall and approached them.

"I'm so sorry. He must've terrified you. He's been beside himself ever since Johnny died."

"We understand." Her voice quivering with residual fear. She could still see and hear the scythe slicing through the air.

"Please, don't report him. I think he's gone a little mad. But it'll pass. Please!"

"By rights I should have him carted off to jail. He'd no right to attack my wife." Anger still evident.

"I know but please…." Desperation manifest in her voice.

"Okay, I can understand how upset he …, both of you must be. I'm not sure how I'd react if I lost a child. Still, that's no justification for attacking my wife. Now take him home and make sure he never does anything like this again. I'll not hesitate in future."

"Thank you, thank you." Almost kissing his hand.

"Take him off before I change my mind." Quickly returning to her husband, she lifted him in an embrace and led him out of the stable yard. Though convulsed with tears, they could still hear him indistinctly muttering. What was he saying? 'T's t'r faut. Ty gon pay. Mak sur cant do tis no on else.'

"Are you all right sweetheart?"

"Yes, I think so. Oh, Richard, I was so scared. I do not think he really knew what he was doing. He was like a man possessed."

"That's no excuse. Anyway, as long as you're all right, I'll let it go."

"Yes I am. I feel so sorry for them."

"So do I, but that's still no excuse. I love you and don't know what I'd do if you were taken from me." So reassuring to hear the sincerity of those endearing words.

"And I love you. Just the thought of losing you makes me ill." She suddenly vomited.

"Sweetheart! Are you okay?!"

"Yes, sorry."

"That wretched man. He's upset you. Must be the fear."

"No. It has nothing to do with him. I did not want to tell you until I was sure."

"Sure of what?!"

"I am pregnant again."

~~~~~~~~

A week later she was still vomiting excessively. Why? The others had not been like this. What was different? She had never felt so worn and ragged.

"You really are not well are you Katherine?" Helina asked, unable to hide her concern.

"I do not understand why, but the sickness has been far worse this time. Perhaps I am just getting older."

"No, I think it is more than that. You are hardly old yet. Richard better have a look at you."

"He is so busy. I do not want to bother him with this. I am sure it will pass soon, as always."
~~~~~~~~

"I am not so sure. You are losing weight, and I think there are signs of dehydration. We better make sure. This can be dangerous. We need to ensure you and the baby are both well."

"Richard has been asking. But I did not want to worry him, so said I was fine and it was just a passing phase."

"I think we both know it is far more than that. He will be very cross if anything happens and finds you have not told him."

"I suppose so."

"Come on Katherine, be fair. It is his child as well. Besides which, he loves you very much. He would never forgive himself, or me, if anything happened." She still was not entirely sure, despite his recent actions and reactions. But at the same time had to admit he had been more attentive since the incident with Peter Woodcote.

"Yes, I expect you are correct."

"Ah! Here he is." Glancing out of the window. "I will ask him to come and look at you straight away." Giving her a reassuring pat on the hand, she left the room. Within a couple of minutes, she returned with her son.

"Mother tells me you're not well."

"It is nothing really. Just I have been vomiting far more than I did with the others."

"That's not good. Let me have a look at you." She lay back against the sofa cushions while he examined her. The sensation of his fingers against her flesh awakened her love and longing for him even though she had not the strength to react to it.

"Um. How long has this been going on? You look dehydrated."

"Since the beginning. I have lost count of how many times I vomit in a day."

"I thought there was something wrong. But each time I asked, you told me everything was fine. I'd noticed your weight loss but, as you said nothing, just thought it due to the heat." The last weeks had been very warm.

"I am sorry. I did not want to bother you. I thought it would pass quickly."

"I think you may have hyperemesis gravidarum."

"Oh! That never crossed my mind."

"What is that Richard?" Helina asked, clearly worried.

"It's when a pregnant woman's vomiting becomes severe and prolonged. It can lead to all sorts of problems. Dehydration and weight loss, as in Katherine's case. But it can also cause liver damage and blood disorder. We're going to have to be careful."

"What can we do?"

"As Katherine knows well, she'll have to rest and take a lot of fluids. It really can be dangerous both for her and the baby."

"Katherine! Why did you not say something sooner?"

"I honestly thought it would pass. Hyperemesis gravidarum never crossed my mind. I should have realised. We nurses and doctors often overlook the obvious when it comes to ourselves."

"Take her straight to your room Richard. I will ask Martha to make some broth. I will bring it up as soon as it is ready."

"Sweetheart, why didn't you tell me? You must've known something was wrong."

"I am sorry darling. I really did think it would pass, and I did not want to trouble you. You have enough to do without worrying about me."

"You and the children are my life. I don't know what I'd do without you. You must never hide things from me. How do you think I'd feel if something happened and I could've prevented it?"

"I am sorry. I did not think about it like that."

13

Danger

The day's labour had been hard and demanding and, as always, after such exertion, he felt exhilarated. His whole being tingled with anticipation as he looked forward to an evening of pleasure. Thankfully, his love had improved markedly and was now able to reciprocate his desires.

"What's wrong sweetheart?" She'd greeted him at the door with a look of deep concern.

"Roger has sent a note to say his friend is on his way. He has invited us over on Friday. Apparently, his friend can only stay a couple of days."

"Bother. I'd hoped he might forget."

"You must have known he would not."

"I suppose so. But there's no harm in hoping."

"What are we going to do?"

"We'll have to go. I'll try and steer the conversation away from Knights Serpent as much as possible, but his friend will no doubt want to talk about it. We're going to have to play dumb and maybe even lie a bit."

"I hate that."

"I don't see we've a choice."

"No, I suppose not. Do your best to minimise the discussion."

"I will."

"It is all so childish."

"I know. But we've had sufficient experience of them now to realise things aren't going to change. We're just going to have to be careful. It's a damn nuisance. Well, there's nothing we can do about it tonight, so let's forget it for now." Kissing her full on the mouth, his earlier anticipation returning. Lifting her in his powerful arms, he carried her to their bedroom. Then, having placed her on the four-poster, began slowly unbuttoning her dress while she pulled his shirt over his head. It was all he could do to hold himself back, longing for the sensation of their joined bodies. Love and desire surged through his now taut body as he lay with her.

"Darling."

"Sweetheart."

~~~~~~~~

A knock on the door disturbed their enjoyment of a relaxing cool pre-dinner drink on the veranda. It was one of Richard's rare early evenings home.

"Come in!" Martha entered.

"I'm sorry to disturb you, but there is a gentleman downstairs asking for you, Mr Palmerstone."

"Who is it?"

"Mr Harris."

"Okay. Show him to the drawing room please, Martha. I'll be down in a minute."

"What do you think he wants?"

"I've no idea. Maybe it's about his friend. You going to come down?"

"No. I feel far too nervous. I doubt I could hide it."

"All right. But you're going to have to do better on Friday."

"I know. It is just the unexpectedness of his visit. I will have more time to prepare myself on the evening."

"I'll be back as soon as I can. You better rest. You're looking quite pale."

"Good evening Roger. Katherine and I were just discussing Friday." Struggling to smile and convey a light sense of pleasure at seeing him.
~~~~~~~~

"That's what I've come about. I've just had a note inviting me to a selection interview. It's short notice, but apparently the existing incumbent has been taken seriously ill. They doubt he will return and need someone to replace him quickly. Elections are due soon."

"No worry, we can always come another day."

"No, it's not that. I'm supposed to meet Peter when he arrives in town on Thursday. My appointment is for quarter to one and he's due to arrive at one. Would you meet him for me please?"

"Of course. How will I recognise him?"

"Just ask for Mr Peter Lucca. I'll send a note telling him you'll be there instead of me." His shock must be evident!

"Hum, okay." He couldn't bring himself to say more.

"Thanks, I appreciate it. You'll like him, I'm sure. He can tell you far more about the benefits of Knights Serpent than I can. He's been with them for years and has moved up the ladder."

"I doubt it'll make any difference to my decision, Roger, so don't get your hopes up."

"We'll see. I'm already benefiting with my political career. A few have already put in a good word for me with the powers to be."

"That's good."

"Yes, well, I better get back. Jennifer hates me being late for dinner."

"Okay. See you Friday." How were they going to get out of this?

"Richard! It cannot be him!"

"No mistake unless there are two men with the same name and both in Knights Serpent."

"What are we going to do?!"

"Try to stay calm, sweetheart. I don't want my parent's getting suspicious. We mustn't involve them in this."

"No, you are right. Oh Richard, I am afraid of what he may do. He really was quite nasty."

"Well, short of telling Roger the whole story, which I don't want to do, I can't see we've much choice. I'll have to meet him and try to talk some sense into him."

"Do you honestly think he would listen? Remember what he was like when you saw him in the city."

"I'll just have to try. I'm hoping he may've calmed down a bit now he's had time to think on what I said. After all, I really have been no threat to them."

"I doubt he will see it that way. You were no threat before, but that never stopped him. Shall I come with you? Two are better than one. He might behave if a lady is present."

"It didn't stop him chasing us in Venice. No, I'd rather you weren't there. If he becomes aggressive, I'll be able to deal with him better if I don't have to worry about you."

"I suppose you are right. But I am scared."

"I know. I'm sorry."

"It is not your fault darling. Owe! Oh, not again!"

"What's wrong?!"

"I think the baby is coming."

"It's not time yet. Are you sure?"

"Time or not, it is coming."

"Blast and damn that man. Must be the shock. Blast!"

"Richard! Get Martha. Quickly!"

"Mother! Martha!"

"It's a BOY!" The announcement echoed throughout the house.

"Well done sweetheart." Richard, though he loved the girls dearly, more than happy to have a son at last.

"Let me see him." Helina pushing the blanket down a little, to give her a better view, brought the little treasure to her bedside. "I would like to hold him please."

"All right dear. Here." Gently laying the tiny bundle in her daughter-in-law's arms.

"He is gorgeous."

"We'll call him George." Richard announced with uninhibited joy.

"That will be a little confusing. When summoned, neither your father nor our son will know who is being called."

"That's easy. He can be Georgie. Then there'll be no confusion."

"All right darling, if that is what you would like."

"Yes, I think it is."

"His grandpapa will be pleased." Helina affirmed with one of her broad, beaming smiles.

~~~~~~~~

"Richard, I am worried about you going to meet him." It was Wednesday evening.

"What else can I do? If I suddenly refuse, Roger will want to know why. What would I tell him? No, I'll have to go and hope for the best. I really don't want Roger finding out."

"But he is bound to tell Roger what happened."

"Not necessarily. If I can make him see sense, then I hope I'd also be able to stop him telling Roger."

"Do you honestly think he will 'see sense'?"

"It's a long shot I know, but I can't see any way round it."

"And if he does not? What will we do? He will know where we live and no doubt would inform other members. We would never be safe again."

"I don't know. Damn it, if only I hadn't let Ronaldo talk me into joining."

"It is not fair to blame him. He was hardly to know what was going to happen."

"He could've told me more. Or at least explained the consequences of not playing along."

"Well, it is too late to worry about that. Remember, it will not just be us who are in danger. I am worried about the children and your parents. What if they decide to take revenge on them also?"

"It's me they want, not them."
~~~~~~~~

"Maybe, but this Peter Lucca appears to be quite vindictive. Is there no other way out of this?"

"I can't see one. Even if I leave the area while he's here, Roger's still bound to tell him who we are. He'll just come back another time. I'm just going to have to try and talk him down."

"I am frightened Richard. Actually, I am terrified."

"I'm sorry sweetheart. This is all my doing. You shouldn't have to suffer because of my stupidity."

"You were not stupid. Perhaps a little naïve, but that is all."

"Sweetheart, you're so understanding. I don't deserve you."

"Nonsense." Then, silently standing in each other's arms, they looked out across the peaceful valley. If only they could share in that peace.

"What's wrong sweetheart? Can't you sleep?" She had been agitatedly twisting and turning all night.

"I am sorry darling. I tried not to disturb you, but I am worried. I cannot stop thinking about tomorrow. I cannot see Peter Lucca being amenable."

"Try not to worry. I plan on discussing the situation with him. He's a grown man now, not some spotty student. He's bound to see reason."

"You think so? As far as I could see, he was never a 'spotty student', as you put it. He appears to have been fully aware of what he was doing. I am worried he may try to hurt you again."

"I doubt he'll try anything in public. There'll be a lot of people round when I meet him."

"That did not stop him in the city."

"True.... I'll just have to be careful. If I think he's going to try anything, I'll leave him there. He'll have to find his own way to Roger's."

"Even if he does not try anything in town, there are long stretches of quiet lanes on the way to Roger's house. He may attack you then."

"That's possible. I'll have to judge matters after I talk to him. If he's implacable, I'll come straight home for you and the children. There'll be no choice but for us to leave. We'll initially go to Portside. From there, if necessary, we can leave the country. Perhaps go to my friends in Sweden."

"I hope it will not come to that. Anyway, it would not be fair to let your parents face him on their own. He may hurt them!"

"I can't see any other way out. We'd have to explain before leaving."

"Would you really leave them to confront him?"

"No, I suppose not. Well, at the very least, I'd get you all away from here. Then try and deal with him myself."

"No Richard! He would kill you."

"Don't be so sure. I ran from him in the city because I didn't want to get into a fight. But I'm no weakling. I'm sure I could beat him in a fair fight."

"He will hardly fight fair. Will he?"

"Perhaps not, but if it came to it, I reckon I could get the better of him."

"What about asking Roger to help?"

"I doubt he would once he knows the full story. He's ambitious and wouldn't want to spoil his chances with them."

"But surely he would not fight you?!"

"Probably not, but I don't think he'd intervene either."

"This is ridiculous!" Tears gathering in her eyes.

"I know, and I'm sorry. But I can't think of any other way out of this mess except to face up to him. As you point out, running wouldn't achieve anything."

"But even if you beat him, we will never be safe. He is bound to tell others in Vienna and here."

"Maybe, but I think we're jumping the gun a bit. Never know, he may listen and see things sensibly."

"I cannot see that. But you are right, we are jumping the gun. Nevertheless, it still worries me."

"Let's forget it for now. You need to try and get some sleep. Anyway, I'm sure I'll be able to deal with him." Though he spoke with the semblance of confidence, he had serious doubts. Lucca was as tall and broad as him and, as evidenced in the city, fit. They would be on a par if it came to a fight and Lucca had a viciousness he didn't possess.

Standing slightly back from the window, so as not to draw attention, she watched the man who meant everything to her, preparing to leave. They had agreed it best for her to remain in their room rather than alarm the others with her agitation. Feeling as if her rapidly beating heart would choke her any moment, she wondered. Will I see him again? Had this morning been their last one together? No! Must not think like that. He is strong, fit and sensible and probably right about his ability to overcome Lucca if it came to it. Oh Lord, why has it come to this? Fighting the tears as he moved across the stable yard, she again wondered. Will this be my last sight of him? The closer he got to the gate, the more intense her fear and laboured breathing became. Control yourself! Must not collapse. Must watch until he is out of sight. Oh Lord, please intervene. Please protect him.

Resisting the temptation to look up, he thought of how much he loved her. How she truly is the love of his life. How there really had never been anyone else, even when she'd been difficult. He crossed toward the gate at a steady pace. She needed to see him confident and firm. He debated. Was there any way out of this damned situation? The inevitable confrontation? He'd serious doubts about being able to talk Lucca down. The man was a demon who'd manifestly not stop at anything. Insane! Would he be able to get the upper hand if it came to it? Or would this be his last day on earth? Would he be able to kill him if he had to? To protect his family, perhaps. But would he be able to live with it? So many hypothetical questions. Well, not long before he'd know. Better get on with it. No turning back now. Don't look!

What is that?! A movement in the lane having caught her attention. Struggling to see through the tearful mist, she watched with bated breath. Within seconds, a teenage boy appeared by the ready open gates. Who is that? What does he want? Without hesitation, the lad made a beeline for Richard. What is going on?! Stopping in front of her beloved, the out of breath boy, taking deep gulps of air between words, hurriedly spoke. What is he saying? Is something wrong? Being much taller, Richard had bent to listen. She could not see his expression. Please Lord, what is happening?! She strained to hear through the tense vibration in her eardrums, but they were too distant. An eternity passed. Time stood still. Breathing almost ceased. Dare she hope?

While patting the lad's head, Richard took something from his pocket and gave it to him. Like a dawning sun, the boy's face instantly brightened with a beaming smile of gratitude. As he ran off, her beloved turned, and looking up, gave her a jubilant wave. Had they been spared?! Oh Lord, please! Nearly tripping over the hem of her dress, she rushed from the room and down the corridor. Almost colliding at the top of the stairs, they fell into each other's arms.

"Sweetheart!"

"Darling! What has happened?"

"Lucca can't make it. He's been detained by some business. Roger thinks he may have to return to his home."

"Oh darling!" Almost screaming with relief and joy.

"Shush! We mustn't alarm anyone."

"Sorry. I am so happy. I thought I may never see you again." Her tears would not be restrained this time. Half lifting her, he led the way back down the corridor and to their room, where he allowed her to sob until calm.

"Better rinse your eyes and tidy your hair before we go down. We don't want to alarm anyone."

"No, we do not." Sitting in front of the dressing mirror, she commenced the repairs. "Do you think we can forget all about him now?"

"I doubt it. Roger will probably invite him again. We'll just have to wait and see."

"So we cannot relax." Deep disappointment registering.

"We should be able to for a while. If Lucca has to return to his home, it's unlikely he'll be able to visit for some time. So let's just try and forget him for now."

"I hope you are right. But I cannot stop worrying. If only he would go away altogether."

"I'm sorry sweetheart. I never intended to put you through this."

"There is no need to keep apologising darling. I am not upset with you. You thought you were doing the right thing. Someone should have explained better, but that is immaterial now. If only we could find a way out of this forever."

"Try to put it to the back of your mind for now sweetheart. As I said, it's likely to be a very long time, if ever, that we have to face this again. Perhaps things will blow over before that." Hoping the falsity of his confidence wasn't apparent.

"All right, I will do my best. We better go down now, otherwise Helina and your father will think something is wrong." Each practiced a smile in the mirror before leaving their room.

14

Reprieve

"Dorcas, are you all right? You look washed out." Despite her pregnancy, she appeared to have lost some of her homely bulk and looked very pale.

"I don't know what's wrong. I've had six with no problems, but this one's being a right .... um..... nuisance."

"How do you mean?"

"I've never been so sick before. And my back's killing me. You'd think after having had six of the blighters it'd be easy now."

"This does not sound like you. Would you mind if I have a look?"

"Of course not. To be honest, I am a little concerned and would welcome your medical opinion. I know I can trust you to be truthful with me. Sorry about my dress. My work's too messy to wear anything decent."

"It does not matter. Anyway, I think it is pretty." She knew full well other than one slightly less ragged dress the poor woman only had her Sunday best. "Now if you would lie down please. It will make it easier for me to check you all round." She examined Dorcas's stomach, ribs, lower back, and sides. "You said your sickness has been worse this time. Do you mean you are sick more often?"

"No. It's just been heavier when I am."

"Good, well, not good, but I do not think you need to worry unduly. I was concerned you may have what I had with Georgie. But you do not appear to be dehydrated, which is good. Though you have lost some weight."

"Is the baby okay?" A note of urgency in her voice.

"I will need to ask Richard to confirm, but I think it is going to be a breach."

"Oh! I hope not. I've seen how difficult that can be. Peggy's last was a breach, and she went through hell."

"Yes, I am sorry, but I am fairly sure. I will ask Richard to come and see you in the morning."

"Thank you." With a troubled expression, she got up and straightened her tattered dress. "There's nothing else, is there? You're not hiding anything from me?"

"No, I would not do that to you. I am fairly sure it is just the way the baby is lying. You will need to take it a little easier and rest more often. The baby is going to make you very tired at times."

"Ye, I realise, it already does. I'll rest when I can, but it's easier said than done."

"You must try. Remember, if I can help in any way, you are to let me know."

"Thank you. You're always so considerate and understanding."

"I wanted to ask you about Mary. I have not been to see her since Johnny's passing. After what happened, I am not sure what to do, whether I should call in to see her or not."

"Mary's okay. She knows neither of you was to blame. What Peter did upset her a lot. Of course, she's still very distressed about Johnny and misses him terribly. It's not just he was her son, but he was also such a nice boy. I can assure you she would love to see you again. But it'd be best if you go when Peter isn't there. He's still not come to terms with it. I think he may still be a little out of his head with grief."

"I am so very sorry. We did all we could. Richard tried all the treatments and changed the medication to more strident ones, but the pneumonia had taken too firm a grip."

"We all realise. Such a shame, but we also all know how pneumonia takes a lot of people. Peggy's still in a state about it. Still worrying one of hers may succumb."

"Oh dear. Can I help at all?"

"Not really. We just have to try and assure her it's unlikely any of her children will get it."

"I could try. Perhaps in view of my nursing training and experience she may listen to me."

"I doubt it. She respects you, but at the same time, Johnny died despite your ministrations. No, I think it best to leave her to us for the time being. I'll call you if I think she is making herself ill over it. She'll probably calm down as the weather warms up. Even she knows there is less danger then."

"All right. I understand. But you will let me know if I can help at all."

"Of course."

Standing on the threshold, allowing her eyes to adjust from the darkened interior to the brilliant sunshine, she listened with delight to the happy music of the children's' infectious laughter. As always, they were playing on the green. She was about to step onto the path when Mary and her husband came along. Good, could not have asked for a better opportunity.

"Good morning Mary, Mr Woodcote. I hope you are both well."

Neither spoke. Nevertheless, Mary's warm smile was reassuring. However, Peter's glare of bitter, vengeful hate sent a shiver down her spine. As they neared, he appeared to lunge toward her, but Mary, taking a firm grip on his arm, steered him away. Her smile replaced by a look of miserable sadness. As they went past, she could hear him muttering under his breath: 'Murdrers.' 'Desev to die.' 'I'll see to em!' 'I'l mak em pa!' Glancing back, he bestowed another hateful look. Noticing his action, Mary turned her head and gave a weak, sorrowful smile and then pushed her husband on. So sad.

"Is something wrong sweetheart?"

"No, not really. I bumped into Mary and Peter this morning. Although Mary seemed pleased to see me, he was not very friendly. To be honest, he frightened me a little."

"Why?! What did he do?!"

"Nothing. It was just the way he looked at me and the things I heard him muttering under his breath. 'Murderers'. 'Deserve to die.' Etcetera. He obviously still holds us responsible. I also got the impression he is determined to revenge himself on us."

"He better not try!"

"From what I saw, Mary has him under control, so I do not think we need to worry unduly. It is just I found it a little unsettling. Silly really. Sorry I bothered you with it."

"No, you must always tell me when something like this happens. I'll be very cross if you don't." His agitation bordering on violent anger.

"All right darling, please do not upset yourself."

"You're to promise! Now!"

"All right, I promise. But I really do not think there is anything to worry about."

Excitement continued to fill the house long after Georgie's birth. His grandfather, normally a quiet, reserved man, was unusually vocal and Heline went about with a permanent broad, beaming smile. Even Martha and the other staff, unable to resist the infectious atmosphere, sang to themselves as they went about their work. George, ecstatic with the birth of the long-awaited heir, insisted the christening, which normally would not take place for some time, be brought forward. The subsequent weeks were occupied with writing invitations and arranging a sumptuous banquet. Grandad was going to make the most of it.

On the day Katherine was grateful that, unlike the majority before him, Georgie, rather than scream and cry, simply giggled and laughed when the priest poured water over him. It really was a joyous occasion. Back at the house, the party quickly got underway with relatives and friends exuberantly congratulating parents and grandparents. Throughout, Richard and Katherine ensured their daughters did not feel ignored by paying them due attention. Thankfully, most of the guests did likewise. Some even insisting they dance with them, which the girls loved. All was happiness and joy. They doubted the birth of a royal prince would have been celebrated more enthusiastically.

"Jennifer! You should not have. You are always giving the children presents."

"You know I love to spoil them. Anyway, these are from Roger as well."

"You certainly do spoil them. Thank you, these are beautiful. What do you say girls?" Besides a set of silver tea wear for Georgie, she gave each of the girls a gorgeous doll.

"Th..ank you." Each uttered in their shy manner.

"Where is Roger? I would like to thank him as well."

"Here somewhere. Ah, there he is talking with Richard."

"Oh yes." Hoping her anxiety did not show. The serious, concentrated look on Richard's face was worrying. She could see he was trying hard to smile through it.

"Great party Richard."

"You can thank my parents for that. They've made a real fuss of Georgie since his birth. Father's really pleased. He was worried he'd not witness the birth of an heir. I don't think I've ever seen him so jubilant."

"Can understand that. He's waited a long time for this. And I'm sure you're more than just a bit elated yourself."

"Yes, of course. Katherine and I are very happy. Two lovely girls and now a son. What more can a man ask for? But my parents can be a little over the top. They're for ever doting on him. Sometimes I can hardly get them to attend to other matters. To be honest, I'm a little worried he'll grow up thoroughly spoilt. That'll never do."

"I'm sure you'll see that doesn't happen."

"I'm going to do my best, but I don't want to upset them. They love him so much."

"You'll manage. Now, I'm sorry you didn't meet Peter. You would have liked him. And he could have explained so much more than me."

"No worry Roger. As I told you, I doubt I'd have the time for something like that."

"Maybe, but they really could help increase your business."

"It's doing really well as it is, thank you. In fact, it's all I can do to keep up."

"Nevertheless, I'd still like you to meet him. He did have to go back to his country, but I've extended an open invitation. So whenever he's free he'll be able to visit. Though it'll probably be months, perhaps even longer, before he can."

"We'll just have to wait and see. Now come on, we're missing out on the buffet. This lot's going to eat the lot if we don't watch it." Trying hard to camouflage his relief, even though it was probably only temporary.

"Ha! Good point."

After all the planning and hard work, it was no surprise the party proved a great success. Everyone utterly spoilt Georgie and his sisters which, all three clearly enjoyed. The inevitable excitement affected them so much that while the last guests were taking their leave, they all began to yawn.

"Good, they are all asleep at last. I did not think I would get them to settle."

"I think my parents have worn themselves out too. They're both dozing in the drawing room."

"Good. Now, what were you and Roger talking about? I could see something was agitating you."

"He was saying how sorry he was we did not meet Peter."

"If only he knew."

"I know, and I hope he never does."

"Anything else? I do not think you have told me everything."

"He's extended an open invitation for him to visit anytime he wishes."

"Oh! So we still have reason to worry."

"Sort of. Roger doubts he'll be able to come for several months, perhaps longer. We can only hope he never does."

"Yes, I suppose hope is all we have."

"There's no point making ourselves ill over it. If it happens, we'll just have to face it at the time or try and find some way out."

"I had hoped we could forget all about him. But that was obviously too much to ask for."

"Let's not talk about it anymore. We'll put it to the back of our minds for now. May take a bit of effort but there's so much more for us to concentrate on. The children, for starters. And father, though he tries to hide it, is deteriorating."

"I had noticed. Do you think your mother has?"

"Bound to've. She's very observant, and after all, they've been together for a long time. I'm sure she realises but says nothing so as not to upset him. It's not as if he's ill and we could do something about it."

"No. It is sad to see. We will just have to make them both as comfortable and happy as we can."

"You've certainly made them happy by giving them three wonderful grand-children."

"And are you happy?"

"How can you ask? I'm thrilled. I'd never thought it possible to be so happy."

"Good, I am glad. Now, the others are not the only ones who are tired. I'll make sure Martha locks up early, then we can all have an early night."

"Okay sweetheart."

~~~~~~~~

"Congratulations Dorcas! Do you know what you are going to call him yet?"

"Peter after an uncle of mine. A nice man."

"Oh. Why not your father?"

"As you know, we've already named Michael after Adam's father. It so happens my father is also Michael. I didn't want two of them, it'd be far too confusing. So we decided on Peter."

"He is very lively."

"Yes, hasn't stopped since he was born. Also has a terrific set of lungs. Never had a baby like him."
~~~~~~~~

"You look tired. Is he keeping you up at night?"

"Unfortunately. I do my best to stop him waking the others, but does mean I often have to sit up with him. Just don't understand. Do you think there may be something wrong with him?"

"He looks healthy enough. As far as I can see, there are no indications of anything untoward. Let me hold him for a moment so I can have a closer look." He immediately started kicking, squirming, and squealing.

"I'm sorry. He's always like that whenever someone else tries to hold him."

"There is no need to apologise. He obviously prefers to be with his mummy." While struggling to keep him steady, she examined his tiny body. No bruises, cuts, damaged bones or swelling that she could see. Holding his head as firmly as she dared, she looked into his eyes and, as best as she could above his screams, listened to his little heart. "I cannot find anything wrong. He really appears to be quite healthy. I have occasionally come across babies like him. Their lively behaviour is often indicative of an active and bright intellect. Unfortunately, for the parents, these children usually require less sleep. Consequently, they are alert from early morning until late at night. Can be quite a drain."

"Thank you for having a look. I didn't think he was ill, but you know how we mothers will worry. So you think he's going to be an intelligent boy?"

"Yes, I think it very probable."

"Will he ever quieten down?"

"I cannot tell you. Some do, but then others do not. It is just a case of wait and see. I am sorry I am unable to tell you anything more definite."

"That's okay. As long as he's healthy. That's all I can really ask for."

Stopping at the top of the hill, as had become her habit whenever passing that way, she turned to look across the valley. Even after all the years, she still loved it. There may be other interesting and exotic places, but this was home and so beautiful. Breathing in the view as if it were a cool draft of some refreshing drink, she turned to continue her way home.

"Oh! Jennifer! You surprised me."

"Sorry, I didn't mean to startle you. You weren't at the house, so I assumed you'd been down to the cottages. I thought I may catch you here. I wanted a word with you."

"Are you all right? Do you need something? You are not ill, are you?"

"No, no, nothing like that. It's just I've some news I wanted to share before anyone else told you."

"What is it? You are not .....?"

"Oh, no!" Jennifer broke in before she could finish her sentence. "Maybe later. Well, I hope so anyway. No. Roger and I are leaving."

"What do you mean 'leaving'?"

"For the sake of his career, we need to move to the city. We're leaving next week."

"Oh. How long will you be away?"

"It looks like it's going to be permanent."

"Oh Jennifer! I had no idea you were thinking of something like this. Why did you not say anything before?"

"We weren't certain until a few days ago. I admit I hadn't anticipated this when we married. But if he's to get on, we have to go."

"I am going to miss you."

"And I you."

"Are you all right with the idea?"

"I think so. Well, in truth, I'm not sure. But he's my husband and for better or worse this is it. I want him to get on and have always been prepared to support him, no matter what. It's just I hadn't expected this. All my relatives and friends are here. I don't really know anyone in the city."

"I quite understand. It is going to be hard on all of us. I really am going to miss you. After all, we have known each other for most of our lives. But you will come back from time to time. For holidays and family events, I mean."

"I hope so, but Roger says we may not be able to leave the city whenever we wish. You know what he's like. Once he has the bone in his mouth, he'll not let go."

"But that is hardly fair on you, or us."

"I know, but my place is by his side. I do want him to be a success. So a small sacrifice on my part is only fair."

"I suppose so. It is always we women who have to make the sacrifice though."

"Roger's leaving his own family too."

"I appreciate that, but it is different for a man. What do they say about it?"

"His mother's upset, but the rest wish him good speed and success. I think his father quite fancies having a high level politician in the family. You know what a snob he can be at times."

"Ha! Ha! Yes I do. We will see you before you leave?"

"Yes, I'll make sure of it. You will write and let me know all that is happening here, won't you?"

"Of course. And you must write and let me know how you are."

"Hello darling. Good day?"

"Not bad. We cleared the north eastern copse, so it's now ready for breeding pheasants and perhaps a few partridges."

"Good. You look fit and healthy even if a little tired."

"The work was harder than I expected, but I enjoyed stretching myself. You and the children okay?"

"Yes. I have some news."

"What's that?"

"Jennifer came to see me earlier. She and Roger are moving to the city."

"For good?!"

"Virtually. Apparently, he needs to be there if his career is to go in the right direction."

"You'll miss her."

"Yes I will. But you know what this means?"

"What's that sweetheart?"

"Oh, wake up Richard! We no longer have to worry about that Peter Lucca coming to stay."

"Oh yeah. Hadn't thought of that. Good. I don't suppose there's any danger of Roger bringing him down here when they visit?"

"Jennifer thinks it is unlikely they will come back often. Roger reckons he won't be able to leave the city very much."

"Great. So let's forget all about that bas......... Sorry didn't mean to say that out loud."

"It is all right darling. I quite understand and totally agree with your sentiments."

"Well, hadn't expected that today." He went and cleaned up prior to them joining his parents for dinner. That night, their passion knew no bounds. Neither had really appreciated how the threat of Peter Lucca had been hanging round in the back of their consciences.

15

Weil's

"Goodness Peter has grown Dorcas. I can hardly believe he is already seven."

"I know. The time's passed so fast. Seems only yesterday I had him. But he is such a difficult child. Completely different to his brother and sisters."

"How do you mean?"

"He's always bad tempered. Constantly argues. Is always upsetting the others. Frequently picks fights and not only with his brother and sisters. I'm sorry to say he's quite unpopular."

"I am sorry Dorcas. Can you not stop him?"

"No matter what his father or I say or do, he won't listen. There seems to be no stopping him. I'm at my wit's end as to what to do."

"Does he explain or give any reason for it?"

"No. He'll often try shouting at or arguing with us and frequently just stomps off. I'll not have that. But no end of smacking changes anything."

"Would you like me to try and talk to him?"

"Thank you, but I don't think it'd make any difference. He's often rude to people and I don't want you to have to suffer his bad moods."

"Shall I ask Richard? Perhaps he would listen to him."

"I doubt it. He'll not listen to his father or any of the other men. No, I think we'll just have to battle through and hope he grows out of it."

"I am sorry Dorcas. With everything else you have to do, this is the last thing you need."

"Well, God knows. He'll give me strength. How's your boy?"

"Lively. He enjoys going off on his own and I often lose him. I do worry, but he always returns safely. I do not want to break his spirit or to mollycoddle him too much. But I do get anxious as I am not always sure what he is getting up to, though I am confident it is nothing wrong. I think he is going to be quite self-sufficient when he grows up. I would rather that than someone who constantly depended upon me. Nevertheless, it can be worrying at times."

"I agree. But at least when they're like that, we can be reasonably sure they'll be able to take care of themselves when we're no longer round."

"Yes. We have to consider their future even if it gives us heartache in the meantime."

"How's little Maria getting on?"

"Well, thank you. It is hard to believe she will be four in a few weeks."

"Really! My goodness, how the time has flown. I thought there was a larger gap between my Peter and her."

"I know. Both of them seem to be leaping ahead. In her own way, she is just as active as the others."

"Are you going to have anymore?"

"I do not want to. To be honest, we had not planned on Maria. But I do not regret it. She is such a wonderful child. But I really hope she will be the last. Four are quite enough for me."

"As I've often said, more the merrier as far as I'm concerned. Mind you, Peter has caused me to have second thoughts. Anyway, I'm getting to that age now."

"I am sure you cannot be there yet. Still plenty of time if you want more. I still do not know how you manage with the ones you have. I am sure I would have gone mad by now."

"It's not that difficult, really. Besides the elder ones help when I need it. They're so good."

"I am glad to hear it. Now, I better get going. I promised to be back in time for lunch."

~~~~~~~~

"Wow! That's great!" Georgie could not help shouting with joy as he swung across the pond. Twisting round to swing back, he suddenly lost his footing on the muddy edge. At the same time, his sweaty hands lost their grip on the rope and he went sliding down the bank. The sharp rocks dug into his young flesh as he landed backside first at the edge of the pool. "Agh!" No, he wasn't going to cry. Drawing back the tears, he struggled to stand, but slipped again. His arm struck the jagged point of a large stone and blood spurted out, turning the water a dark pink. Rinsing his sore hands and the cut in the water, he decided it was time to go home. Anyway, the rumbling tones erupting from his stomach told him it was time for dinner.

"What have you done Georgie?"

"Nothing."

"Georgie."

"Ooh. Just a small cut."

"That is no small cut! And you have rope burns on your hands. What have you been up to?"

"I was just playing down by the pool."

"Doing what? Why did you need a rope?"

"I was swinging across."

"How many times have I told you to be careful? What would you do if you were hurt and could not move? Hardly anyone goes down there these days."

"It's okay Mama. I know what I'm doing. And I've done it lots of times without getting hurt."

"Not today! Where did you get the rope?"

"I found it in one of the old stables. I didn't think anyone would mind me taking it. Looked like it's been lying there for some time."

"It could have been rotten. You really must be more careful."
~~~~~~~~

"Sorry Mama. I'll be more careful next time."

"There will not be 'a next time'. You hear me. I do not want you taking risks."

"But Mama!"

"That is enough. No more. You hear me?"

"Yes Mama."

"Now come here. Let me clean up those wounds."

"Are things any better with Peter?" On one of her frequent visits some days later.

"Not really. But we battle on. I just wish I understood what makes him so hateful of others. He won't talk about it, no matter how often I ask."

"That is difficult. Talking of difficult I saw Mary's Peter yesterday. I tried to talk to him, but he just ignored me. You know he has not spoken to Richard or me since Johnny. Just as on other occasions, when we happened to see each other, he went off muttering under his breath."

"Despite the years he's not got over it, I'm afraid. So far, 'time' hasn't helped. I doubt he'll ever come to terms with it now. Mary does her best, but he's become increasingly morose and withdrawn. None of the children will go near him."

"That is sad. He still appears to hold us responsible. I am sure I heard him say we had no right to live, Richard and I, I mean."

"I'm sorry dear, but in his confused mind I think you may well be right, and that he does still think it's your fault Johnny died. But don't worry, we'll watch him." But she did worry. The look in his eyes the day before had borne deep malice, and she was sure he could act upon it.

"So sad. I wish there was something we could do to help."

"Everything has been tried. I think he's one of those whose grief will stay with him until the end. Anyway, enough of that."

~~~~~~~~

"Richard!" Thankfully, he had not left the house yet.

"What's wrong sweetheart?" The hysterical note in her voice had him there within seconds.
~~~~~~~~

"Georgie is ill."

"What do you mean? What's wrong with him?"

"He is feverish and yet sometimes appears to have a chill. He is also complaining about a bad headache and that his muscles ache. His eyes are also inflamed. I have not seen symptoms like this before. I am scared Richard."

"Okay sweetheart. Let me have a look at him." He examined his son while the child moaned and groaned, unable to speak coherently.

"What is it?!"

"Not sure. But he's definitely not well. I'll consult some books." His worried expression as he left did anything but reassure her.

"Well?" Returning a half hour later, he looked no happier.

"I think I'll get your father. He's had far more experience than me. He may recognise the symptoms."

"You know something, or at least you are guessing at something. I can see it in your eyes, so do not try to deny it."

"Well .... I think I may have an idea." He'd not wanted to say anything until he was sure. Nevertheless, he knew better than to try and put her off with a lie. She always saw through him.

"What is it?! You are frightening me!"

"I recently read in one of those journals I receive about the findings of a man called Adolf Weil. He's been looking at infections he thinks have been caused by bacteria. There's one where the symptoms appear to be similar to what Georgie has. Doctors have started referring to it as Weil's disease. But I don't want to say more until your father's had a look. I may be wrong."

"Papa has not been very well. I am not sure he will be able to come to the house."

"It's okay. I'll take the carriage. If need be, I can carry him into it. I'm sure he'd like to see to his grandson."

"He will. But I am worried it may take too much out of him."

"Don't worry, I'll look after him. You stay with Georgie while I go for him. I'll ask mother and Martha to come and sit with you both while I'm out."

"Is there anything I can do for Georgie while we wait?"

"Not really. Just try to keep him calm. Put some damp cloths on his forehead if the fever gets too bad. I'll not be long."

"Do you know how we can treat it if it is what you think?"

"Let's just wait until your father has had a look."

Georgie twisted and turned as the fever and chill alternated. One moment his temperature soared with the fever and the next plummeted with the chill. The three really did not know what to do other than attempt to cool or warm him as the need arose. Time stood still. The hour it took for the men to return an eternity.

"Hello Papa. Are you all right?"

"Never mind me. Now step back and let me have a look at Georgie." Obediently they all moved back a pace. "Hum. I think you may be right, Richard. It does look like Weil's disease."

"What is Weil's disease?" Concern for her son escalating.

"It is caused by a bacteria, usually carried by animals. Very often in their urine. Has Georgie had contact with anything where rats may have been?"

"I do not think so. Oh! Maybe. He has been using some rope from one of the old stables for a swing."

"A swing?"

"Yes Richard. He has been throwing the rope over tree branches and using it to swing over the old pool."

"I assume there are rats in the old stable?"

"Yes sir. We've been trying to clear them but it's taking time." Shooting an annoyed glance at his wife.

"Katherine, has Georgie had any fresh cuts on him?"

"Yes. He fell off the rope and cut his arm and hand on some rocks. He also had rope burns on his hands."

"That is it then. I do not think there is any mistake. It is Weil's disease."

"Is it dangerous Papa?" Struggling to keep the tears back.

"I am afraid it is darling. We will have to treat it as best as we can, but only time will tell."

"How dangerous?" Did she really want to know? Did she want to ask? "Could he ...." Did she really want to hear the answer? "...... die?" She hardly had strength to whisper the question.

"We do not need to consider that for now." Desperately trying to alleviate his daughter's concern.

"Could he!"

"Yes." Richard grabbed her as she went to faint.

"Is there any treatment sir?"

"There is Richard. There is no modern medicine, well not yet, but some of the old remedies have apparently proved effective. Katherine and Helina here should be able to make some up."

"What do we need?" Helina taking charge. Her daughter-in-law's dazed and fearful condition leaving her little choice.

"There are certain fungi moulds and plant extracts which, when combined, have apparently helped. Let us leave Katherine and Richard with Georgie while you and I go down to the outhouses. I will explain what needs to be done."

"Oh Papa. He will be all right?"

"Yes, of course dear. He is a healthy boy. Now you just look after him while Helina and I get the remedy made up." The two left the room.

"Richard, I cannot bear the thought of him suffering, or worse."

"Come on sweetheart. You heard what your father said. He seems confident it can be dealt with." Not wanting to say anything about the deep look of worry and concern he'd seen on her father's face as he and his mother had left the room.

"You are not confident, are you?" Helina had waited until they reached the top of the stairs before asking.

"I am sorry Helina. But it does not look good. This disease is evil. But as I said, the remedy we are going to make now has had positive effects on some."

"But not all?"

"No. Many die."

"How long before we will know for sure?"

"He will be ill for a few days and then appear to recover. But it will be short-lived, two, maybe three days. Then the second stage will set in."

"What are we to expect then?"

"There could be severe kidney and liver damage. And there may be symptoms similar to those you see with meningitis."

"How will we know if his kidneys and liver are affected? I am sure I would recognise the other symptoms if they arise."

"He will be jaundiced. His skin and the whites of his eyes will have a yellow colour."

"And then?"

"There will not be much else we can do except make him as comfortable as possible. I am afraid it would then just be a matter of waiting for the end."

"Richard and Katherine would be devastated."

"I know. I do not think any of us will cope very well. Georgie is precious to all of us."

"No, I doubt we will. George would be more than upset. As far as he is concerned, the family's future is tied up in Georgie."

"Yes. But best we do not jump the gun yet. The remedy may have a positive impact. I was not lying when I said he is a healthy boy. He has a fairly robust constitution and may rally. But I wanted you to be aware of the possibilities, so, if it comes to it, we may be ready to help support the others."

"Here we are." Helina and Katherine's father returning to the sickroom an hour and a half later.

"I nearly sent Richard to look for you. You have been so long."

“Sorry dear, but we had to make up the potion. Thankfully, we were able to find everything we needed. How is he?”

“The fever and chill still alternate. In the brief moments when he can utter anything, he complains about the headache and his aching joints.”

“Poor little thing. Come on Georgie.” Helina lifting the small frame so Katherine’s father could administer the remedy.

“Now what?” Richard almost demanded, finding it hard to restrain his fears. But for the sake of Katherine and the others, he did.

“Now it is wait and see.”

“I am sorry to have kept you here Martha. I think we are all right now.” Throughout, Martha had quietly remained in the background in case she was needed.

“No trouble Mam. Will little Georgie be okay?”

“We are going to have to wait and see. We have done all we can for now.”

“I’ll get some fresh sheets and bedding Mam. His are soaked through with his sweating.”

“Thank you Martha.”

No one really got any rest or sleep over the following days and nights.

“Richard!”

“What is sweetheart?!” Having run to her in Georgie’s room, fearing the worst.

“He is better. Look, he no longer has a fever or a chill!”

“That’s good.” Dare he hope it had passed? “Mother!”

“What is it dear?!” Out of breath from the sudden excursion, Helina rushed into the room a couple of minutes later. “Is Georgie all right?” Fear their constant companion.

“Look! He’s better!”

“Oh! Thank the Lord.”

“Yes!” Unable to control his joy or relief, he hugged his sweetheart and mother, almost squeezing the breath out of them.

“We must send a note to Katherine’s parents. To let them know.”

"Okay. Will you do that please, Mother?"

"Of course. I will go and write it straight away." Helina left the room with very mixed feelings. She had not forgotten what Katherine's father had told her about a temporary recovery. But she did not consider it right to bring it up with the others now. She would include a request for him to come to the house later, hoping he would be up to the short journey. He would know how best to handle the situation.

"Papa! Georgie's much better."

"So I understand."

"You do not look too happy about it. Why? Is there something you have not told us?"

"I am sorry dear, but I did not want to tell you before it was necessary."

"Tell me what?!"

"This is how the illness goes. There is always a short period of apparent recovery before the second stage of the disease sets in."

"What are you telling us? Do you mean Georgie is not really better?"

"Yes, I am afraid I am saying that."

"You should have warned us Papa."

"You are right. I should have. But I did not see any point in making matters worse before necessary."

"Oh Papa! I would not have got so excited if you had."

"I am sorry dear. At the time, I thought it for the best. Perhaps I was wrong."

"Yes, you were." Struggling not to let the bitterness she was feeling come through. "What are we to expect now? Is he going to be very poorly again?"

"He is. In fact, it will probably be worse."

"Is there anything we can do?"

"Just keep on giving him the potion. I assume you and Helina have been able to make more."

"Yes." She dared not say more whilst her emotions were so strong. They all spent the rest of the day sitting round little Georgie's bed. Martha came during the afternoon and helped wash him and change the bedding. There having been no change, for better or worse, in the boy's condition her father left late evening stating he would return first thing in the morning.

"Are we going to lose him?" She asked her husband that night as they sat alone with their son, the tears flowing down her face.

"I don't know sweetheart." Fighting back his own tears. Nevertheless, she could not mistake the shine in the corners of his eyes.

"Good morning Papa. Oh Mama, I am glad you have come." Collapsing into her mother's arms with deep sobs.

"I wanted to see Georgie and you. How is he this morning?"

"Restless." Doing her best to stem the tears.

"Oh, I hoped this would not happen." Her father had been carefully examining Georgie.

"What Papa?!"

"He is jaundiced."

"I thought he was. Is it very bad?"

"I am afraid it is. It means the disease has attacked his kidneys and liver and may be affecting his nervous system."

"Can we do anything?"

"Only continue giving him the medicine you have made."

"Is there nothing else?"

"I am sorry dear, but no. We now have to wait and see."

"How serious is it? And this time, please do not hide anything."

"No, I will not. It is very serious. He may not recover."

"Do you mean ......?" Unable to utter the word, but everyone understood.

"Yes." A universal gasp arose with the brutal statement.

"NO!!"

"Darling." The two grandmothers fighting to subdue their own shrieks while attempting to comfort the distraught mother.

Katherine leaned heavily on Richard's arm as they followed the tiny white coffin. Her precious Georgie could not be in that box. No, no, it is impossible. Collapsing on her knees by the graveside, she groaned and wailed with the agony consuming her. Richard, tears flooding down his own face while holding her convulsing shoulders, also knelt beside the undersized grave. Grandparents, each holding a hanky to their own eyes, stood slightly aside, allowing the distraught parents' room to express their inconsolable grief. Friends, workers and villagers, many in tears, stood further back. The boy had been a favourite with all. Theirs was a small, fairly tight-knit community and the loss of a loved one, let alone a child, always affected them. All, let alone the family, would take a long time to come to terms with Georgie's passing. For sure, none would ever forget him.

16

Fire!

"Happy anniversary sweetheart." His apparently disembodied voice emerging from behind a massive bouquet of gorgeous roses.

"Happy anniversary darling. I can hardly believe it has been fourteen years. Where has the time gone?" Taking the bouquet, she placed it to one side and kissed her adorable husband. "Thank you, these are lovely." The years had been kind to them. Neither having really changed since their first encounter in Vienna.

"Who cares? All I know is how happy I am. I love you so much. I'm looking forward to the next fourteen."

"And just to think if you had not knocked me over."

"I know. It's terrible to think we could've never known each other. I'm sure it was meant to be." Both laughed at the recollection.

"Well, whatever, I am very pleased we did meet. God must have been in it."

"Would you like to go out for the evening? We could go to Berties."

"I would prefer we made this a family occasion with the children. Would you mind?"

"Of course not. You know how I love us to be together."

"Yes I do. Good, but thank you for thinking of it."

"What're you two up to? Those are lovely flowers. Is it something special?"

"Yes Ellen. It is our anniversary. We have been married fourteen years."

"What a long time. You must really be old. I mean, it's longer than I have been alive."

"Thank you dear. Very kind. It is not really that long. You will understand when you grow up."

"Ooo! Pretty flowers!"

"Hello Maria darling. Papa bought them for mama."

"That is nice of Papa." Running across the hall and, unable to reach further up, hugging his legs.

"Hello sweetheart." Lifting her in his arms and kissing her on the head. "What have you been doing?"

"I have been putting Amie, Billy, Cocky and the others to bed." Giggling as she recalled how Billy, her pet goat, had head butted her when she told him it was time for bed.

"Will you please sing to us after dinner Maria?"

"If you would like me to Mama."

"Yes I would. It would be a nice way for papa and I to celebrate our anniversary. I will accompany you on the piano and Ellen and Andrea can sing the chorus."

"All right Mama."

Taking her place, Katherine prepared to accompany her daughters. Maria stood beside her while Ellen and Andrea positioned themselves in front of the family's grand piano. Their father, anticipating the sweet melody of his daughter's combined voices, rested back on the sofa. He couldn't be happier. Her hand, raised in readiness to strike the first note, froze mid-air as a loud vicious banging erupted from the front of the house. 'Bang! Bang! Bang!' 'Bang! Bang! Bang!' 'Bang! Bang! Bang!' 'Bang! Bang! Bang!' Continuing without respite. Instinctively jumping up, all rushed into the hall where Martha was just opening the front door.

"Quick! Come quickly Sir!"

"What's wrong?"

"Fire Sir! One of the cottages is on fire!" The man shouted back as he ran off with no further explanation.

"I better go and see what's going on."

“I will come with you. Someone may be hurt. Martha, please take the girls back to the drawing room.”

As they ran out of the house, both noted the orangey glow dissipating the blackness of night they had anticipated. Then, without further hesitation, they followed after the messenger. The further down the hill they got, the brighter the sky. The fire must be substantial. Putting aside all fear of tripping in the darkened undergrowth, they increased their pace. Upon reaching the edge of the hamlet, both stopped in their tracks, horrified.

“Oh, no!” Before them stood a cottage fully engulfed by flames. A human chain of men, women and older children stretched from it to the well on the green. Water spilt as buckets hastily passed from one to the other. Richard immediately went and spoke to one of the men who appeared to have taken charge.

“I’m going to help them. You see if anyone needs medical attention.”

“All right.” She called back as he returned to join the human bucket chain. Looking round, she noted a group of women standing off to one side with the younger children and babies, most of whom were crying.

“What happened? Do you know?”

“No. We were just clearing up after our evening meal and getting the children ready for bed when someone saw a bright light through the window. The next thing we knew people were running round shouting fire! We all rushed out to be greeted by what you see now.”

“Has anyone been hurt?”

“We’re not sure. I think all of us here are okay.” Glancing round at the other women, all of whom nodded agreement. “But there’s so much confusion and we’re still trying to account for everyone.”

“That is Dorcas’s cottage. Have you seen her or the family? I cannot see them anywhere.”

“Not yet, but as I say, it has all been rather chaotic.”

“I can see Peggy over there. She may know. Hers is the next cottage.”

"You can try, but she's in a right state, as usual." Peggy uncontrollably twisting her hands, stood a little way off with her own children gathered round.

"Peggy, have you seen Dorcas or Adam or the children?"

"We'r gon lose evrting! Me ome! Me ouse! Evrting! Wat we gon do?!" Screaming hysterically, her elder children watching in terror and the younger ones in tears. Have to do something. Her hard slap across Peggy's cheek brought a sudden and in some ways terrifying silence. Grabbing hold of her skirts, the elder children's already terror-stricken expressions intensified. The younger ones ceased crying, frozen by fear. The eerie silence continued while Peggy remained mute. Then she appeared to come to life.

"Uh, wat? Oh! It ye. Wat yee say?"

"Have you seen Dorcas and the family?"

"Uh.. no. No itea wre tey be. Wat I gon do! Me ouse! Me ome!"

"All right Peggy, calm down. Take the children and join the other women over there." Peggy, looking confused, she pointed. "Over there in the corner. I will see if I can find Dorcas and the others." She had thought to ask Mary, but had not seen her either. Then she spotted her helping in the water chain. It was not a time to interrupt.

"Watch it doesn't spread to the other cottages!" He shouted above the sound of splintering wood and crashing timbers. "Better douse that cottage as well." Flames leaping perilously close to the roof of Peggy's.

"Richard, do you know if the family are safe? This is Dorcas's cottage."

"I haven't seen anyone. No one seems to know what happened. I expect they're on the green or over on the edge somewhere."

"I hope so. They're not with the others. I will look for them. You be careful darling."

"Yea okay, you too. Better stand back, the roof's about to cave in completely and there're sparks flying everywhere. I'm worried they may set something else on fire."

"All right. I will see you later."

Searching round the perimeter, the green and the cottages on the far side, her concern for Dorcas and her family grew. They were nowhere to be seen. Where could they be? Perhaps they have been found and are now with the others. Making her way back across the green to check, a slight movement caught her eye. What is that? Moving closer, she discovered Peter, Dorcas's young son, crouched by a large rock intensively watching the burning building. His soot covered face held a strange expression. Sullenness and blankness appeared to be amalgamated with a smirk. Very strange. Must be shock. It would be foolish and unkind to speculate on what was going on inside his little head at this stage.

"Peter." No reaction. "Peter!" His head turned slightly this time. "Peter, are you all right?" No response but to stare at her blankly. "Where are the others? Do you know?" No response but to turn back to face the now ruined cottage. That odd expression still on his features. Shock, must be shock.

"Come on Peter. Come with me." Bending to pick him up. He backed away. "Come on, Peter, you know who I am. You cannot stay here." Gently, yet firmly, taking hold, she lifted him in her arms. He did not resist, but putting his hands round her neck shifted so he could still watch the flaming mass. "My Peter, you have grown. You are quite heavy now." Still no response. Never mind. Will have to wait for the shock to wear off.

"Where was he?"

"I found him by that large rock over there. He seems to be in shock."

"What about the others?"

"I cannot find them."

"Oh! Do you think they didn't get out?"

"They must have. Peter here did, so why would they not?"

"I expect you're right. They're probably sheltering somewhere."

"I hope so, but where? I have looked everywhere I can think of. Besides, I would have expected to see Adam with the others dousing the flames."

"He's probably looking after the family. It wouldn't be a time to leave them alone."

"Yes, but where? If they are not on the green, with the others or at one of the other cottages, where are they? But they must be safe!" The alternative too horrific to contemplate.

"We've found some bodies." Richard joining her for a moment,

"Oh no. Who is it?"

"Hard to tell. But one is definitely an adult and there're three smaller ones."

"Oh, Richard." The heaviness in her heart carrying through into her weakened voice.

"We've almost got the fire under control. There's not much left of the cottage, but we managed to stop it spreading. Once the flames have died down, we'll be able to search more thoroughly."

"Peter here got out, so some of the others must have." Glancing down and hugging the child closer to her breast. "He is clearly in shock, so it is probable the others are also. Goodness knows where they may have wondered off. I will have another look round."

"Okay, but be careful. I hope you find them. I better get back." Leaving Peter with one of the women, she made a further two circuits. This time extending her search into the edge of the surrounding woods. Some of the others must have got out. Surely it cannot just be Peter. But there was no sign of them. Reluctantly giving up her quest, she returned to the group.

"Any one?"

"No." Unable to bring herself to say more.

"Oh dear. That's terrible. They must've all been trapped."

"I do not understand how. If Peter managed to get out, some of the others must have also."

"Perhaps they were overcome by smoke."

"I hope not." A shudder passing down her spine.

"Richard! Are you all right?" Looking at his blackened face and clothes.

"Yes. We've found another three bodies. With the four we already had, that's seven. There were twelve in the family, weren't there?"

"Yes. Dorcas, Adam and ten children."

"Okay, so with Peter here, that leaves four unaccounted for. We won't be able to search further until the fire dies down completely."

"Oh Richard. Surely they cannot have all been trapped. Some of the others must have got out."

"Did you find any of them when you searched just now?"

"No, and I went round a couple of times. Maybe they have wondered further off. They must be in shock, just as Peter here is. He was quite shaken when I found him. Look, he still is." The child sitting by the feet of one of the women still gazed intently upon the smouldering remains. His expression still confusing. Was it shock? It did not look like it. So what was it? Bewilderment, that must be it. He is bewildered, and yet. "The others are probably in a similar condition."

"I'm sorry sweetheart, but I don't think you should build your hopes up. It really doesn't look good."

"Excuse me sir!" One of the men indicating for him to go over to where he was standing.

"I'll see what he wants. You wait here." Over his shoulder as he quickly crossed the green. "Yes, what is it?"

"We've found the others."

"How many?"

"Four. We've laid them all out on the far side of the green."

"Show me." He followed the man. "Oh God! No one should see this. Cover them up. I saw some sacks over by the well. Use them." Leaving the man to get on with the ghastly task while he returned to his wife.

"I'm afraid we found the others. Two adults and nine children by the looks of it, though it is not easy to tell."

"No. It cannot be. How come none of them got out? Peter managed to."

"I don't know. But I can tell you, the fire was intense and there must have been a lot of smoke. They must have been overcome. Perhaps Peter was near a window or door where the smoke may have been disbursed by a breeze or something."

"Perhaps."

"They've been laid out on the far side of the green. I'm having them covered with some empty sacks. It's not a sight anyone should see."

"This is terrible. How on earth could it happen?"

"I don't know. We'll have to wait until morning to have a better look."

"There is no point in me staying here any longer. None of the others appear to be hurt, and at least their homes are undamaged. Some may be in shock, but I will have to let them sort themselves out for now. I think it best I take Peter away from here. He really should not be seeing this. Anyway, it is almost dawn."

"Sensible idea. I'll stay for a while just to make sure everything is damped down properly. We don't want any sparks flying off into the other cottages or woods."

"All right darling. You be careful."

"I'll. See you later."

"Martha!" She came running from the drawing room.

"Oh, my goodness!" Shaken by the sight of the soot covered child. "What's happened?"

"There has been a fire. One of the cottages. I do not want to talk about it now." Glancing surreptitiously down at the boy in her arms. Martha acknowledged with a discreet nod.

"Peter here is going to stay with us for a while. Please have a bedroom made ready and bring him a warm drink and something to eat." The child, shy of Martha, buried his face into her shoulder.

"Right away. Would you like a drink?"

"No, I am fine, thank you. Oh, better have a bath made ready. He is a little grubby."

"Of course. I'll be back with his drink and food as quick as I can."

"We will be in the library. I do not think this is a time for him to have other people round. Please tell the girls to remain in the drawing room."

As they entered the library, he raised his little head from her shoulder and appeared to take in the new surroundings. The books in particular seeming to attract him the most. Of course, he had never seen so many, if any at all. Kathrine mused. At least he recognises we are somewhere different. Good, maybe tonight's trauma has not caused him to withdraw completely from reality. That hopefully means, with a little time, his emotions should surface. Be a shame if they remain buried to fester. Who knows what the result may be if they do? In danger of dropping her heavy load, she immediately moved across the room, intending to seat Peter in the comfortable cerise armchair by the fireplace. However, he refused to loosen his grip from round her neck, leaving her little choice but to sit with him on her lap. The opening of the door made him jump. Martha, quietly entering with his drink and food, set it down on the occasional table next to the chair. "Thank you Martha." Indicating for her to leave again. Taking the cup she offered, he twisted further to look round the rest of the room, but still would not leave the protection of her arms. Despite the uncomfortable weight, she decided it best to allow him to remain where he was. Drinking and munching in a distracted manner, he continued to look round. Taking opportunity of this distraction, she carefully examined him. First his head, face and neck. Though the previous eerie expression had gone, there remained a bewildered, no, not the word, 'wild', 'stark' look in his eyes. To her surprise, he did not appear to have been crying. Must be shock. Continuing down the rest of his small frame, she could detect no physical injury. Neither did he appear to be suffering from smoke inhalation.

"How are you feeling Peter?" Turning back and staring straight into her eyes, he made no response. "All right, we do not need to talk now. Have you had enough?" He no longer drank or eat. No response. Assuming he did not want more, she shifted his weight, got up, and left the room.

"There, that is better." Having bathed him, she wrapped a warm towel round his small but sturdy frame. "Time for bed now. I expect you are tired." As before, he just looked without saying anything. She tucked him in and then sat beside the bed until he slept. Quietly leaving, she ensured the door remained open a little in case he woke frightened or needing anything.

"Are you all right darling?" Descending the stairs as her beloved came into the hall.

"Yes. Just a bit smoky."

"But you are limping!"

"Oh that. Nothing really. Peter Woodcote accidentally dropped a bucket on my ankle. It's bruised."

"It would be him. Should I look at it?"

"No need. It's really just a small bruise. Should be fine in no time. Have to say though I'm not entirely sure it was an accident but there. How's Peter?"

"Silent. I think he is probably still in shock. Do you have any idea of what happened?"

"No. None of us can work out how it started. We can only guess a log from the fire or something off the cooker fell on to the floor. I'll go back in the morning. What am I saying? It's already morning, well, in a couple of hours. I'll then see if we can get a better idea."

"Are they really all gone?"

"I'm sorry. I'll send one of the lads to the undertaker later. We'll have to arrange the funerals. There doesn't appear to be anyone else."

"How sad. I will come with you when you go down. Peggy was, understandably, in quite a state. I would like to see if I can help her at all. And I would like to check on Mary and the others. Besides, I also want to know what happened."

"I'm sorry. You really liked Dorcas, didn't you?"

"Yes." Tears coming into her eyes.

With heavy hearts and damp eyes, they followed the procession of coffins from the church. The sight of so many, especially so many little white ones saddening all gathered. That one event had almost obliterated a whole family staggered each person present. Holding his small hand in hers, Katherine observed Peter's features. Again, he did not cry. His expression bore a sullenness and detachment mixed with something she could not fathom. Residual shock, presumably. As the coffins were lowered, he almost looked malevolent. Sad to see in someone so young. Perhaps bitterness at the loss of his family. Who knew what was going through that innocent little mind.

"What are we going to do about Peter?" Back at the house. "I have asked about, but no one knows of any relatives."

"I've to go into town tomorrow, so I'll ask there and see if anyone knows anything. In the meantime, you check the church records. There must be someone somewhere."

"I hope so. It will be sad if he is all alone in the world."

"Don't worry sweetheart. We'll make sure he's taken care of."

"Thank you darling. I did not want to see him just left to fend for himself. He is so young."

"You know I'd never allow that. Besides, my parents have always insisted all our workers and their families are cared for and brought me up to do the same. For the time being he'll remain with us. You okay with that?"

"Yes, of course. It is the least we can do."

"Did you find out anything?" He had just returned from town.

"No one knows of any other relatives. However, some told me about a place that takes orphaned children. But I don't think we'll want to send Peter there. Apparently, it's more like a workhouse than a home. I'm told the accommodation and food is poor and the children are made to work all hours for no additional reward."

"Sounds terrible."

"Yes, I thought so too. No, we'll definitely not be sending him anywhere like that. Did you have any luck with the church records?"

"No. They confirmed what I had been told, that both Dorcas and Adam were only children. But it also turns out their parents were also only children, on both sides. So even if there had been any others, they will be long gone. I asked the priest if he knew of anyone, but no. What is going to happen to him?"

"I'll give it some thought. Perhaps one of the other families would be willing to take him in."

"Though they may want to help, I doubt most will consider themselves in a position to do so. Peggy is far too highly strung, and Mary has her hands full with her Peter and daughters. Anyway, I would rather he is not exposed to Peter's morose attitude. The rest already have so many children. I doubt they would feel up to coping with another not their own."

"Okay. I'll have a think. Don't worry, we'll find a solution. I'll ask my parents. Perhaps they'll have some ideas."

"Good morning darling." Cuddling into his warm body as the sun peeped through a gap between the curtains.

"Good morning sweetheart."

"I have been thinking."

"What about?"

"Peter. I have an idea, but I am not sure what you will think of it."

"What's that?"

"Why do we not adopt him?"

"Uh!"

"Why do we not adopt Peter?"

"Oh!"

"In some ways, he could make up for us not having Georgie here."

"Um, I need to think this through."

"I know, it came to me during the night. I must admit it surprised me, but the more I thought about it, the more sense it made. You could teach him all about the business so he could carry it on after you."

"You've obviously thought this through."

"I could not sleep after the idea came to me, so have had most of the night to consider it. What do you think?"

"I'm not sure. The idea never occurred to me. I'll give it some thought through the day and ask father what he thinks."

"What do you think of Katherine's idea father?"

"Well, it is not something that would have immediately come to my mind. But she has a point about him being a substitute for Georgie. How would you feel about an heir who is not your own blood and flesh?"

"I'd hoped we may have another son, but it increasingly looks unlikely. Yes, I suppose I could live with it. Not what I expected, but it would resolve the issue of who will inherit the estates. Would you be okay with it?"

"I think so. If only we had not lost Georgie." Drawing back the rising tears. He missed his grandson and the joy he had brought him.

"Yes .... I still miss having him round." Forlornly looking down at his clasped hands.

"Welcome into the family, Peter Palmerstone." Richard shaking his hand a month later.

"Yes, welcome Peter." Hugging and kissing him.

"Welcome brother." Each with a sweet smile.

"Thanks." Though still not talkative, he had at least started giving one-word responses.

"There, that's all settled. Now you all go off and play." The children dutifully left. "Happy sweetheart?"

"Yes darling. I am glad we have done this. We can now give him a good life and ensure his future is secure. I would have hated to see him sent to one of those horrible places. I feel it is the least we could have done for Dorcas."

"Good. Well, I can't sit here idle. There's work to be done."

17

Changes

"Ah, good you have come." Opening his frail eyes to look upon his son, but unable to sit. "I wanted to speak to you before it is too late."

"No need to talk like that sir. You're just tired today. You'll be up and about in no time."

"Come on Richard, we both know that is not true. I have not got long. But I wanted to tell you how proud I am of you."

"Thank you sir."

"Not only have you got a good grip on the business, but you have also caused it to grow more and more successful each day. But it is not only that." Stopping to catch his breath. "You have also shown yourself to be a sensible and kind man. You are respected and looked up to throughout the district. The family name is truly safe in your hands." Again stopping to rest for a moment. "And yet again it is not just that. Richard, I love you. I hope you have always known that."

"Thank you sir. I have. And I love you. No one could ask for a better father."

"Thank you son. I wanted to make sure you knew before I leave. Now I would like to speak to your lovely wife. She really is quite a treasure."

"Yes, she is. I'll fetch her right away."

"No. I wish to see her on her own."

"Very well sir. I'll send her to you." The old man closed his eyes to rest as his son left the room.

"Good morning sir."

"George please."

"Sorry, of course, good morning George. How are you today?"

"As you see."

"I am sorry. May I do anything to make you more comfortable?"

"Thank you Katherine, but no, nothing. I wanted to speak to you while I still can."

"Please do not talk like that. You will be fine soon."

"Come Katherine, I expect better from you. I am not afraid, but admit I do not like the thought of leaving you all. But this is all part of life, as we both know."

"I understand."

"I want to thank you for making Richard so happy and for giving us such lovely grandchildren. Also, for you willingness to put yourself out and help with house, business, clinic and workers. I realise it is not always easy, but you never complain." Closing his eyes to rest. "I never expected to have a daughter-in-law like you and am truly grateful for you." Again stopping for a moment. "Though Richard understands, I did not want to say too much in front of him. I will not be with you much longer and wanted to ask that you please take care of Helina for me. Though she presents a strong front, she will not cope well with my passing. We have been together a long time and I am very fortunate to have had someone who loves me so much and whom I love. Many have not been so blessed."

"Of course, there is no need to ask. I love you both and would always do all I can to make you both happy."

"Thank you. Please also continue to give Richard the benefit of your sensible guidance and bring the children up to respect their family name. Shame Georgie is no longer with us to carry it on. At least, though the blood line will effectively end, it will continue with Peter. I hope he will do it justice."

"Richard and I will do our best to make sure he does. Now I think you better rest. All this talking is tiring you."

"Time enough for rest soon. Thank you for everything, Katherine. I love you."

"I would also like to thank you for making me so welcome from the start and for making my life here a happy one. I will miss you very much." Unable to restrain the tear in her eye.

"Come, come, none of that now." Weakly patting her hand. "Please ask Helina to come to me."

"Right away."

Within a week of his passing, Helina was confined to her own bed. It had been all Richard could do to support her at the funeral and within a short time she had also failed.

"Richard, my darling son. I miss him so much."

"I know Mother, we all do. But you need to concentrate on getting better. We need you, the children need you."

"No, no, you will all be fine without me. Katherine is more than capable. I am so pleased you married such a wonderful woman. She really is a treasure. Never forget that."

"Come Mother, there's no call to talk like that. You'll be up and commanding the house again very soon."

"No Richard. I miss him too much. Never forget how much I love you." Then, closing her eyes, she let her last breath pass.

Both funerals were attended by all in the district. George and Helina having been loved and respected by everyone they had any contact with. Never haughty or proud, despite their wealth and high social standing, they had always sought to ensure no one was left in need. It helped Richard and Katherine cope with their great loss to see such genuine outpourings of sympathy and condolences. It was quite a reputation they were to live up to. After the funerals and initial mourning period, they sought to return the household to normal, though the loving grandparents would be sorely missed by all.

"Give it back!"

"Stupid, get it if you can!"

"Stop it, you'll break it!"

The commotion had her heading for the drawing room within moments. What is wrong now? Opening the door, she was greeted by the sight of Peter swinging a doll by one leg above his head and Andrea jumping up and down, trying to reach it.

"Stop Peter!" The unexpected suddenness of her voice momentarily freezing him. Turning with a defiant look, he meant to challenger her, but then thought better of it.

"Here you sissy!" Throwing the doll at Andrea, who catching it, ran from the room in tears.

"Why do you keep teasing and bullying your sisters?"

"Stupid a girl of her age playing with dolls."

"You know very well she collects them. You also know how fragile the porcelain heads and bodies are. And how precious they are to her."

"Stupid nonsense."

"Peter, I do not understand you sometimes. You have been with us for eight years now and yet continue to argue with and bully your sisters. Why?"

"They're not my sisters!"

"They are. You are our son and, therefore, they are your sisters."

"Humph. I'm no ...." Stopping mid-sentence, he looked down and kicked at the carpet.

"Now, please stop behaving like this. Go and apologise to Andrea and then go to your room. You may come down again for dinner, but not until then."

"Hello Peter. Katherine tells me you've been bullying the girls again."

"They're always playing stupid sissy games."

"I'll not have it. Do you hear?"

"Ye."

"Ye what?!"

"Yes, sir." Scuffing his shoes as he did whenever being told off.

"That's better. Now I wanted to have a word with you. You're now fifteen, going on sixteen, and it's time we discussed your future. As we have always made clear, you, as our son, will be an equal beneficiary with your sisters. Nevertheless, responsibility for the estates will fall to you as the only male. So I think it's time you started to learn the business. Okay?"

"Do I have to? I'm not interested in all that."

"I'd noticed. But you seem happy enough to take the horses out and to spend money in town with your friends. Where do you think it all comes from?"

"Estates suppose." Mumbled while staring at the floor.

"Yes, that's right. Well, unless the estates are maintained, there won't be any. There's no one else but you. So if you want to carry on enjoying your lifestyle, you better start learning."

"Why can't the girl's husbands do it, when they marry?"

"The estates will belong to you, not them. They'll have their dowries and a small share of the inheritance, but other than that, it will all be yours."

"I'd rather live in a city. I hate the countryside."

"But your biological family were land workers and happy in it."

"And poor. I want more. I don't intend to scrabble around in the dirt for a living. I'm for better things than that."

"You hardly 'scrabble around in the dirt', as you put it. You have a comfortable life, don't you?"

"Suppose so."

"Okay. You obviously need to think about this. I'll not pressurise you now but we're going to have to start your training soon. You can go now." With gaze still averted toward the floor, the boy left.

~~~~~~~~

"How did it go?"

"Not good. He's saying he's not interested in the estates."

"Oh dear. What are you going to do?"

"I told him, if he wants to continue enjoying the life he has, he better think about it."

"And?"
~~~~~~~~

"He didn't say anything. Just went off in his usual huff. Expect it's just his teenage years. But I must admit I'm disappointed by his attitude."

"You are probably right, and it is simply his age. I am sure it will pass soon. But I wish he would stop teasing the girls."

"I hope you're right sweetheart and that it does pass. He's always been a bit morose. But we've always made allowance, putting it down to his terrible experience that night. But honestly, it's time he grew out of it."

"We do not really know what damage that night did. It must still play on his mind. Do you think anyone really gets over something like that?"

"I don't suppose they do. I certainly doubt they ever forget. But that's no excuse for him behaving badly, especially to the girls."

"As you say darling, must be his age. Should pass as he grows older."

"Let's hope so."

"Hello darling. Good day?"

"Not bad. I've been over at the north end. We're going to need more grazing. The livestock really have been producing at quite a rate."

"That is good. But I suppose it means you will have to be out more often, and later." Her disappointment manifest. "I already miss you as it is during the days."

"I'm sorry sweetheart, but they do need my attention. And I'm afraid I'll have even less time for the clinic."

"That is all right. I can cope as long as you are still available on Wednesday and Friday mornings and whenever your doctor's ministrations are required."

"Let's be honest, most of the time you really don't need me. Your knowledge and experience are usually more than enough. Of course, I'll still be in the office for Wednesdays and Fridays, but in truth, most of them really don't require me. It's usually minor ailments or, more often than not, they simply want to talk and be reassured they're okay. It's just some are a little snobby and think it below them to see anyone less than a doctor. You'd actually probably be better for them. And of course there are the hypochondriacs."

"Do not be unkind. Whether they are hypochondriac or just need to talk, it is still a need you can meet. We both know illness or perceived illness is not always physical. We did decide we wanted to help anyone we could, and this is all part of that."

"You're right, of course. But I sometimes get irritated with their self-obsession. Most of them could do with finding an occupation. Well, enough of that. I better getting going. I'm off to see about buying that extra grazing land."

"Now?!"

"Yes. Most of the landowners I want to see will be enjoying an evening drink together, and we really need to get extra land as quickly as we can."

"All right darling. Will you be back in time for dinner?"

"I hope so, but it'll probably take a couple of hours or so to agree on a realistic price. I really miss father on these occasions. He was a brilliant negotiator."

"I miss him too and Helina. The house still seems strange without them. And the children miss them. I still find Maria sometimes forgetting and going to their room, expecting to see them."

"Yea, I think it's going to take us a long time to adjust. Well, better get going. If I'm not back in time for dinner, go on without me. I'll grab something out."

"Martha could put something aside for you."

"No need to bother her."

"How did you get on?"

"As usual, they were asking ridiculous amounts. And as expected, I had to bargain for a couple of hours, but I eventually got them down to a sensible price. I'll have to go back in the morning to finalise everything."

"There, that's all settled." Having returned from his morning business meeting.

"And you are here for lunch. Makes a lovely change."

"Yes it does. But I'll have to go straight off after. Now we've got the land, I need to get it fenced. I want to move the livestock onto it tomorrow if I can."

"Excuse me interrupting Mam, but a letter has arrived for you."

"Oh, thank you Martha." Taking the proffered letter from the old gnarled hand.

"Is Martha okay. She looks tired."

"Yes she does. I am a little concerned. I think her age is starting to tell. I asked if she wanted to retire after your mother passed, but she said, if I did not mind, she would rather continue with us. Of course, I told her I did not mind and we would love to have her remain. To be honest, I do not think she has anywhere else to go. She has been a part of this household from an early age and I think truly sees us as her family. And she really loves the children and they love her. I have noticed, though, that she is quietly teaching Catrina. When she does eventually retire, I think we should keep here with us. Like a great aunt to the children. What do you think?"

"I agree. She was like a second mother to me when I was growing up. I'd hate to see her leave."

"Good. I will not tell her yet. She may feel I am forcing her to retire. But when the time is right, I will make our intentions clear. I am sure Catrina will not mind and will help care for her in old age."

"Great, that's settled then. Who's the letter from?"

"Oh, I nearly forgot it." Picking it up from the table. "Looks like Jennifer's handwriting." Turning it over to open.

"What does she have to say?"

"Let me see." She pursued the flowery lettering across the pages. "They are both well. She is enjoying the social life. Apparently Roger has made many contacts and there is a constant round of dinners, balls and outings. It took her a while, but she has finally become accustomed to hosting large social events in their home."

"How's Roger getting on with his politics?"

"Quite well by the looks of it. He has been seconded to the ministry for shipping. Apparently, he will have to spend some time in Portside. She hopes they may be able to visit while there."

"As long as they come on their own and don't bring any unwelcome 'friend' with them."

"Quite. Thankfully, there is no mention of Knights Serpent. Perhaps Roger has got over his infatuation with them."

"Let's hope so."

"I wish we could forget all about them, but it looks like it will haunt us for the rest of our lives."

"I don't think we need to worry much after all this time. I doubt we'll ever have contact with them again."

"I hope you are right."

"Talking of troublemakers, I saw Peter Woodcote on my way to town. He still doesn't appear to like me. He waved his fist at me and muttered something I couldn't make out."

"Such a shame. People I speak to think he has gone slightly mad. I am told the children are still a little nervous of him. Apparently, some will not go anywhere near him."

"As long as he doesn't try anything again. If he does, I'll have him dealt with. Confined if necessary."

"I do not think there will be any need for that. Mary, I see her occasionally, though not when Peter is around, seems able to keep him under control. I am sorry for her though. That innocent, sunny nature of hers is gone. She always looks sad these days. It must be difficult. Dorcas would have been able to help, but the others have no patience with him."

"Though I'm also sorry for her, she better keep him under control. I'll not hesitate if it comes to it."

"All right darling. I understand. I will keep an eye on things."

"Okay, but be careful. I don't want you endangered again."

"I will. As I say, I do not go to Mary's if he is about. No point in irritating his mind further."

"Okay. Now let's get on with lunch. I need to get over there and organise that fencing."

"I am sorry darling, I'm still not feeling too well."

"You haven't 'felt well' for a while!" Becoming irritated by his increasing frustration.

"No, I am sorry. I have been having painful cramps in my abdomen. I think it may be dysmenorrhoea. And my menstruation has not started properly yet. It really is very uncomfortable."

"Okay!"

"I am sorry. I have been taking one of the old remedies, but it is taking time. I am sorry."

"Blasted nuisance. Okay. No need to keep apologising." Punching his pillow into shape as he turned away.

"Sorry." Still a very handsome and physical man, she again worried. His needs still required satisfying, which she had been unable to do for a little while. Though now certain of his love, she could not deny the increasingly visible frustration and irritation. Aware that many of the less discreet women continually flirted with him and he tended to respond, she wondered if he may be tempted. Nothing short of absolute satisfaction would do. Partial release was never enough. As sad as it would be, she knew if he did go elsewhere, it would not mean much. He loved her, of that there was no doubt. Enough! No more of that thinking! Despite her concerns, she smiled to herself. She also had her admirers, though had never encouraged them or flirted back. All will be fine. No need to worry. Certainty and hope battled each other.

18

Inheritance

"Twenty-one already. How time has flown."

"I know it hardly seems creditable. It certainly doesn't feel that long since we adopted him."

"Well, it is, and here we are getting ready for his party. Ellen and Andrea's coming-out balls were wonderful, but somehow this feels more special. I only wish it could have been Georgie's. I still miss him. Not that I do not love Peter, it is just ...... well, you know."

"Yes I do sweetheart. I miss him too. I think we always will, no matter how many years go by."

"Yes. But I do not want Peter to think we love him less because of it. He may have been a difficult child, but after what he went through, I think it is understandable. It obviously had a deep impact upon him."

"I suppose so, but it does make me cross. Nevertheless, I love him as a son. I love you all. You're all special to me. I just can't imagine life without you all round me."

"There were times when I wondered if you still loved me."

"I've never stopped since the day we met. But I've to admit when things were difficult between us, I was tempted to go elsewhere. I never did, though I came close to it a few times. You know what stopped me?"

"No, not really. If I am honest, I sometimes thought you had found comfort elsewhere. However, you never brought it home, so I said nothing."

"As I said, there were times when I was severely tempted. But each time I considered it, my love for you surfaced with force. I really do love you."

"Deep down, I always believed you did. Nevertheless, I could never have blamed you if you had given in. Your physical need and frustration must have been intense at times."

"That's all in the past now. I never did give in. I also know you didn't, though many handsome men have, understandably, flirted with you over the years."

"I had not realised you noticed. Anyway, that is all it was, flirtation. I must admit it was flattering and reassuring when you were paying me less attention. However, I was never really tempted. I have always loved you and remained loyal."

"I know sweetheart." Bending and gently kissing her mouth and then the tender flesh of her neck. The years had not dampened their ardour or enjoyment of each other.

"Better stop that right now, Mr Palmerstone. We have a party to get ready for." Sensing his increasing passion, not to mention her own.

"Spoil sport. Teaser." Both laughing at their teenage behaviour.

"Besides Georgie, the only thing I regret is neither of our parents are here. They would have enjoyed seeing Peter come of age."

"I know. I'd always thought they would both live to ripe old ages. Mother would've, but father's death hit her hard. She didn't want to go on without him."

"They were so devoted to each other. I think it was similar with Mama. She found it difficult seeing Papa's health failed so quickly and, the same as Helina, do not think she wanted to go on without him. Sad, but we must push all that to the back of our minds now. We do not want to spoil Peter's party by being miserable. It would not be fair to him or the others."

"It wouldn't. Okay, you go and see to the arrangements. I've some accounts I need to deal with."

"Looks like our first guests are arriving." Alerted by the sound of carriages in the yard. "Is everything ready Catrina?"

"Yes Mam. All organised."

"Good. Have you seen my husband?"

"He was in the study last I saw. Shall I ask him to come?"

"No thank you, I will get him. But if you would please ask Master Peter to come down."

"Right away Mam." Catrine hurrying upstairs while she went in search of Richard.

"Darling, our guests have started arriving." Moving to him at the desk and caressing his shoulders.

"Oh, okay. I can finish these later."

"Welcome. Thank you for coming. Oh, how kind of you. Presents are being collated on the table over there." Indicating one already laden with packages in the far corner of the entrance hall.

"Martha dear, please put that tray down. You are a guest tonight."

"But it feels wrong. I should be helping."

"Not at all. Catrina has everything under control. You really trained her well."

"Thank you. This is a nice party. Mistress and Master would have been proud."

"I believe they would have."

"I miss them. Sorry, I didn't mean to imply anything by that."

"I know you did not. We all miss them. But come on now, this is a party. We must not spoil it for Peter."

"No, of course not. Thank you for inviting me to join you all and for making me feel part of the family."

"You always have been Martha. Richard refers to you as his second mother and you helped bring Peter up. It is only right you be here."

"You are very kind. Thank you."

"Ah, there is Mary Woodcote. You know her, do you not?"

"Yes, such a nice girl, well hardly a girl anymore. Shame about her husband."

"Yes. He has never been the same since Johnny's death."

"That was sad. He was such a nice boy."

"Yes. Let us welcome her." Leading the way across the crowded hallway.

"Hello Mary, I am so glad you could make it." Gazing past her through the open door into the yard. "No Peter?"

"No, I thought it best if he didn't come tonight. Anyway, the girls aren't quite old enough to be left on their own yet."

"Of course."

"Happy Birthday Peter." He passing by.

"Thanks." Moving on.

"Shame Dorcas couldn't be here to see this. She'd be very proud of him. You've been very good taking him in, giving him a good education and providing a nice home. She would have appreciated it very much."

"As he had no other relatives, we felt it was the least we could do."

"Still, very generous of you both."

"Come on in and help yourself from the buffet. Martha can show you where it is. And remember Martha, you are a guest. I do not want to catch you working. All right?"

"Yes Mam. Thank you."

"Katherine please." But Martha could never bring herself to be so intimate with the family. The adults, at least.

"Hello sweetheart. The party seems to be going really well. Well done."

"Catrina did most of the work."

"But you planned, organised, and sent out all the invitations. There'd be no party without you."

"I wanted his to be as nice as the girl's balls. If anything, I think we have been more lavish with him. I hope he is enjoying it."

"I'm sure he must be. I've not seen him since it started."

"Come to that, nor have I."

"I just need to go and finish those accounts. I need to have them ready first thing."

"Oh Richard. Surely they can wait."

"Don't worry sweetheart. It'll only take me a few minutes. Fifteen, twenty at the most."

"All right, but no longer. After all, you are Peter's father and should be circulating among our guests."

"I promise. See you in a moment." Heading toward the study and she turning her attention back to their guests.

The sound of the door opening caught his attention. Looking up from the papers on his desk, the sight of Peter standing in the opening greeted him.

"Ah, hello Peter. Enjoying your party?"

"Now I'm of age I want my inheritance." Totally ignoring the question.

He sat stunned, as if struck by some solid object, struggling to comprehend, unable to respond.

"Well!"

"What do you mean?" Trying to shake his head clear of the confusion.

"What's there not to understand? I'm of age! I want my inheritance!"

"In good time you'll have your share along with your sisters." Overcoming his intense shock by pure force of will. But still unable to believe what he was hearing.

"Hu!" The disdain in his voice cutting deeply. "I want my money while I'm young enough to enjoy it. I don't want to be old like you before I get it!"

"All of us have to wait for our inheritances. You'll have to wait like the rest."

"I want it now!"

"No. Anyway, it wouldn't be fair to your sisters to give you anything now."

"What do I care? They're not my sisters!"

"What are you saying?! Of course they're your sisters."

"No they're not."

"Yes they are." Desperately trying to subdue his rising temper. "You're our son. Okay, by adoption, but nevertheless we have loved you, brought you up as our own and made you an equal member of the family. As far as your mother and I are concerned, you are our son."

"You're not my 'mother' or 'father'!" A sour, bitter, and vicious intensity in his voice.

Feeling as if he'd been winded, he took a moment to recover, certain a dagger plunged into his chest could not have hurt more. "I see." Almost inaudible. Then collecting himself; "If that's how you see it, I must assume you don't consider yourself our son. In which case, there can be no inheritance. Well, not as far as you're concerned."

"You used my family as servants, worse, then took me when you had the chance. No doubt you thought you'd make me do what you wanted in place of that boy of yours! Well, you can't! And you took all they had, all of which should've been mine! You owe me! I'm going to have what's mine!"

"Who's been putting such nonsense into your head? First, we never 'used' your family. They were employed by the estate and paid a salary the same as everyone else. Second, they had very little. Yes, we took what there was and added the salary they were owed to it. We then invested the lot in your name so it would earn you some interest. We didn't even take any for the funerals, your education or your clothes. We paid for everything. Third, they were our friends. They'd be very upset to hear you talking like this. We've given you everything we could. And yes, finally, to some degree, we did consider you to be making up for our loss of Georgie. But that was never our motivation. Even if he'd still been with us, we would've adopted you and considered you our son."

"Liar! You took everything and thought you'd be able to use me as cheap labour. Well, you can't. I want what is rightfully mine!"

"Have I ever made you do anything you didn't want? Have I ever made you work on the estate? Yes, as I told you a little while ago, I would like you to learn the business. As our son, you'll inherit the majority of the estates as well as the family business and need to understand all that's involved. But I'd never force you into it."

"You only adopted me to ease your conscious! I want what's mine! And I want it now!"

"No! You'll have to wait like the rest!"

"Give me my inheritance!"

"No!" Struggling to restrain his increasing anger and the temptation to give his son a good beating. "I don't understand what's brought this on Peter, but you really disappoint me. Now, go back to the party before you say anything else you'll regret."

"If you don't give me what I want now, I'll kill you and that woman you call 'mother'!" His bitter tone not desisting. "Then we'll all get our inheritance."

"For goodness sake Peter! Why are you behaving like this? I can't tell you how sad you're making me. Please stop." Attempting to come to terms with this unwarranted behaviour.

"I don't care! I want my money NOW!"

"Peter," refusing to allow the tears gathering behind his eyes to show, "even if I agreed to give you any money, you'd probably squander it. Then what would you live on?" Hoping reason would bring him round.

"I'm quite capable of looking after myself! I don't need you telling me what to do! Give me my money NOW!" Raising a clenched fist in apparent readiness to strike.

Though not a man to be intimidated by anyone, the shock of this encounter bewildered him. It even felt as if his heart may break any moment, not a sensation he was accustomed to. How could their love and care have resulted in this? It was beyond belief. What to do? He clearly didn't wish to remain with them. At least if he has money, he should survive and not end up on the streets. He still cared. Unable to bring himself to say more, he simply nodded.

"When!"

"It'll take me a day or two. I don't keep large amounts handy."

"Tomorrow! The sooner I get out of here, the better."

"I'll see what I can do, but can't promise."

"Get it!"

"Peter, for goodness sake."

"Don't try soft talking me! Just get it!"

"I'm finding it hard, after all the love and care we've shown you, that you'd behave like this. You really disappoint me. Now get out of my sight you ungrateful wretch!" No longer able to control his anger and hurt.

"TOMORROW!" As he stomped out.

Shock, disappointment, disbelief and other emotions he didn't recognise combined to suspend him, almost as if he were in mid-air. Then, deflated, he collapsed back into his chair. He shook his head. Surely he'd imagined it all. He couldn't have heard such words coming from his son. But, no, it was all true. He had heard. Overcome by the enormity of it all, he sat with head in hands staring, sightless, at the papers on his desk.

"Such a lovely party Katherine."

"Thank you Margaret. I am very pleased you are enjoying it."

"Hardly seems credible Peter is twenty-one already."

"I know. Richard and I were saying the same. The time has passed so fast."

"Well, you have certainly done him proud this evening. He really is a fortunate boy to have you adopt him."

"Thank you."

"Where is Richard? I have not seen him."

"He had to see to some business. He should be back any moment." Wondering, in fact, where he was. It was over a half hour since he went to the study. She went to find him.

"Darling, you have been a long time. People are asking after you." Embracing his shoulders and kissing the back of his neck as he sat looking down at the papers. "What are you reading?" But then noticing he was not reading, but just blankly staring. "What is wrong?" The lack of any reaction alerting her to his unusual demeanour. "Darling?"

"Oh, just feeling a bit tired." Coming out of the mist and fog surrounding his thoughts. The slight shake in his voice, however, betraying him.

"There is something wrong." Moving round to face him.

"There's nothing wrong. Reckon the busyness of the last couple of weeks has just caught up with me." His tone still betraying the reality.

"Come on darling, I know you better than that. Something is not right." Concern escalating.

"Everything's okay. I'm just tired." Irritation beginning to register. Wishing to protect her from the truth for now.

"No it is not. I can tell something is bothering you."

"That's enough!" The suddenness and strength of his aggression surprising and disturbing him. "Go back to the party. You're neglecting your duties as hostess." His tone resolute and commanding.

"Very well. But we must talk later." Now truly anxious, but knowing better than to argue when he adopted that tone of command. She was unhurt by the sharpness, fully aware he only spoke that way when there was something serious.

Forcing a smile, she returned to the party, hoping anyone who knew her well would not look too closely. Though the cheerful celebratory atmosphere helped lift her spirits slightly, a concerned debate continued at the back of her mind. What could be wrong? What could have happened? He was clearly very upset. She sighed. Just have to wait for their guests to leave. Curbing her anxiety and impatience, she circulated and chatted.

"That was a wonderful party Katherine." At last, the final guests were departing.

"Thank you. I am glad you enjoyed it." Trying to hide her impatience.

"Good night then. We must get together again soon."

"Yes, we must. Good night." As the door closed, she quickly gave Catrine clearing up instructions and then rushed back to the study.

"Now, what is wrong? And please do not pretend there is nothing. I can see something has upset you." Hands on hips, determined not to be brushed off this time.

"Okay, yes, you're right. Peter came to see me earlier." The recall causing him to choke up for a moment.

"What is it?" He then recounted everything. "Are you sure? He could not have said all that. You must have misheard him."

"I'm sorry. Though I doubted my ears at first, there's no mistake."

"Oh darling, I cannot believe it. Why would he say those things? None of it is true."

"I know, and I told him so. But he wouldn't have it. In fact, he was barely willing to listen."

"What are you going to do?"

"I've already told him I'll get him the money. He wants it tomorrow. I couldn't promise, but I'm going to see what I can do in the morning. The sooner he's out of here, the better."

"Darling." Seeing how upset he was.

"After all we've done. And he must know we love him. I just don't understand."

"Someone must have put these ideas in his head."

"He denies it. He's really hurt and disappointed me."

"It is hard to believe you are talking about our Peter."

"I know, but I am." Neither able to any longer hold back the tears, they fell into each other's arms and wept. "What about the girls? Hadn't you better go and see to them?" Drawing back the tears.

"No need. Catrina will see to them. Anyway, Martha, despite them being that much older, still likes to tuck them in at night. They will be all right. Besides, I do not want them to see me like this."

"Okay, as long as you're sure." Tears flooding down again, unable to restrain his sorrow further.

Morning dawned without either noticing. "I better make a move. I'll have to sell a couple of acres to raise sufficient cash." Bitterness more than evident in his voice.

"We should talk to Peter before you do that. He may have come to his senses overnight. Things always look different in the light of day."

"I doubt it. He made himself very clear. Anyway, after this I'm not sure I want him in the house."

"But darling, we should try."

"No point, I assure you. I tried last night, but he's made up his mind. No, the sooner I can get the cash, the better. I'll go straight away."

"Are you sure? Is there no hope of reconciliation?"

"I'm sorry sweetheart, but no. You didn't hear the hate and bitterness. It was truly ugly."

"Really?" A shiver passing through her as she tried to imagine what had taken place.

"Really."

"All right, if you must, you must. But you cannot go out looking like that. You are a mess. We both are. Have a wash and change while I get some breakfast."

"I don't want anything. I'll change and then leave."

"At least a cup of tea, please darling. You must have some nourishment."

"Okay, if you insist. Some tea but nothing to eat, I couldn't stomach it. I'll be upstairs."

"How long will you be?" Setting the teacup down on the dressing table.

"I don't know. Mark Faber and Charles Fontain have been pestering me for some time now to sell them land. Both want to expand their crop growing capabilities. Mark wants the field in the north-east corner and Charles has his eye on a strip along the west boundary. I've refused them so far but now ......" Leaving the sentence unfinished.

"I am sorry darling. I know how much the land means to you."

"At least it means I won't have to find buyers." Sidestepping the issue. "I'll go straight to the business section. They'll more than likely be there. I'm not the only one they're trying to buy land from. After that, I'll have to go to the bank and get the balance."

"Shall I come with you?" Worried about him being on his own in his current disturbed state.

"No need. Anyway, they'd not expect a woman to be present. Wouldn't look good."

"If you are sure?"

"Yes. Now I don't want you going anywhere near Peter while I'm out. Okay?"

"But I could try to talk some sense into him. He may listen to me."

"No! You didn't see him. I didn't tell you, but at one point, he even went to strike me. I don't want you anywhere near him and his violent temper. Do you understand?!"

"Oh. All right if you insist. What shall I tell the others?"

"Nothing. There's no point upsetting them. We'll tell them everything after he's left. I know it'll be difficult, but you'll have to behave as if nothing has happened. I doubt Peter will say anything. He'll probably remain in his room till I get back. If you do see him, just behave normally, as far as you can."

"If he asks after you?"

"Just tell him I've gone to town. He'll understand. Then you're to leave him to himself." No mistaking his firm, insistent command. "The others probably won't ask. They're all used to me leaving before breakfast."

"Very well. I wish there was something I could do."

"I'm afraid it's gone beyond anything you or I can do. He's really intent on divorcing himself from us."

"I just do not understand. What can have caused this?"

"I don't know. But he's made his decision. The sooner we get this over with, the better. Okay, I'm off now. Remember, you're not to try anything. Just leave him to himself. I'll be as quick as I can."

"All right. Please take care darling." His agitated condition still worrying her.

With heavy heart and troubled mind, he slowly made his way. Though he felt the urgency of getting it over with at the same time, he could not bring himself to hurry. How had it come to this? Was all their love truly unrequited? What evil had got into him? The more he thought, the more the full weight of the situation oppressed him. But mustn't let it undermine his resolve to be rid of the ungrateful boy.

"Good morning Mark, Charles." As expected, he found them negotiating with others.

"Hi Richard. You okay? You're not looking too good?"

"Yea thanks. Just a late night." Hoping they'd not see through his deception. "I've decided to let you have the land you both want."

"What?! That's a change of heart. You were emphatic the other day you'd not sell to us."

"I know, but I've changed my mind."

"Okay. How much do you want?" Both astonished but not going to argue.

"Make me an offer." His response further surprising them. They, as customary, offered the lowest possible amount, anticipating the pleasure of a negotiation.

"Okay." Too depressed and discouraged to bother bargaining.

"Are you sure?" In unison, unable to believe he'd accept such low offers.

"Yea. The only condition is you have the papers drawn up and the cash to me before lunch. If you can't, I'll go elsewhere."

"We don't usually rush things like that." Still bewildered by his easy compliance with their ridiculous offers.

"That's my condition. Take it or leave it. I need to know now."

"Okay, we'll see to it."

"Good. I'll meet you back here in a couple of hours. Remember, I want cash, not a banker's draft."

"Okay." Both staring at him in disbelief but glad to have got the land at such a low price.

With sagging shoulders and bent head, he headed for the bank. His hopes and aspirations for the future of the family estates and business evaporating as he did so. What had his father and he worked for, if this was to be the end?

"That's a large amount, Richard." The bank manager surprised by his request.

"It's just a business transaction for which I need cash this time."

"Very well. It's only you normally ask for a banker's order."

"Yes, but there's a tight deadline on this one."

Illogically, or at least so she thought, feeling vulnerable without him there, she wondered why. Was she afraid? Was she frightened of her son? No, and yet. Richard's account of the previous evening's encounter was unsettling. Why should Peter behave like that? It made no sense. She will speak to him. He will have come to his senses by now. It must have been a misunderstanding. But no, must not. She had promised. Unable to sit still, and knowing Peter would probably be leaving later, she busied herself preparing a food parcel. He was still their son, and she still loved him. Could not bear the thought of him going hungry or suffering.

"Are you all right Mama? You are not looking well."

"I am fine, thank you Andrea. Just tired after all the arrangements for last night's party." Discreetly pushing the parcel out of sight and hoping she would accept her explanation.

"It was a nice party." Bouncing off to the drawing room.

"Oh good, you are back. How did you get on?"

"Mark and Charles were more than happy to get the land and to complete it all this morning. I got the rest of the cash from the bank."

"I am sorry darling. I know how much the land means to you."

"It's hard parting with it after all father's, and my, efforts to build up the estates. But at least we can get him out of the house today."

"Are you sure he cannot be talked round?"

"Yes. Catrina!"

"Yes Sir."

"Please ask Master Peter to come to the study."

"Right away Sir."

"Please try not to lose your temper darling."

"I'll do my best."

"Have you got MY money?!"

"Peter, why?" Tears in her eyes. Unable to speak further.

"It's my right!"

"But we love you and we have been happy together for so many years. Why not stay and continue those happy times? We really do love you. We can forget all about last night." For a moment, he appeared to weaken. She could see it in his eyes. He knew full well they loved him and how much. But then a hard selfishness returned.

"They've not been happy years for me! You've just been using me to appease your guilty conscious for taking everything my family owned."

"Peter! You know that is not true. Do you realise what would have happened to you if we had not adopted you? You would have been sent to one of those awful places. Then, as you got older, you, as an orphan, would have been made to work in the fields as a low paid labourer. We only ever wanted the best for you. As for your family's possessions. There was not very much. We invested what there was for you and paid for everything you needed from our own pocket."

"I've already told him." He'd been standing quietly, knowing this was the first opportunity she'd had to talk to their son.

"Well, have you got my money?!" Ignoring her, which hurt.

"Yes." Handing over the cash, feeling deflated and yet angry.

"Good, I can get away from here now." Some sort of harsh recrimination in his tone.

"Peter, please. Why are you behaving like this? We love you. We have truly only ever wanted the best for you."

"Huh!"

"Where will you go?" Tears now streaming down her face.

"None of your business!" Brutal and bitter. "I don't know." Kinder and more gently, her distress obviously getting through to him.

"Please do not go. We can get over this. We will forget all about it and be happy as we were before."

"Too late for that. He's made his decision. Let him go." Anger now starting to rise to the fore. Frightened, he may actually strike him if he didn't leave immediately.

"Yea tis." Turning to leave.

"Peter, here you are. Some food for your journey." Tearfully handing the package over.

"Uh! Oh, thanks!" Avoiding her eyes, but giving Richard a final, belligerent look as he left the room.

"Oh darling!" Collapsing into his arms, sorrow now overcoming her totally. He also let his tears flow as they tightly and lovingly held each other.

"Has this all been some awful nightmare?" Twenty minutes later, breathing back her sobs.

"Afraid not. It's all too real. Anyway, he's gone now."

"What are we going to tell the others?"

"Nothing for now. We'll tell them over lunch."

"They will be upset."

"Rightly so. But we'll just have to help them come to terms with it."

"I am worried about how they are going to react."

"Another reason I want us to wait. The longer we leave it, the further away he'll be."

"He had no right!"

"The ungrateful wretch!"

"Is that why he was always nasty to us, Mama?"

"We are sorry dears. But we had no idea he would do this. We thought he was happy here with us."

"Papa, why did you give him the money? He had no right to it?"

"I know Ellen, but he'd made up his mind to go. And I thought it best to let him. He would've only caused trouble if he'd stayed."

"But was that not also our inheritance?"

"No, yours is safe. I only gave him the portion he would've eventually received."

"Still, it is very mean and unkind of him."

"I know. But we must now forget all about him. He's no longer part of this family." Struggling to control his own sadness at losing another son.

"And none of you are to harbour any ill feelings. As papa says, we must forget him and not allow bitterness, recriminations or any other negative thoughts to spoil our lives." Knowing full well neither she nor Richard would ever be able to forget, but that must not be allowed to spoil the children's lives.

19

Prodigal

"It will be Peter's birthday soon. Hardly seems possible a year has passed since he left." Unable to prevent the tear in her eye.

"That's of no relevance to us anymore. He's no longer a member of this family. You must try to forget him."

"But he is part of us. He is our son."

"No son of mine. He gave up any right to be considered such. Now stop talking about him." Nevertheless, unable to hide his own residual pain, sorrow and distress.

"I still do not understand."

"That's enough sweetheart. No more talk of him. Our priority must be the girls. I want them to grow to appreciate and value the family name without having the sense of a smear upon it. Shame it won't continue with them."

"Yes, of course, you are right. But I cannot just close my heart to his existence. I wonder where he is."

"I'm sorry sweetheart, I know you miss him, but he's gone. I wish we could forget, but that's not going to happen. We must therefore push all remembrance of him to the back of our minds. Please try."

"I will." Her heart, though, continuing to ache with their loss.

"Now, I think it's time the girls learnt a little about the business. After all, in the absence of anyone else, they're the ones who'll inherit it."

"I suppose they will. But it will be difficult for them as women. And what will happen when they marry?"

"Well, there's no one else. I've no cousins or anything. Anyway, I'd rather it all stayed within our branch of the family. I'm hoping at least one of their husbands will have the interest and ability to take on the estates and business."

"Assuming they do marry."

"Of course they will. Why shouldn't they?"

"No reason, just a thought. Not all women do."

"Humph."

"Well, whatever happens, at least we do not have to worry about their relationship with the estate staff and families. They have thankfully developed friendships with many of them, though it has taken time. I was concerned for a while because, initially, after Peter's behaviour, Ellen and Andrea were reluctant to spend any time with them or really to have anything to do with them."

"Why?"

"They thought they would all be like him. I explained just because one person turns out bad, it does not mean the rest are. Bright Andrea came back with 'When an apple rots in a barrel it normally affects the others.'"

"Clever girl."

"Yes she is. Anyway, in the end they accepted my explanation that as humans we have intellect, willpower and individual souls and therefore because one neighbour may go wrong, it does not mean we have to."

"Good explanation."

"Since, they have not only established friendships but also frequently help me take care of the sick and poor. They have even started going down on their own."

"I'm glad. The family's a long tradition of caring for our employees and making sure they don't go short. It would've been sad to see that go."

"Yes it would have."

"How do they get on with Peter Woodcote? He still gives me evil looks whenever I pass him."

"Well, yes, they do not really like him. Apparently, he remains very morose and many still consider him off-balance. Such a shame. I would have liked them to be good friends with Mary but, because he is usually about when they go down, they do not call in to see her."

"Good, I'd rather they kept away from him."

"Yes, I suppose it is for the best. Such a shame though. By the way, before I forget. I think Michael Hermann will want to see you soon."

"Why?"

"Have you not noticed how he has been visiting more often?"

"Has he?"

"You can be frustrating at times. Yes, he has. I think he is going to ask for Ellen's hand."

"Oh! How long's this been going on?"

"Some time."

"Why haven't you told me?"

"I was not sure how serious it was, but I have noted a definite change recently."

"He seems a sensible lad. I think he'd be quite good at running their portion of the estates. Perhaps he and the other's husbands could run it all between them."

"I doubt that will happen. Michael is training to be a lawyer."

"But he could do both."

"I do not think so. His father would like him to take over the family firm when he retires. And in the meantime, I understand he has been offered a position with one of the top city firms. So even if he had the inclination it would not be possible."

"Shame. Do you think he'd be a good match for Ellen?"

"As far as I can tell he truly loves her, and I know she is very fond of him. And, as you already pointed out, he seems to have a level head. Yes, I think it would be a good match."

"Me too. Any idea when he's likely to ask?"

"Soon I expect. I think he is probably still building up courage to ask."

"I'm not so much of an ogre, am I?"

"Of course not. He is just a little shy of you."

"Do you want me to talk to him?"

"No. I think it best to let him approach you when he is ready."

"Okay, I'll wait for him. Andrea hasn't got any suitors you haven't told me about, has she?"

"Not yet. But I doubt it will be long. They are both pretty girls."

"Yes they are. At least I'll not have to worry about Maria for a while. She's too young."

"Ha! Ha! Yes she is."

"Darling, what we were talking about earlier, you know, starting to involve the girls with the business." Relaxing together before dinner.

"Yes, what of it?"

"Well, now the harvest is in, it will not be long before we carry out our annual review. Why not start then?"

"Good idea."

"Maria may not understand very much, but the others are certainly old enough to comprehend. Well, some of it at least."

"We could start by simply comparing production with sales. They should be able to understand that much. Then, over time, we'd introduce the more complex matters of wages, underlying costs, transportation, etcetera."

"Makes sense."

"I don't think I've ever told you how much I appreciate you taking the time to learn about it yourself."

"I knew you had planned on training Peter to undertake some aspects while you concentrated on the day-to-day requirements. With him gone, it would have been a considerable strain for you to have to continue doing everything. Anyway, in some ways it was a selfish decision. You are away far too long as it is. I did not want us to see even less of you than we do now."

"But you already have the clinic, the sick and poor and the house to see to."

"As you well know, the clinic, sick and poor do not really take up much of my time. And Catrina is more than competent at running the house. I was therefore grateful for the opportunity to not only help you but also to have something else to do. I hate sitting idle."

"I doubt you'd ever do that. You'd always find some good cause or need to manage."

"Ha! Ha! I suppose I would. But, as they say, 'charity begins at home' and I am glad I am able to help."

"I'm truly grateful. Most wives wouldn't bother getting so involved."

"We are family darling. Of course I want to be involved."

"Thank you sweetheart. I love you so much. And not just because of the business."

"And I love you darling."

"Excuse me Mam."

"Yes, Catrina, what is it?"

"Mrs Harris is here."

"Jennifer! How lovely! Please show her in. And please bring some tea."

"Yes Mam."

"Jennifer my dear! What a lovely surprise!" Reaching out and embracing her lifelong friend.

"Hello Katherine. Good evening Mr Palmerstone. I hope I find you both well."

"Good evening Mrs Harris. Yes, you do. Thank you for asking, and you and Roger?" Looking to see if he was hovering in the background.

"We are thank you." Then noting how he looked over her shoulder. "Roger couldn't come I'm afraid."

"That is a shame, but it is so good to see you. It has been far too long. No doubt Roger will join you later or on another occasion. Now come and sit with me and tell us all about your life in the city."

"First, Roger insisted I pass on his personal regards and apology. He really had hoped to come, but his duties wouldn't allow it."

"That's very kind of him. As Katherine says, we'll no doubt see him another time. But please be sure to give him our regards when your return." Not certain if he was grateful or not for his absence. "How's his career going?"

"Thank you, Mr Palmerstone, I will. He's getting on quite well. In fact, the reason I've been able to come down is because his current responsibilities made it necessary for us to spend a few days in Portside. As it isn't too long a journey, I decided to take the opportunity and visit my relatives. But of course I couldn't miss calling on you also even if it is briefly. I have to get back this evening."

"Oh, that is disappointing. I thought you would stay for dinner."

"Thank you, but I'm afraid I can't."

"Such a shame, but before you have to leave, tell us all about life in the city."

"At first I wasn't too sure about it and for a while felt a little lost and lonely. Roger, while he got to grips with his new responsibilities, had to be out most days and for a good many evenings."

"That must have been difficult."

"It was, but after the first two or three weeks, people, having got to know Roger better, started inviting us to dinners and parties."

"Good."

"Yes it made a great difference to me. In addition to his political colleagues, there are his Knights Serpent friends. He's really pleased he joined them. Not only do we enjoy a full social life, but many of his contacts there have really helped with his career. He tells me it's surprising how doors that would've probably remained closed to him, now open."

"That is good." Both struggling to maintain impassive expressions.

"Yes. I think, with their help, he'll really go far. You know how ambitious he is."

"Yes. He and I used to joke about it." Doing his best to retain a casual light tone.

"So much for Roger, now what about you?" Hoping to steer the conversation away from Knights Serpent. "Have you made any actual friends rather than just social acquaintances?"

"A couple. But if I'm honest, life in the city, especially in political circles, tends to be rather superficial."

"Must be difficult. Any thoughts of a family?" With a mischievous twinkle.

"Not yet." A slightly embarrassed giggle escaping. "Roger's current life doesn't really allow for it. We've decided it best to wait until he's more established in his career."

"I hope you do not leave it too long. Our girls are a true blessing to us. Now tell me all about the latest fashions."

"It was a shame Jennifer could not stay for dinner. I would have enjoyed more time with her." In the drawing room after dinner.

"You miss her a lot."

"Yes. We have been friends for most of our lives and I still have not really got used to the fact she is not here."

"At least you'd a good chat today and it shouldn't be too long before she visits again. She said she'd like to see more of her family."

"Yes she did, but it really all depends upon Roger and his career. You realise he is bound to come with her at some stage. What are we going to do about Knights Serpent? He is obviously very involved with them now and is bound to bring the subject up again."

"As before, we'll just have to pretend ignorance and hope for the best. At least, from what Jennifer said, he won't be able to visit for long, so he's unlikely to bring any 'friend' with him."

"I hope you are right. I am still worried what may happen if he finds out."

"He's unlikely to now. Anyway, nothing's going to happen any time soon. So let's just forget it. Where are the girls?" Concerned lest the recall of Knights Serpent would start to play on her mind again.

"I think they have just popped up to their rooms. They should be here in a moment."

"I know we said we'd wait for our annual review, but why don't we start telling them a little about the business this evening? Be good to get some idea of how they feel about it."

"All right. But please remember, Maria is still very young. She may not understand."

"She is, but it wouldn't hurt to let her hear what we're talking about. She's quite bright and rather than having to explain everything from scratch, as we're doing with the others, it should help her gradually grow into it."

"She may find it boring."

"Perhaps, but it won't do any harm to make her part of it. After all, it'll be a family event and she likes to be part of those."

"Yes she does and she would be upset if we left her out. She could play with........." A couple of resounding knocks from the front door interrupting her flow. "Who can that be at this time of night?"

"No idea. We'll have to wait for Catrina."

"Mama! Mama!" A hysterical Andrea bursting through the door.

"What is wrong darling?!" Jumping from the sofa.

"Mama! Horrible! Horrible!" Pointing back to the hall with trembling hand, her hysteria not abating.

"I'll see what's going on while you try and settle her."

"Come and sit with me darling." Hugging her delicate convulsing form close. "Oh dear." A commotion having erupted in the hall. "I better go and see what is happening. You stay here darling. All right?"

"Yesss Mama." Curling into the corner of the sofa for protection.

Richard, Ellen, Maria and Catrina, together with other household staff, stood in a group violently gesticulating and all talking loudly, shouting really. The sight alarmed her. Unable to hear words through the cacophony of voices, she wondered what could be amiss. Then, a gap opening between the agitated forms, she spotted a bearded, greasy, long-haired, dishevelled, dirty, unkempt man. A shiver of disgust passing through her as she attempted to peer through the grime. "No!" In an undertone to herself. It could not be! "Pe...ter.!" Inaudibly. No wonder Andrea was in such a state.

"Quiet!!" In the commanding voice he only used on extreme occasions. All fell silent, though Peter continued to lash out while spinning round like some wild animal, fire in his eyes. "Welcome." Exercising the full measure of his considerable self-control, but in reality, just wanting to demand what he thought he was doing by coming back. "Would you like to clean up and then come and tell us about your adventures?" Continuing the struggle to subdue his rising anger.

"Don't you patronise me!" Spat out with a snarl. "You didn't give me enough! I want more!" Violent recrimination in his eyes.

"Papa, he has no right!" Ellen loudly objecting while Maria timidly held on to her father's legs.

"That's enough! Quiet!"

"Why do we not go to the study? This is no place or company for such a discussion." Intervening in an attempt to prevent any further escalation.

"Yes." Turning and moving toward the study door. "Catrina, please stay with the girls in the drawing room. The rest of you can go." His commanding voice deterring any possible question or objection.

"You didn't give me enough! I want more!" Repeating himself once through the study door.

"You've had your share. There's no more. But, .." the sight of Peter having reawakened his dormant love for this prodigal son and feeling he had to make a decision quickly, "... though you don't deserve it, I'm prepared to let you come back and live with us as part of the family."

"You're not going to fob me off with that. Anyway, why would I want to live with you in this dump?! I want more money!"

"There's no more!" Anger now showing red in his face.

"Give me my money!"

"Need I remind you that you were given your inheritance when you asked for it, even though it was unfair to the others to do so? They're going to have to wait until your mother and I have gone. As far as you're concerned, there's no more." Continuing the struggle to retain self-control while the residue of his love for the boy disintegrated into loathing.

"You're not my father! You took everything that should've been mine when you took me! I want it all, NOW!"

"You've had everything. That's it! No more!" Self-control abandoned.

"Peter, we would love to have you back with us. You would have food, clothing and a comfortable home. You would also have employment helping run the estates and business. Please come back and let us stop all this arguing dear." Tears hovering in her eyes. Peter, taken aback for a moment by her gentleness in the midst of the aggression, appeared to soften, but then seemed to summon some demon from deep within.

"If you don't give me more ..." Turning back to face Richard. "... I'll hang round and make myself a real nuisance. I'll tell everyone how you took everything my parents had and used me as a servant. None of you will be able to hold your heads up again."

"But that is all lies!" Unable to contain her shock. "Everyone knows how we took care of you after what happened. And how we have given you all the advantages we could. No one will believe you."

"Think not?! People are always ready to gossip about people like you. Your close friends may not believe it, but the rest will simply think, 'There's no fire without smoke.' You'd be ruined."

"How can you be so ungrateful and cruel?" Even her love struggling to survive through this onslaught. He made no response but to stare sullenly at her.

Richard, a bitter, angry expression on his face, remained silent for a while. Then straightening himself. "Regrettably, I'm inclined to believe you'd actually do such a thing. You really are the most ungrateful wretch I've ever had the misfortune to come across. Therefore, for the sake of the others, I'm prepared to give you some more money."

"Richard!" Though not wishing to see her son destitute, neither did she think it right to give in to him.

"Okay sweetheart." Holding his hand up. "As I said, I'm prepared to give you more, but there're conditions."

"What?!"

"Once you've the money, you're to leave the district altogether and NEVER return. Though we still, just about, consider you our son I never want to see you again. Do you understand?"

"Yea." Virtually grunting his acceptance while fire remained in his eyes.

"Very well. Go and wait for me in the stables." Fearing he may completely lose control and give him the beating he deserved.

"How long?!"

"Just go and wait."

"Don't be long!" Moving toward the door.

"Not that way! I don't want you disturbing the others any further. Use the French doors."

"Huh!" Stomping out onto the lawn.

"Richard, as much as I still love him and do not want him to suffer, you cannot give in. It would not be right or fair to the others."

"It's the only way we'll get rid of him. Do you want him staying and spreading his lies? You know as well as I do he's right. People will listen and believe. I don't really mind about myself, but I'll not have the girls' reputations damaged."

"But ......"

"Enough." Holding his hand up to silence her. "Anyway, he's agreed never to come back."

"Can we believe him? We never expected him to return this time."

"It's a risk I accept. But what else would you have me do? I'll make him give me his word again before he leaves and hope he keeps it."

"And if he does not?"

"I'll have him thrown off the estate no matter what threats he makes."

"Oh darling, how did we ever get to this?"

"I honestly don't know." The weight of their joint sadness dragging them both down. "Thankfully, I've some money on hand. I was going to pay Arnold in the morning for that land he's selling me, but I can give it to him later in the day. He won't mind." Gathering the bundled notes from his desk drawer.

"Right, before I give you this, I want you to repeat your understanding and acceptance of the conditions I set."

"Yea, yea, okay."

"Repeat them!"

"I'm to leave the district altogether and never return. And I'll be glad to."

"I meant what I said about us still considering you're our son, but never wanting to see you again. You've hurt and disappointed us more than you can ever know."

"Yea, yea. Where's my money?"

"You really are an ungrateful wretch. Here!" Throwing the wallet at him.

"Good riddance!!" Glaring at his benefactor as he pocked the money and marched off. Richard watching his receding back with a heavy heart.

"He's gone."

"Oh." Now allowing her restrained tears to fully flow. "What are we going to tell the others?"

"Leave that to me. But you must agree not to tell them about the money. There's no point upsetting them further. Okay?"

"If you say so. What a miserable evening this turned into. Nevertheless, I still cannot help loving him. To me, he will always be our son."

"I know sweetheart. And, despite everything, he'll always be a son to me, but we've to be realistic. He's clearly shown what he thinks of us and has made his decision. All of us now have to live with it."

"Yes, we will."

"Better get it over with." Taking her hand and leading the way to the drawing room.

"Where's Peter?" Ellen and Andrea almost in unison. She was disturbed to hear the hint of bitterness in their voices.

"He decided this wasn't the place for him. He's gone."

"Did you give him any money?" Squinting the question at him.

"Just enough for him to purchase a ticket and buy himself some dinner."

"Will he come back Papa? He frightened me." Maria still looking slightly disturbed.

"No sweetheart." Picking her up in his arms. "He doesn't want to be part of our family anymore."

"That is sad Papa. He scared me, but everyone should have a family."

"Yes it is sad, but, as you will come to understand, everyone has to make their own choice."

"Well, though I suppose I feel sorry for him, I am glad he has gone. He was very unkind to us when he lived here. And he was very rude this time." Ellen expressing what they were all really thinking, disappointing as it was.

20

Unforeseen

"Do you know what it is?" Having waited to return to the house before asking.

"I'm not entirely sure. Two of them definitely have pneumonia, but I can't quite make out the others. I think it's possible they've consumption, but it's still too early to be sure."

"I really hope you are wrong."

"So do I. But at this early stage, some symptoms between severe pneumonia and consumption are very similar. For now, I'm going to treat them all as if they've pneumonia. But it won't be long before I'll know for sure."

"Poor little dears. What about Mary's daughter?"

"I'm reasonably sure hers is pneumonia."

"Mary will be devastated if anything happens to her. Losing Johnny was bad enough, but to lose another, well, does not bear thinking about."

"I think she'll be okay. It doesn't appear to have got too strong a hold on her. Not yet, at least. I'm expecting her to respond to the medication fairly quickly. By the way, how did you get Peter away from the house? I'm not sure he'd have let me in if he'd been there."

"That was Mary's doing. Of course, despite his distracted state, he understands Alex is not at all well and requires medical attention. Mary appreciated he was unlikely to let you into the house, so sent him to one of the other cottages with Naomi, their other daughter. She told him it was probably best if they got her away from Alex. One of the other more tolerant ladies is prepared to have him in her home. Most would not even consider it."

"I'm going to have to see Alex again to ensure the treatment's working. Will she be able to get him out of the house each time?"

"I think so. She has arranged for Naomi to stay with the other family for a few days until you know for sure what Alex has. She will send Peter there, on the pretence of making sure she is all right, whenever you are due to visit."

"He's bound to find out sooner or later it's me who's been seeing to Alex."

"I know, but Alex will hopefully be on the mend by then and you will no longer have to go to the cottage. I can deliver any further medication if it is required. For some reason, he now seems to tolerate me visiting, though Mary and I have agreed I will try not to call in when he is there. Just in case. We do not want to cause him any additional, or unnecessary, aggravation, if it may be avoided."

"You be careful. I don't trust him. He continues to give me the evil eye whenever he sees me."

"He appears to hold you primarily responsible for Johnny's death, even though it was me he attacked. Mary thinks that happened because you were not around at the time. In all honesty, no one really knows what is going on in his mind. So sad."

"Well, just try to see as little of him as you can."

"I will."

"We'll go down again in the morning. Their symptoms should've developed sufficiently by then for me to be sure what each has. In the meantime, I don't want Maria going anywhere near them. She doesn't have a fully developed immune system yet. And, if the others go down, though I'd rather they didn't, they're to take proper precautions. Make sure they wear masks and wash their hands thoroughly after any visit. And make sure you also do the same."

"Of course darling. Though I would also prefer not to expose them, Ellen and Andrea really want to help, for which we should be grateful. They have really started to recognise and take on their role as the future estate owners."

"That's good to know, despite the potential danger."

"Yes it is. Now, while we are talking about the estates. I know the harvest is not due for another three months, but I was thinking it may be good to start our annual review now rather than wait. It is less than a year since we involved the girls and it may be easier for them to understand if we continue to build their knowledge in stages."

"Makes sense. But let's deal with this breakout first. There's no point confusing or over burdening them with too many things at the same time."

"I agree. I am pleased to say, in their desire to help those who are unwell, they have shown a keen interest in learning the old family remedies. It would help if they have clear, uncluttered minds while they do so."

"Good, but I have to say overall, I don't think Ellen and Andrea are really medically inclined. They may show some interest now, but that's more than likely because it's people they know who are suffering."

"I think you are probably right about them. However, Maria, despite her young age, has shown a very keen interest and ability, often asking why a disease affects people and how to treat it. I think it is quite possible she will want to train as a nurse later."

"Yes, I've noted it too. Though it's early days, I think it possible she may have the ability, and inclination, to go beyond nursing and become a doctor. I'd like it if one of them kept the clinic running after us."

"So would I, but she is still very young. We must wait and see."

"I better get off. The eastern meadows need some attention."

"Good morning darling." Waking to the brilliant dawn penetrating through the curtains.

"Um... sweetheart."

"Come on, lazybones. We need to go down and check on the sick children, poor little dears, before you go off for the day."

"Um..." Stretching. "... Yea okay." Reluctantly throwing his legs over the edge of the bed.

"No, as I suspected, hers is definitely pneumonia, but it's far more severe than I anticipated. Nevertheless, it should be treatable."

"Are you sure?"

"At this stage, yes. Though you can never be certain. We'll have to wait and see how she responds to treatment. But she's a fairly robust little girl."

"I am worried about Mary. If anything happens, she will not only be devastated herself, but may also have difficulty controlling Peter. Something like this could easily throw him completely over the edge."

"As said, I expect her to recover, but if not, we'll have to deal with the outcome at the time."

"Yes." Though her worries about what Peter would do continued to play in the back of her mind.

"Okay, as far as I can see, I'm not needed here anymore today. I'll leave you to administer the necessary medicines. I must get going, they're waiting for me. Unfortunately, there's far more to sort out in the meadows than we realised."

"That's better. I feel human again." Having washed out the grime and changed after his unusually dusty hard day's labour. "What have you got there?" Noting her concerned expression as she read what appeared to be a letter.

"Um. Oh. A letter..." Briefly looking up but then returning her gaze to the flowery writing. "... from Jennifer." In an undertone clearly bothered by something she read.

"Something wrong?"

"Um. No, not really."

"How are they?" Something obviously still bothering her.

"Roger has been appointed an undersecretary in the ministry for agricultural."

"I thought he was in the shipping department."

"He was, but that was only a secondment. This is an actual appointment."

"Sounds like he's doing well. So what's troubling you?"

"They are expecting to come back here for a few months."

"Why?"

"Apparently the government is considering the introduction of new legislation but before deciding want Roger to carry out some research into current practices and opinions."

"So why here?"

"The research will need to be conducted within an agricultural community. Therefore, as the primary occupation round here is agriculture, he thought it may as well be here as anywhere else. It will mean both of them can spend time with their relatives."

"You'll be glad to have Jennifer back here for a while." But seeing her clouded expression. "Wouldn't you?"

"Yess but ....."

"But what?"

"You realise if they come for so long, Jennifer says it could be six months or more, they may have visitors."

"Oh, I see. You mean Peter Lucca?"

"Yes. And Roger is bound to start on to you again about joining Knights Serpent."

"I've already put him off once, so, especially after all this time, I reckon I could do it again."

"Maybe, but what about that horrible man? What if he does visit?"

"I can't see he'd still hold a grudge, especially as I'm no longer involved, but if he does, I'll have to try and talk to him, as I planned to before."

"And if he does still hold a grudge and will not listen?"

"Damn the man. And damn Roger for joining them."

"Well, what would we do? I am worried about what he may do. Will the girls be safe?"

"When are they coming?"

"Jennifer is not certain, but thinks it may be soon. They are just waiting for Roger to be fully briefed."

"Damn and blast. Okay, I'll think about it."

"I am frightened darling. What are we going to do?"

"Try and remain calm sweetheart. Nothing has happened yet, and it's not certain they'll invite Lucca to visit. Even if they did, he may not be able to. Remember how he couldn't come last time?"

"Yes, but what if he does?" Her agitation now getting the better of her.

"They're hardly going to invite him straight away."

"I know! But!" Her agitation now bordering on hysteria.

"Okay sweetheart, calm down. I'll give it some thought. There must be some way out should it come to it."

"Could you not explain to Roger?"

"I'd rather he didn't find out. And from what Jennifer said last time, he's obviously very in with them. Where would his loyalty lie if it came down to it? After all, he has a vested interest. And no doubt he takes those ridiculous oaths seriously."

"But surely, as a friend, he would do the right thing."

"I'm not so sure. His ambition really knows no bounds and they've obviously helped him a lot. He may see it as his duty to uphold their philosophy, traditions and oaths."

"Oh, Richard, what are we going to do?" A note of hysteria still vibrating in her tone.

"All right sweetheart." Embracing her in his protective reassuringly powerful arms as he would a young child. "Nothing's going to happen now. And it may never. But even if they do invite him, we've plenty of time to consider what to do. I'm sure there's a way out if it comes to it. Now you need to calm down. You don't want to alarm or upset the girls or anyone else, do you?"

"No." Trying hard to calm herself by taking deep breaths. "Of course you are right. It may never happen. But I cannot help worrying, not just for ourselves but also for the girls. Would he harm them?"

"I very much doubt it. Even if he's still as bloody minded, it's me he want's not you or the girls."

“But I don’t want you hurt or worse!” Her imagination running wild with potential scenarios.

“Okay sweetheart, okay.” Holding her even tighter, hoping to subdue her rapidly escalating fear. “I doubt it’ll come to anything serious. And I’m sure I’ll be able to deal with him if I have to.” Masking his own uncertainty about the outcome of such an encounter.

“Sorry darling. I cannot bear the thought of losing you.”

“You won’t. Now come on, the girls will be here in a minute.”

“Yes, of course. Sorry.” Again, taking deep breaths while drying her eyes.

“Good. Now try and forget about it. We’ll be okay. I’m sure.”

“I hope so.” Taking command of her emotions, forcing the fear down.

“Have you been crying Mama?” Ellen as always more observant than they would have liked.

“No, it was just some dust in my eye.” Hating the need to lie, but accepting it was for the best.

“Was there nothing we could do?” Knowing full well there had not been but emotionally needing the reassurance. Feeling as if they had let the families down.

“I tried everything, but you know how resistant consumption can be.”

“But three of them?”

“To be honest, I’m surprised it has been so few, though I think two of the others may follow soon. They’re not responding to treatment either.”

“That is terrible. Will there be any others?”

“I think we’ve been able to contain it now, so I’m hoping not. Nevertheless, a couple of others have fallen ill, though I’m reasonably certain they’ve pneumonia and not consumption. Their symptoms aren’t as severe.”

“Oh dear, so many young deaths in such a small community. It is going to be hard for them to come to terms with it. How about Mary’s Alex? Is she going to survive?”

"I think so. I was right, she doesn't have consumption. However, the pneumonia is severe and isn't responding to the treatment as quickly as I'd like. We'll have to wait a few more days."

"She must get better. For Mary's sake, if nothing else."

"I'm sorry sweetheart, but it's now effectively out of our hands. I've done all I can. We'll just have to wait."

"I suppose so, but it is difficult."

"I know, but we really have done all we could. Now I'm sorry to leave you, but I really do need to get on."

"All right darling, I understand. I think I will spend the morning doing my best to comfort the bereaved families and see if I can help them with the funeral arrangements. You will make time to attend the funerals tomorrow? I think they would appreciate us both being there."

"Of course I will. I'm going to give everyone the morning off so they can attend and the families themselves the whole day. It's a very sad time for all of us."

"Thank you darling, they will appreciate that."

"Right I'm o..." Demented screaming interrupting him. "What the hell?!" Turning to see a demonic-looking Peter Woodcote running toward them across the green. "Get behind me!" Placing himself before her.

"Peter! Come back!" A terrified Mary running after her husband. "Help! Someone help! Please!"

"Murdr..rs! E D..vil.s! E Murdr..rs!" Eyes aflame. Arms gesticulating.

"That's enough Peter!" Two men shouting at him while running up and then forcibly restraining him by grabbing an arm each.

"I'm so sorry." An out of breath Mary. "He doesn't know what he's doing. I'm sorry. He didn't mean anything by it."

"It is all right Mary. We understand." Looking to her husband to confirm.

"Yes, it's okay Mary. But you must control him. I'll not have a repeat of last time."

"I understand. I'm sorry. It's just the worry of Alex that's set him off again. I'll make sure he doesn't trouble you anymore."

"You better. I'll not tolerate it if he does. I'll have him committed."

"E Murdr..rs!" Twisting to stare at them over his shoulder while trying to free himself from his captors as they dragged him away.

"I'm sorry!" Running after the agitated group of men.

"Oh dear. I was hoping this would not happen. I think Alex's illness may have sent him over the edge."

"I don't care. I meant what I said. I'll not tolerate any more from him. If he tries anything, just once, I WILL have him carted off."

"I am sure Mary, with the help of others, will get him back under control. Poor dear."

"Okay. Now I really have got to go. I'm not sure I want you staying here while he's like that."

"I will be all right. The men will keep him under control for now. Anyway, I do not feel I can desert the families at this time. I may not be able to do a lot, but at least I may offer some comfort."

"Okay, but take care. I don't trust him."

"I will. Now you better get going. I will see you this evening."

21

Full Moon

"Mr and Mrs Harris Mam."

"Oh! Um ... please show them in Catrina." Then turning to Richard. "They have only been back a matter of days. I had not expected them to visit yet." He simply responded by raising his eyebrows. "Jennifer, dear, how nice. Mr Harris." Moving across the room to great them as they entered through the door.

"Roger please."

"How kind .... Roger."

"I'm sorry we've called so late, but I didn't want to wait any longer before seeing you." Jennifer sensing the impropriety of such a late visit.

"That is all right Jennifer. You know I am always pleased to see you. I just thought you may need a few days to settle back in."

"Not really. My family had the rooms all ready and prepared. Other than unpacking, there was little else for us to do and I really wanted to see you."

"Ah Richard, good evening." Roger shaking Richard's proffered hand and acknowledging him with the socially accepted bend of the head that his host reciprocated. "I'm glad you're here. I've a friend I'd like you to meet." He and Jennifer then moved aside to reveal Peter Lucca standing in the doorway behind them.

"Good evening Roger, Jennifer." Struggling to mask the shock reverberating through him while Lucca glared at him with utter hatred.

"Mr Richard Palmerstone, may I introduce Mr Peter Lucca, a very good friend of mine. You may remember he was due to visit us before, but had been called away."

"Yes, I recall you mentioned it. Good evening Mr Lucca." Moving to shake his hand, having quickly decided it best to put their plan of ignorance into practice for Roger and Jennifer's sake.

"You!" Whispered as Richard took his hand and while his friends were engaged in answering Katherine's enquiry about their health.

"Come and have a seat." Katherine leading Jennifer to the sofa with Roger following close behind. Lucca, however, holding back with Richard.

"I wondered when Roger told me your name. It seemed too much of a coincidence. After all, how many Richard Palmerstones can there be? Don't think I've forgotten. I'm going to make you pay." Still whispering.

"This isn't the time. We'll talk later." Whispering in his turn.

"What are you two whispering about?" Roger taken by the strange, almost aggressive expressions of both men.

"Nothing. It's just we think we may've seen each other somewhere." Hoping Lucca would support the lie, for now at least.

"Yes. Vienna probably." Roger having thrown an enquiring look at his friend.

"Please have a seat, gentlemen." Trying to defuse the obvious tension between the two, as well as her own trauma and fear.

"Thank you." Smiling gratuitously at her. "Out of respect for Roger, I'll not do anything now. But you're going to pay for your treachery. Don't think you've got away with it." Again discreetly whispering as they made their way toward the seats and whilst the others had returned to their own conversation.

"As said, we'll talk later." Whispered back.

"How do you find your new appointment Roger, congratulations by the way?" Debating within herself how she might divert that horrible man from his very apparent intention of hurting her husband. She could see it in his eyes.

"Thank you. I must admit I'm very proud to be appointed to such a position so early in my career. My friends at Knights Serpent have indeed been more than helpful." Glancing a smile toward Peter Lucca.

"Oh, really?" Kicking herself for opening the discussion so as to allow the inclusion of that terrible organisation.

"Yes. They have truly proven to be good friends. To be an undersecretary so soon is really quite an achievement."

"And do you like the work? If I remember correctly, you were with shipping before." Hoping to steer the conversation away from Knights Serpent and to more amenable topics.

"Yes, I was and yes, I do like my current occupation. My secondment to shipping proved interesting and useful. It enabled me to learn how things work within the ministries. But this is more to my liking. After all, my family has been involved with agriculture for generations. I am the first to have broken away for many years."

"Were they disappointed?" Intent upon keeping the conversation to such non-controversial subjects.

"Yes and no. Of course, as the elder son, they had expected me to continue with the family business. But then, at the same time, they were proud of my appointment to parliament. Besides, my younger brother, who has always had more of an interest in the day to day running of the estates, can carry on the family tradition. He'll also be the means of continuing our name within the district. My career is likely to mean I'll spend the rest of my days in the city."

"I can understand their pride, especially now you have been appointed to such a responsible and prominent position. I suppose it may have been more difficult for them if it had not been for your younger brother. Now Jennifer, you must tell us all about the latest fashions, and of course the gossip..." with a twinkle in her eye, "... circulating round the city. I am sure there is much we 'country bumpkins' have not heard about." With a further little smirk. Jennifer then regaled them all with the latest city news. Katherine transfixed, not only with genuine interest but also in hope of making Knights Serpent a forgotten subject. The men simply sat back with bored expressions.

"Goodness, what is that?!" A loud commotion having erupted in the hall.

"Sorry Mam, Sir!" A clearly shaken Catrina bursting through the door.

"What is going on Catrina?"

Glancing at the guests, she bent to speak to her mistress. "Peter's in the hall." Quietly, so as not to be heard by the others.

"Oh." In an undertone while trying to cover her surprise and distress. "Very well." Audibly, at the same time indicating for Catrina to leave. Then leaning toward Richard. "Please excuse me Jennifer, Roger, Mr Lucca." Attempting to keep her expression passive. "Richard, Peter's in the hall." Again, in an undertone.

"Please excuse me, something just needs my attention." Rising from his seat. "My apologies. Shouldn't be long." Like his beloved doing his best to hide, in his case, the instantaneous anger that impacted upon him.

"I thought we'd agreed you'd never return! We certainly have no wish to see you again."

"You never gave me enough! How was I supposed to live on those pittances?!"

"You've had far and above your share. We've been more than generous with you. You should've taken care of it. I assume you've squandered it on so called 'high' living, as well as gambling and other immoral pursuits. Well, that's you fault!"

"I want everything! All you own, the entire inheritance! You owe me! You took advantage of me and my family and now I want retribution. I want what is mine!"

"How many times must you be told we did nothing of the sort?! In fact, we've done the opposite. We gave you everything we could and even invested for you. How dare you accuse us of having done otherwise. We owe you nothing! Now get out of here!"

"NO!! YOU OWE ME! I WANT EVERYTHING!!"

"Oh dear. I am sorry. I think I better go and see what is happening. I do apologise." The increasing volume of voices having penetrated through the drawing-room door. "Please make yourselves comfortable. I will ask Catrina to bring some drinks." All three looked at her quizzically, but said nothing.

"Oh, my goodness!" Having set eyes on her dishevelled son, who she recognised without difficulty this time despite the long greasy hair and beard, ground in grime, wild look and strange long ragged dirt covered coat he wore. Though the sight saddened her, it did not shock her as previously.

"Catrina, please give our guests drinks while we deal with this."

"Very well Mam."

"Peter ..... how nice to see you." Not sure how to react.

"WELL!!" Glaring at Richard while totally ignoring her.

"Peter, please dear, this is not the place. Let us all go to the study where we may talk privately." Gently and lovingly taking hold of his arm, but he violently shaking her off.

"What do I care about privacy! It's time people knew what you're like! It's time I had all that's mine!"

"That's enough!" Unable to restrain his temper any longer. "I've a good mind to have you kicked out right now!"

"Richard, remember we have guests."

"Damn! Okay, suppose we better go to the study. Get in there you ungrateful wretch!" Restraining himself to raising his hand in warning, though in truth wanting nothing more than to beat the ungrateful boy to a pulp. Then, realising his temper was getting out of control, he took a deep breath and led the way to the study. As they moved, she noticed Peter walked with a stiffness, but thought little of it, assuming it was the result of him living rough, which he had obviously been doing.

"WELL!" Again.

"There's no more! I'm sick to death of your ungratefulness!"

"Peter, what would your parents say?" Hoping to bring him round, though fully aware it had always failed before.

"What do I care about them! They never gave me what I wanted, always giving preference to the others. I reckon they'd not even have noticed if I weren't there."

"Peter! That is not true. I know for a fact Dorcas loved you. Even when you were being difficult, she never stopped. All she thought about was how to make life good for you."

"Huh! All she wanted was me out-o-the -way. Bloody bitch! Some mother she was!"

"Peter!"

"Ha! Ha! Do you still think the fire was an accident?!"

"What are you saying Peter?"

"I'm glad they're all dead. That's what I wanted. I burnt the bastards!"

"Nooo!" Richard catching her before she collapsed onto the floor.

"What are you talking about you wretch?!"

"I waited until they were asleep and then thoroughly enjoyed watching. Shame the smoke got them. I'd wanted to hear them scream."

"Uhh!!" This time actually collapsing into her husband's arms. Though they had tried to guess at the fire's cause, this scenario had crossed no one's mind. "You are not serious Peter?" Coming round for a minute, struggling to comprehend and speak at the same time.

"Aren't I?!" His laughter on the edge of manic. "Now, I want everything!"

"Get out you wretch!" His need to support his love the only thing preventing him from launching into the evil figure standing before him.

"Please excuse me Roger, Jennifer. I've just remembered where Mr Palmerstone and I met. There is something I need to speak to him about in private." Lucca rising from his seat and heading for the drawing-room door.

"Do you think this is the appropriate time Peter?"

"It can't wait Roger. Now I've remembered it's important we speak as soon as possible. Anyway, just sounds like a family disagreement. They'll probably be grateful for an interruption." The expression on his face, however, raising an unexplained concern within both of his friends.

"I'm not so sure."

"Nor am I. You'll only embarrass Katherine, well, both of them, if you go in now." Jennifer concerned for her dear friend's comfort.

"It's important." Without further hesitation, marching out of the door. Then, unsure where the study was located, standing and listening to see which direction the raised voices were coming from.

Having determined the direction, he moved, grasping the dagger handle beneath his cloak as he did so. No time like the present. No doubt, as with all such occasions, the argument would soon end and he'd have Palmerstone to himself. It was time he paid his debt. After he'd return to the others as if nothing had occurred. Then when his enemy's corpse was discovered, he'd fain ignorance stating he was alive when he left. Could always say there had been some outstanding debt that had to be settled but had agreed to wait until the following day. However, upon entering the room, the obvious aggressive and violent situation surprised even him.

"I want my money now!"

"There's no more!"

"GIVE IT ME!!"

"No more! Now get out!"

The sudden violent shattering of glass as the French door windows exploded into the room took them all by surprise. Conversation ceased as all looked with horror, including Lucca now standing in the doorway, upon the cruel honed brilliant edge of the scythe slashing through where the glass had once been. None could mistake the "Murd..rs, d..vils, butch..s." coming from the other side of what remained of the doors. Then the appearance of the wild, bedevilled man crashing through while lashing out in all directions with the evil implement led to each instinctively stepping back.

"Ahh!" Having recovered from her earlier faint, but now almost breaking into hysterics at the sight of the horrific weapon.

"What do you think you're doing Woodcote?!"

"E Murd..rs! E D..vils! E ain't gon kil no on els!" Continuing to push his way through the debris.

"Put that down!"

"No til I finis..d e! E no kil no one els! Murd..r!"

"Come here Peter!" Two men rushing through the broken door and grabbing him while a third concentrated on getting the scythe out of his hand.

"I'm sorry Sir. He's gone completely mad tonight. I'm sorry!" Mary beside herself, running in behind the men. "I saw he weren't right, but he got away before I realised he were doing so. Sent these three after him soon as I noticed. Sorry Sir, so sorry."

"All right Mary." Katherine, regaining some composure, moved to comfort her distraught friend.

"Get him out of here!"

"Yes sir." Two of the men, each holding an arm, dragging him back out while the third followed behind.

"Secure him! And make sure he doesn't come back."

"Yes Sir."

"I'm sorry Sir. It's just all the children dying and our Alex having been ill."

"We'll talk about this tomorrow Mary. Now go!"

"Yes Sir."

"Please do not be so harsh darling. You can see how upset she is."

"I don't care. I told you before I'll not have this again. Now leave it. We'll decide what to do tomorrow." His already raised anger reaching new heights. "Make sure you bind him tight and lock him up securely for the night." To the receding backs of Woodcote's captors.

"Now!" Turning back to face his son, but then seeing Lucca in the doorway. "What're you doing here?!" Noticing as he posed the question how Lucca's hand grasped the dagger handle. "What the hell! What's got into everyone tonight? Is there a full moon or something?!" Lucca gave no response but simply glared while Peter stood inert, clearly astounded by all the action. But then recovering.

"I'm not going to wait any longer. Give me what's mine NOW!" Meanwhile, Lucca remained in the doorway, trying to make sense of what he was witnessing. Then, fully sensing Peter's aggression appreciated he wasn't the only one who had it in for this traitor.

"You've had all you're going to get and I regret having given that to you. Now get out! I never want to see you again!"

"GIVE ME MY MONEY!"

"THERE'S NO MORE! GET OUT." Stepping forward. His temper now completely out of control.

"MAKE ME!" Drawing out a shotgun from under his strange coat.

"PETER NO!" Through her intensified trauma, still trying to comprehend it was her son behaving this way.

"MY MONEY NOW!"

"NO! YOU DON'T INTIMIDATE ME YOU LITTLE WORM!" Moving to grab the gun while Katherine stared in horror and Lucca stood bemused.

'BANG!' Firing straight into Richard's chest.

"AGHHH!!" Grasping her collapsing love as he, with a look of utter disbelief, slowly descended on to the floor. "HELP ME!" Looking to Lucca.

22

Running Wild

"YOU HAVE KILLED HIM!" Tears, anger, shock, grief all mixing to send her to the edge of sanity. "Why Peter?! Why?!"

"Good! Now if you're also out-o-the-way, we'll all have what's our due!" Bringing the shotgun up and aiming it at her.

"Peter!! What are you doing?!" Fear now combining with her anger temporarily overriding her other intense emotions of loss and grief. She stared up at this devil who was her son, unable but to think of him as such despite what was happening. While still on her knees, holding her one and only true love's now lifeless corpse, her inner sense of self-preservation emerged, causing her to debate inwardly. Should she try to grab the gun or should she run? Yet she remained motionless, stunned with utter disbelief. It was all so unreal. "Why Peter? Why?" More to herself than anyone, looking down and caressing her love. A surreal haze of doubt, disbelief, sorrow and more suppressing her ability to accept or to think straight. Then, for some unknown reason, her focus cleared, and she looked up again to see the two barrels of the shotgun being aimed at her. "Peter......" Not actually pleading but deep down hoping to bring him to his senses. For a few seconds, both remained transfixed, looking directly into each other's eyes. Then a demonic darkness blackened his and she knew there was no hope.

Lucca, still standing in the doorway with dagger in hand, looked on, slightly doubting he had actually witnessed what he had. But, after a few moments, appreciated things were happening as seen. A smirk then crossed his features. Well done that boy! Saved him the bother. That traitor had it coming, served him right! No sorrow. No regret, except for not having been the one to make him pay. No sympathy.

Instinctively rising, through the foggy mist that had returned, she felt torn between her innate desire for preservation and not wishing to leave her beloved alone on the floor. However, no longer doubting her son's intentions, she turned and ran. The resounding shot tore through what remained of the frame to the French Doors as she passed through. Cursing her luck, Peter expelled the spent cartridges, quickly reloaded and set off in pursuit. Seeing his opportunity, Luca speedily moved to check whether his enemy was actually dead. If not, he could finish him. No one would know.

"What's going on?!" Roger and Jennifer running in, the sound of the shoots having alerted them. "What?!" Spotting Richard's immobile body by Lucca's bent figure.

"There was some man, boy here. I think they called him Peter….." Discreetly returning the dagger to its scabbard.

"He's Richard and Katherine's adopted son."

"Well, he's just killed Mr Palmerstone and is now chasing his wife."

"Why didn't you stop him?!"

"First, I didn't know who he was or what he was about. Second, why should I've?"

"What do you mean? Of course you should've."

"Not really. He was a traitor."

"What're you on about?"

"He and I had met before. He was inaugurated as a knight of Knights Serpent in Vienna. But he betrayed our secrets."

"You mean all the time I was telling him about us he was already a member?"

"Yes. And a traitor!"

"But he said nothing."

"He wouldn't. He knew his tongue and heart were forfeit. No doubt he'd hoped to keep you in the dark."

"What're you two talking about? Katherine never mentioned anything to me. She would've told me if Richard was already a 'knight', as you like to call yourselves."

"She wouldn't. Our paths had already crossed before. She knew her husband was a marked man."

"But why didn't you tell me Peter?"

"Until tonight, I wasn't entirely sure it was him. Though I'd my doubts, there may have been another Richard Palmerstone."

"So, what were you going to do?"

"Make him pay of course."

"You're not serious?!" Jennifer feeling rather shocked never having come across such an attitude among the Knights Serpent families she knew.

"Of course I am. His tongue and heart were forfeit. That boy has simply saved me the trouble."

"Peter...." Roger struggling to make sense of what he was hearing. Though he knew and had taken the same oaths, he too had not, until this moment, considered them more than ceremonial.

Where to go? Where would she be safe? Could she outrun him? Reaching the other side of the lawn, she took a moment to look back. Seeing him push his way through the debris of smashed glass and wood, she decided it probably best to get out of the gardens. There was no real shelter within them. The fields, that will be her best option. He had never taken any interest in the estates, so there was a good chance she could lose him. By now, Catrina or someone should have sent for the police. Just needed to keep safe until they arrived. Better not run in a straight line. Richard had always explained how they had difficulty hunting when their prey zigzagged.

While running for the fields, she tried to make sense of what had just happened. Had it happened? Was it some terrible nightmare? No. It was all too real. Tears welled up as she recalled the still body of her beloved. What had happened to bring them to this? How could the son they had both loved and done everything for have done this? Did he really mean what he had said about killing his family? What had made him so evil? What had they done wrong to cause this? Why was he repaying their love like this? Why was he now also trying to kill her?

Breath catching in her throat as she ran full pelt, she began to realise it was unlikely she could outrun the much younger man. Have to find somewhere to hide. Where? Where would he not find her? Then she remembered the ravine. It lay to one side of the estate and few knew about it. Tall grasses hid it from general view. They had agreed to have one area in which to grow wild herbs and to act as a wildlife preserve. For certain, Peter did not know about it. Changing direction, she headed for the small rock bridge that crossed the ravine in one place. Where were the others? Someone should have set out in pursuit by now. Still running as fast as possible, she strained her ears. But, above the rustle of the tall dry grasses, as she and the evening breeze brushed through them, the only sound was of Peter crashing through the undergrowth behind her.

Still heading for the little bridge, she glanced back. A small hillock hid her from the boy's view. Just what she needed. Quickly going to one side, she found the bridge, crossed within seconds and then re-diverted back, so it appeared as if she had been running in a fairly straight line. Despite the fear, shock, and adrenaline, her mind was working fine. Her sense of self-preservation had truly kicked in.

Spotting her ahead of him as he crested the hillock he stopped, took a firm stance and raised the shotgun to his shoulder. Then, taking a steady aim, tightened his grip on the trigger. 'Bang!' She fell. Great! Better check. Lowering the gun to his side, he set off again at full pace.

As the shot rang out, she felt the ground slopping down from her. Not wanting to fall face first, head-over-heals into whoever knew what, she locked her knees and forced her torso into a backward motion. Grateful for the soft bush she landed upon that also prevented her sliding down the bank, she held her breath and remained as still as she could, listening. What had brought her to this? Why was he behaving like this? That her mind continued on these lines despite the present circumstances surprised her. The shock, sorrow and hurt were obviously having a greater impact than her fear. Her beloved! Oh, her love! No, must not let those thoughts overpower her. She shook her head clear.

Had her ploy worked? She strained her ears further. Then a thud and groan confirmed. Just in case she waited for any further sound of movement. He may not have been incapacitated. After a short period, there being no further indications of any motion, she tentatively stretched her hand out. Besides the moans of pain emitting from above her, there were no other sounds, so, grabbing a branch for initial support, she pulled herself back up the bank.

Being careful not to dislodge any rocks and fall in herself, she peered into the ravine. The scurrying clouds allowed the moon to dispel some of the dark of night. Near the bottom of the ravine was a distorted figure with one leg folded beneath it and an arm thrown out to one side. A glinting moonbeam revealed the shotgun caught on a branch halfway up the opposite bank and out of reach of the immobilised figure. It was obvious he would not be able to climb up to it even if he desired to. Certain now that no harm could befall her, she stood. "Why Peter? Why?" His only reply a groan of pain.

"Katherine!"

"Mrs Palmerstone!" The voices drifted through the air. At last.

"Over here!" Shaking herself from her still shocked and unbelieving mind set. Silence followed for a few seconds.

"Where?! Keep shouting!" She did until a figure appeared on the brow of the hillock that had shielded her from Peter's view when approaching the ravine. She waved with a mixture of relief and sorrow. What would happen to Peter now? He had done an awful thing, but she could not help the love she felt. The figure waved back. She collapsed. Exhaustion, shock, sorrow, love, anger, despair and grief now at liberty to take their toll. Within a cauldron of pain and disbelief boiled with unmitigated ferocity. She just wanted to curl up into a foetus position and forget all that had happened. To be left alone. To wake from this nightmare. None of it could be true. Could it?

The police, having determined her location, ran toward her. Then realising the danger. "Watch out! There is a ravine!" Regaining her equilibrium, she staggered back toward the bridge. What now? What was to happen to her son? Her son? Was he really? Yes, she could not deny it. But what he had done. Her beloved no longer. Was this really all real? Was she dreaming? Had she gone insane? Richard would be here any moment, would he not? Then reality kicked in. No, he would not. He was gone. What hope was there left? What about Peter? What would they do to him?

Having regained the other side of the ravine, she watched as two armed policemen clambered down the bank. One collected the stranded shotgun as they descended and passed it up to a colleague. He then followed his companion who, being that much further ahead, had now reached Peter's twisted body. Roughly taking both his arms, he forced them behind and quickly slapped on a pair of handcuffs. Peter's cry of pain as his injured arm was forced behind him made her heart leap, as it did whenever one of her children was in pain. The two policemen then forced their captor to his feet, resulting in a further cry of agony. Again her heart, despite the anger, sorrow and grief, jumped. Her confused thoughts threatening to engulf and undermine what little resolve to survive she had left.

Catrina and Jennifer reached her just in time. She was on the verge of collapsing again. Within her confused and befuddled mind, she just wanted to let go of everything. To be with her beloved. To spend eternity with him. To forget this now horrible and empty life. But then the sound of Ellen and Andrea's distraught cries reminded her she had a responsibility, with or without Richard. Her children needed her! But what help could she be to them? They would cope without her. But, no, Richard would not approve. He would want her to care for their children. To show them how to live life. The way forward. Do not want to! But! Must! They deserved it.

"Where am I?"

"Home. You passed out. We carried you back." Jennifer spoke quietly and soothingly.

"What happened?"

"Don't you remember?"

"Um. Oh! Peter. Richard. Is he .... gone?"

"I'm sorry Katherine......"

"It is not your fault. So it really did all happen?"

"Yes. I'm sorry. Peter did shoot him."

"Where is he? Peter I mean."

"The police have taken him off to prison. The best place for him."

"Is it?" Still rather bewildered by the kaleidoscope of images racing before her eyes. Had it really all happened? Had her son done what she saw in her mind's eye? Could he have done it? Could he have been so vindictive? All too much to comprehend. She felt herself withdraw back into the blankness, into denial, into unreality. It was safe here. Nothing bad had happened. It was all a bad dream. A nightmare.

"Hello dear. Welcome back."

"Where am I? What happened?"

"Don't you remember?" Jennifer concerned by this repetition, wondering if her friend's mind had gone.

"Oh!" Memories and images rushing back with unrelenting force. No denying the truth this time. It really had all happened. "Ohhhh!" The pain of loss now fully registering and drawing out the agony she had been subconsciously trying to suppress.

"There dear." Holding her head tenderly to her breast in hope of conveying some comfort for her loss.

"Where is he?"

"Who?" Not wishing to aggravate her already agonised condition by mentioning Richard.

"Richard, Peter."

"Um. Richard is still in the study. Peter has been taken away."

"Is ...... Richard ..... really ..... dead, gone?"

"I'm sorry."

"Nooo! It cannot be true."

"I am sorry, but it is. He is gone."

"Ohhhhh!" Greif now fully overcoming.

"I'm sorry." Holding her dear lifelong friend tenderly but firmly as she convulsed in her agony.

"Peter?" Struggling to bring her grief under control.

"Prison."

"Ah." Though comprehending, still trying to come to terms with the two awful truths. "The girls?"

"They're safe. Catrina's with them in the drawing room. Naturally, they're all a little shaken."

"Good." Then summoning her inner strength in the knowledge of what Richard would have wanted. "Please do not let them see me like this. It has been horrible enough without adding to their distress."

"Of course. Catrina will look after them."

"Thank you...." Starting to drift off into unconsciousness again.

"Katherine."

"Um, yes."

"The police are waiting to talk to you."

"Do they have to?"

"Well yes. They need to know what happened."

"Now? Can it not wait?"

"I'll ask."

"Thank you." Drifting off again into the comparative protection of anonymous darkness. An unfeeling, ethereal, black and yet protective corner of life.

23

A Barren Land

"Now Mrs Palmerstone, I appreciate this is difficult for you, but would you please tell the court the events that took place once you were in the study."

"Um...." Hesitating to draw back the tears ready to fall. "Um ... yes." This time doing her best to control the tremors running rampant throughout her being. Her heart feeling as if it would implode with the sorrow and grief that still consumed her.

"It's alright. Take your time."

"Thank you. Well, as soon as we were through the door, my son..."

"Mr Peter Palmerstone, the defendant?"

"Yes."

"Please go on."

"Well, as soon as we entered the study Peter, um.. 'the defendant' started shouting ......" She went on to describe all that had occurred from the shouting match with Richard to her running across the ravine to Peter's eventual capture. Tears flooding down her face throughout her recital.

"Thank you. That was obviously very difficult for you."

"Does the defence wish to cross-examine this witness?" The judge peering over the top of his glasses.

"Yes, your honour." Rising from his seat next to the murderer and approaching the witness box. "I've been given to understand that your husband, Mr Richard Palmerstone, was very intolerant of his son. That ....."

"That is not true! He loved him!" Incensed by the suggestion.

"Please do not interrupt. As I was saying. That he, your husband, frequently provoked the defendant by refusing all his reasonable requests. And that you both ...."

"Why are you saying these lies?! None of it is true! He only refused ......"

"Your honour?"

"Mrs Palmerstone, I must request you do not interrupt council and only answer questions as they are posed."

"But ...."

"Do you understand?" Firm and unyielding in his tone.

"Ye..ss ... I am sorry but ....."

"Please continue." Turning from her to the defence council.

"He refused all reasonable requests and that you both took all the defendant's family had when you adopted him. Those are the facts, are they not?"

"I do not believe this. How can he tell such lies?" More to herself than anyone else.

"Please answer the question."

"I do not know where this has all come from, but none of it is true. We have given everything we could to make life as comfortable as possible for Peter. We went out of our way to give him all the advantages of a good education and a secure family background. The only time his father, my husband, refused him anything was when he asked for his share of the inheritance." She then related the facts of how they had invested what little Peter's biological family had, how they had paid for everything and how they had eventually given him his portion of the inheritance and more.

"I believe your husband threatened to strike his son on more than one occasion."

"No! Even during the most violent arguments he never struck him, not once."

"But he threatened to?"

"No! Well, he did raise his hand once, just on one occasion when Peter was being particularly rude and aggressive, but had no intention of hitting him. It only lasted a couple of seconds and was simply an indication, to his son, of how upset he had made us both. He would never have struck him."

"So he did threaten him?"

"No, as I said, it was simply to indicate how sad he had made us by his behaviour. Especially after all the love and care we have shown."

"So the defendant had cause to fear your husband?"

"No. Why are you distorting the truth? He never had anything to fear from us. All Richard, his father, and I ever wanted was the best for our son."

"So considering your husband's behaviour, the defendant had every reason to think he may need to protect himself?"

"No!" It was all becoming too much.

"Your honour, I object. Council is bullying the witness."

"Council has the right to clarify the facts. Overruled."

"The defendant had every reason to fear for his safety and to think he may need to protect himself from your husband's violent temper?"

"Nooo......." Trailing off, the rising blood pressure causing her vision to blur and her head to feel fuzzy. Her knuckles turned white as she griped the side of the witness box in an attempt to steady herself.

"Yes!"

"How can you thin ......?" All before her disappeared in a misty haze while the strong loud pulsing in her ears deafened her to all sound. Then there was nothing but a blank grey wall. Then total darkness. She collapsed.

Faint light penetrating through the darkness slowly brought her back to consciousness. Where was she? What was this hard, unyielding thing she was lying on? What had happened?

"Mama." Ellen's voice.

"Mama, are you all right?" Andrea.

"Where am I? What happened?"

"You collapsed Mama."

"Oh yes. That horrible man saying all those lies about your papa."

"Try to stay calm Mama."

"I must tell him he is wrong. Surely he cannot believe those lies he is telling." Struggling to sit. Then noticing she was no longer in the witness box. "Where are we?"

"We are on a bench outside the courtroom. The judge asked the bailiffs to bring you here so you could recover. Here, have some water." Pressing the glass to her lips. She drank gratefully, her mouth feeling dry and acrid.

"We have got to go back. I do not want them believing all those lies. They must know the truth about how papa loved and cared for Peter. How he did his best to give him everything."

"It is too late, Mama. Peter has been convicted. Andrea looked after you while I went back in to see what was happening."

"Oh." Falling back onto the bench with a feeling of bewilderment and confusion. "What .... What did the judge do?"

"It was all rather mixed up. Before he would pass sentence, the judge asked for any pleas of mitigation to be put forward. The defence council then continued to argue Peter had reason to fear Papa and therefore it was self-defence. The prosecutor, however, said it was premeditated because Peter had brought a shotgun with him. But then the other man shouted that was because he was frightened."

"Oh goodness."

"Yes, it was not very nice. Anyway, the prosecutor then asked why, if indeed it had been self-defence, he, Peter, chased you with the clear aim of also murdering you, as testified by other witnesses. He meant that Lucca man. I do not like him."

"No, nor do I. What happened then?"

"Peter's lawyer, barrister or whatever he is, said it was simply a reaction after all the proceeding violence and that his client had no intention of harming you."

"Is there no end to the lies?"

"In the end, the judge said enough was enough. The jury had reached their verdict, and it was now time for him to pass sentence. He then went on to explain how the government continues to debate about the death penalty. Whether it should apply to all violent crimes and treason or whether it should only be reserved for the most heinous crimes. Apparently, the current thinking is it should only apply to the worst heinous crimes." Ellen stopped to catch breath at this point.

"What did he decide?" Frightened and yet eager to hear what was to become of her son.

"He went on to say, having listened to all the evidence and council's plea of mitigation, he considered there was probably an element of fear in the defendant's actions. He possibly had believed there was some need, whether perceived or actual no one would ever truly know, to be prepared to defend himself."

"How could he?! Richard would never have harmed him. And he knew it."

"We know that Mama but others do not. Peter has obviously been quite persuasive."

"Yes, I suppose so. But how could he tell all those lies?"

"How could he kill Papa?" Struggling to control her own grief. Not wishing to distress her mother further.

"Yesss........" Still finding it hard to accept recent events had actually occurred. Still hoping to wake from this nightmare, which it must be. Then recalling where she was. "Well, Ellen, what did the judge decide?"

"In view of the uncertainty about whether Peter had cause to fear, the government's current thinking, and the undeniable fact Peter had killed Papa and chased you, causing you considerable distress, he sentenced Peter to life imprisonment without parole."

"Oh good. I am so glad. I could not have born the thought of him being hung."

"But Mama, he deserves to be properly punished." Andrea had remained quiet up to this point, allowing her elder sister to explain all. But she felt her mother's gentle and almost forgiving attitude was too much.

"He is being punished darling. Life imprisonment means he will never be allowed into the open world again. He will have to live within the dark confines of a prison for the rest of his days." A tear she could not help came into her eye. He was still her son after all.

~~~~~~~~

The preceding events and the strain of the court hearing finally caught up. Depression set in with a vengeance. Neither her daughters, nor Catrina, nor the other staff, nor the estate manager, nor her friends, including Jennifer, who had subsequently made a point of returning to the village whenever possible, were able to bring her out if it. There was nothing ahead. Instead of the green, fertile land of hope and happiness they had anticipated together, there now stood before her a barren, dry, arid, lifeless vista. To be in the gentleness of heaven with her beloved would be much better. To feel his caress, his kisses, his love. To press into his strong, protective, reassuring, loving arms. To kiss those manly lips and to gaze into those wonderful, captivating hazel eyes once more. No point in this life now. Time to leave.

"What was that darling?"

"The girls. You must take care of them. They've no one else."

"They are all right. They are clever. They can look after themselves."

"They need you. They need your guidance."

"But I want to be with you."

"In time sweetheart, in time." His wonderful, handsome face, together with his glorious eyes, slowly faded. She then woke. I had all been a dream.

"Are you all right Mama?" Maria's young innocent voice calling her back to reality.

"Um, oh, yes Maria sweetheart. Goodness, it is dark. What time is it?"

"I am not sure. I think it must be getting near to midnight."
~~~~~~~~

"Goodness. How long have I been asleep? It was the afternoon last I remember."

"You came home from the court in the afternoon and went straight to bed. That was nine months ago."

"Pardon?!"

"You have been asleep for nine months. I was worried you would never wake up. But just now, we each take turns to sit by your bed and talk to you, I saw your eyes move and then you gave a little moan."

"I cannot have been in bed for so long. You are playing a trick on me. Your papa liked to do that sometimes."

"No Mama. I am not playing a trick. You really have been asleep for nine months."

"Oh, my goodness. I thought it was a long dream."

"What was?"

"I dreamt I was with papa." Tears gathered as she now recalled what had happened to him. That he would not confidently stride into the room any moment. "I was so happy. But he reminded me you would all need me. For a while at least."

"We do Mama. I was so scared you would not come back to us. I am glad you are back." Leaning over the bed to hug and kiss her dear mama. She then ran from the room to call the others.

"My dears! My darlings!" In a tumbled mass, they all clambered over the bed, hugging, kissing and crying, with joy this time.

"Mama! You are better! I am so glad."

"So am I Mama! I have missed you!"

"I'm also very glad to see you awake Mam." Catrina having waited outside until the initial euphoria calmed a little. "Would you like some tea? And perhaps a little light soup?"

"Thank you Catrina. Some tea would be lovely. I am quite dry."

"Right away Mam." Almost skipping out the door.

"Well dears, you must tell me all that has been going on. I still cannot believe I have slept for so long."

"Are you sure Mama?" Ellen taking control. "You look tired and very pale."

"I do feel a little tired. You would think after sleeping for nine months I would be full of energy. Must be the excitement of seeing you all my darlings."

"It could wait for tomorrow."

"Probably, but just tell me a little while Catrina is getting my tea. How are the estates? Who has been taking care of them? Have they been taken care of?"

"Andrea and I have been helping the estate manager look after things."

"So have I." Maria feeling her sister was unfairly forgetting.

"Sorry Maria. Yes, Maria has also helped."

"But how? Your papa and I had only just started to teach you. There is much for you still to learn. We did not want to overburden you with everything at once."

"We remembered what you had taught us, and using that knowledge did our best to help. We then learnt more as we went along. The estate manager and all the estate workers have been really kind. Everyone has done what they could to keep everything on an even keel."

"That is kind of them."

"Yes it is. No one complained about doing a little extra to help."

"We must make them proper recompense."

"We decided to wait for you to sort that out. We did not think it would be right for us to assume your role as head of the family."

"I had not thought of that. I suppose I am now." Tears returning.

"Come on Mama, do not upset yourself."

"Thank you dear. Let me have a good look at the three of you again." Visually examining each as they stood back for her to do so. "My goodness, you have grown. You look quite mature and proper young ladies." Grateful they had got on and yet saddened their maturing had been accelerated by such terrible events and that she had missed it.

"Here's your tea Mam." Catrina entering with a small laden tray. "And, just in case, I've brought you some of cook's little cakes and biscuits."

"Thank you Catrina, thoughtful as ever." Placing the tray on the bedside table, Catrina gave a modest, but pleased, smile.

"Now come on you three, out with you. Your mama needs to rest." Each, first giving their mama a warm giant hug and kiss, dutifully left the room.

"Thank you Catrina. How are they really? They look well, but are they coping with their papa's death and Peter's betrayal?"

"That wretched, ungrateful boy."

"Now Catrina, that sort of attitude will help no one. He is paying the price for his misdeeds. We will never see him here again." Still unable to stop the tear in her eye.

"He doesn't and never did deserve to have anyone like you. But never mind him now. The girls are doing well. Naturally, they were very upset and a little distraught at first. And, of course, your illness did not help. But they are young and resilient and time has helped them come to terms."

"Good. I am very glad. Thank you so much for taking care of them."

"It's always been and always will be a pleasure. I love them like they're my own. To them I think, along with Martha, I've become a sort of aunt figure."

"Thank you." Eyes now feeling heavy.

"You must rest now. You're still weak. Goodnight Mam and sweet dreams."

"Um ... oh ... yes, they will be."

"Hello Mama. It is nice to see you downstairs." Two weeks later.

"Thank you Ellen. I am feeling much better today. Anyway, I thought it was about time I got out of bed."

"Good. I have been waiting to tell you something, but did not want to do so while you were unwell."

"What is it dear?"

"Michael. Aa, I mean, Mr Michael Hermann wishes to ask you for my hand."

"Does he?" With her mischievous little smile. "I hope you have been behaving yourself." She was definitely feeling better, though the sorrow and sadness were ever present in her heart. But it would not be fair to the others to display her feelings constantly. She must help them get on with their own lives.

"Yes, he does, and yes, I have. As the head of the family now it is your place to approve, or not, potential matches for us. You will say yes. Pleaseee."

"We will see. I knew for a while he was interested in you. I had been expecting him to ask your papa any day before ...." Would she ever get over the difficulty when referring to that awful time?

"Yes, he was going to but, well..." She too still found it hard to recall that horrible evening.

"Tell him he may call whenever he wants."

"Thank you Mama." Rushing from her seat to embrace and kiss her mother. "Um..."

"Something else?"

"Well, yes. Because you were so ill we have waited all this time. So, if you approve, we would like to be married straight away. He is due to take up his new position with the city firm in a month. We would like to be married before then, so I may go with him as his wife."

"So you have already made plans, presuming upon my agreement and approval." Again, with a mischievous spark in her eye.

"Well, yes. I am sorry if that is wrong, but nine months is a long time."

"All right dear. Let me talk to him and we will see what comes of it."

The house was a hive of activity for the next three weeks. Ellen and Michael Hermann were married in the village church amongst great rejoicing. They left the following week to start their married life together in the city. Katherine knew she would see little of her daughter thereafter. A bitter pill after the loss of Richard. Nevertheless, she was happy to know Michael did truly love and would take care of her daughter.

A further year passed with Katherine reopening the clinic and resuming her visits to the estate families. But now, in addition, she had to take responsibility for running the estates and family business. Thankfully, she had an acumen for business and, with the estate manager's help, it thrived. She also continued to teach Andrea, despite her having no real interest in the estates, and Maria. Her youngest was the only one of the three who showed any true regard. She had an empathy with nature and all things living and delighted in their surroundings. She had even once stated, categorically, never to leave the area. She would spend her whole life here, on the family estates in the Lucas valley, whether she married or not. Her husband, should she marry, would have to agree to it, otherwise he would have to go. Katherine smiled at the innocent statement, knowing full well how love could change things within the blink of an eye. But she was grateful for Maria's sincerity.

Within the following year, Andrea was also married to a young man who was to set up his own shipping business in Portside. They too left the village to go and live there. Katherine continued her education of Maria, who not only had an avid interest but proved more than capable of assimilating the information and applying it effectively. However, Katherine was also conscious of Maria's interest in medicine and of how quickly she also assimilated and applied that knowledge. Richard, when he was still with them, had also noticed it. Her heart tore at the mere thought of him. They had agreed, when old enough, and if still interested, Maria should go to Vienna to study for a doctor's degree, having both accepted she had the ability.

"Excuse me Mam. A letter has arrived." The two ladies, Maria, no longer a girl, had just sat down to lunch.

"Thank you Catrina." Taking the letter from the salver Catrina was holding out. "Oh! This looks official."

"Who is it from Mama?"

"I am not sure. But there is an official seal. Let me see." Slicing it open with the paper knife Catrina had also placed on the salver. "Oh!"

"What is it Mama? You have gone quite pale."

"Um ..." Holding the letter in her now limp hand.

"Are you alright Mam?"

"Um ... yes. It is Peter ...." Staring off into empty space.

"What about him?"

"Um... he is dead." Tears gathering in the corners of her eyes. Catrina, seeing how distraught her mistress looked, manoeuvring to be to hand should she faint.

"What? How?"

"Apparently ..." Returning her eyes to the letter. "Apparently, he was in a fight with another prisoner who killed him."

"Oh dear." Despite the cruelty he had shown them, Maria could not bring herself to hate her brother.

"The letter goes on to explain that Peter was always an awkward prisoner who bullied and regularly picked fights with other inmates. The writer, a Mr Nuggett, Senior Warden, says it really was only a matter of time before something like this happened. He offers his condolences."

"Kind of him, especially in the circumstances."

"Yes it is." Bursting into full flood.

"Mama."

"Mam." Moving closer.

"Whatever he did, he was still my son. I still love him." Breaking down altogether this time.

"Maria." A month later.

"Mama?"

"As you know, your sister's husbands both declined a portion of the estates as part of their dowries. Besides their trousseaus, they simply asked for a little cash. Consequently, it will fall to you to continue the family tradition in the district. Unless, of course, your husband shows no interest and takes you away."

"I meant what I said about not leaving here. If anyone wants to marry me, he will have to agree to live on, and work, the estates. I love it here and never want to go anywhere else."

"Things can change."

"Not for me."

"You may change your mind when you see Vienna."

"You did not. You came back, did you not?"

"Yes, but then I fell in love with your papa."

"No. If it means leaving here, I will not marry."

"And if you fall in love with someone from elsewhere?"

"I would have to get over it. I never intend to leave."

Acknowledgments

Thank you Mama, for sharing our family's stories with me,
even though you were reluctant to burden me with the
sadder elements.
I would also like to thank my son for undertaking most of the research required
for some parts of this book.
Also, for his guidance and support during the writing of this tale.
I found his insights invaluable.

About the Author

T. R. Robinson is an independent author of memoir, autobiography and fiction. Her author career commenced upon the realisation that her own and the lives of her ancestors were anything but 'normal'. Readers will find her books inspiring and relevant, often showing the strength of the human spirit and how previously considered insurmountable obstacles and difficulties may be overcome and survived.

Throughout, no matter into which genre a book may fall, T. R. draws upon her own and her ancestors' life experiences, some of which are truly shocking, frightening and surprising. She has had varied employments ranging from managing small electrical components, laboratory assistant, hospital orderly, waitress and much more between, all of which are drawn upon in her writing, whether memoir or fiction.

Other Books by T. R. Robinson

Memoir

Eternally Naïve: A Reluctant Autobiography

Tears of Innocence

Negative Beauty

Lost Dreams

The Hammer

Broom Attack

Novels

Peter

Loving Maria

Short Stories

Her Next Door

Reverse Gear

Snake in the Grass

Off Balance

Felina

Manipulation

The Blonde Brunette

All are either entirely true or heavily based on real events.

Further details available at:

www.trrobinsonpublications.com

with some also available at: www.anickto.com

APPENDIX

A number of different medical conditions are referred to in this tale. I thought it may assist the reader if I provide a little detail about each.

Menstruation (Chapters 11 & 17): The process in a woman of discharging blood and other material from the lining of the uterus at intervals of about one lunar month from puberty until the menopause, except during pregnancy.

Bronchopneumonia (Chapter 12): A type of pneumonia (an inflammation of the lungs due to an infection caused by viruses, bacteria or fungi). – Symptoms: Fever; a cough that brings up mucus; shortness of breath; chest pain; rapid breathing; sweating; chills; headache; muscle aches; fatigue; confusion or delirium.

Pneumonia (Chapters 12 & 20): An infection caused by viruses, bacteria or fungi that inflames the air sacs in one or both lungs. The sacs fill either with fluid or pus and may become solid. – Symptoms (may include): Fever; sweating; shaking chills; cough, which may produce phlegm (mucus); chest pain when breathing; shortness of breath; fatigue; nausea; vomiting; diarrhoea.

Hyperemesis Gravidarum (Chapter 12): Extreme, excessive, and persistent vomiting in early pregnancy. – Symptoms: Main symptom is severe vomiting, which causes dehydration and weight loss.

Weil's Disease (Chapter 15): Weil's disease is a severe form of a bacterial infection known as leptospirosis. – Symptoms (may include): Jaundice (yellowing of the skin and the white part of the eyes); nausea; loss of appetite; weight loss; chest pain; fatigue; swollen ankles, feet or hands; painful swelling of the liver; decreased urine; shortness of breath; rapid heartbeat; coughing up blood; symptoms similar to meningitis.

Dysmenorrhoea (Chapter 17): The occurrence of painful cramps during menstruation. – Symptoms: Dull, throbbing cramping in the lower abdomen that may radiate to the lower back and thighs. In addition, some women may experience nausea and vomiting, diarrhoea, irritability, sweating, or dizziness.

Consumption (Chapter 20): A potentially serious infectious disease that mainly affects the lungs. It is an old and once common term for wasting away of the body, particularly from pulmonary (of the lungs) tuberculosis. – Symptoms: Coughing that lasts three or more weeks; coughing up blood; chest pain, or pain with breathing or coughing; unintentional weight loss; fatigue; fever; night sweats; chills; loss of appetite; it can also affect other parts of the body, including kidneys, spine or brain.

www.ingramcontent.com/pod-product-compliance
Lightning Source LLC
Chambersburg PA
CBHW020500310726
48979CB00016B/2731/J
* 9 7 8 1 7 3 8 5 4 3 5 5 7 *